SPARK

D0059651

Other Books in the Swipe Series

Swipe

Sneak

Storm

SPARK

THE SWIPE SERIES

EVAN ANGLER

BOOK 4

THOMAS NELSON
Since 1798

NASHVILLE   DALLAS   MEXICO CITY   RIO DE JANEIRO

Spark

© 2013 by Evan Angler

Published in Nashville, Tennessee, by Tommy Nelson. Tommy Nelson is a registered trademark of Thomas Nelson.

Tommy Nelson titles may be purchased in bulk for educational, business, fund-raising, or sales promotional use. For information, please e-mail SpecialMarkets@ ThomasNelson.com.

Scripture quotations are taken from THE ENGLISH STANDARD VERSION. © 2001 by Crossway Bibles, a division of Good News Publishers.

Library of Congress Cataloging-in-Publication Data

Angler, Evan.
  Spark / Evan Angler.
    pages cm. -- (Swipe series ; book 4)
  Summary: Nine-year-old Ali, a beggar living in the Dark Lands city of al-Balat, crosses paths with exiled Logan Langly, Chancellor Cylis, and the fierce battle for power that spans reality and the virtual world.
  ISBN 978-1-4003-2198-8 (pbk.) 5240 1002 11/13
  [1. Science fiction. 2. Government, Resistance to--Fiction. 3. Fugitives from justice--Fiction. 4. Christian life--Fiction.] I. Title.
  PZ7.A5855Sp 2013
  [Fic]--dc23

                    2013023033

Printed in the United States of America

13 14 15 16 17 RRD 6 5 4 3 2 1

This one is for Ali,
Who saw the tinchers first

CONTENTS

CONTENTS

A NOTE FROM THE AUTHOR

Dear Reader,

The world is big. And every story has many sides.

This book you have found is the fourth in our ongoing chronicles of the Dust's great defiance. You've already read about Logan Langly and his Markless friends, Daniel Peck, Hailey, Dane, Blake, Joanne, Meg, Rusty, Tyler, Eddie . . .

You've read about Erin Arbitor too, as she at first worked with Logan to thwart Peck and his gang, and as she then worked against Logan once he went Markless himself on his thirteenth birthday.

You've watched Logan travel from New Chicago in middle America all the way to Beacon on the East Coast, in search of his older sister, Lily, who disappeared when Logan was eight. You saw him find the top secret prison where Lily was held, saw him break in, and then saw Lily betray him . . .

You saw the Dust start a Markless revolution across America, with the first signs of hope for a better future. But when a new threat emerged—the bioweapon Project Trumpet—and when Erin began showing the first signs of illness, you saw her and Logan and Peck and Hailey journey out west, to the lawless city of Sierra, desperate to find the Project's engineer and determined to find its cure.

During this time, you watched the American Union, led by

General Lamson, and the European Union, led by Chancellor Cylis, become the Global Union, and you read on in horror as, with the help of Logan's sister, Lily, Cylis unleashed Trumpet across America, killed General Lamson, and became supreme chancellor once and for all.

Overwhelmed in the face of this, Daniel Peck, leader of the Dust, left before the worst of it could hit, because something or Someone bigger than him was calling him away, and because he couldn't stand to lose the battle at hand.

Well.

That battle *was* lost.

Erin did eventually cure herself of Trumpet, along with the rest of the American State, with the treatment she discovered out in Sierra. And she did make it back to the Dust. But there was no real victory there. Cylis had already taken credit for Trumpet's cure, was already beloved by the country he had just destroyed, and had already captured Logan and sentenced him to a traitor's death.

Of course, readers, we alone know that Logan is *not* dead. In a brief and rare moment of pity, Logan's sister, Lily, couldn't bear to kill her brother. So instead she exiled him, trapping him inside virtual reality, in a program of nothingness inside the Ultranet. His body lives on, but his mind is jailed. Even his friends still think he is dead. And absolutely no one is looking for him.

Meanwhile, Cylis's IMP army runs loose, doing their best to put down Markless resistance at every turn. Our friends in the Dust lie in wait, biding their time until their next steps are clear.

And yet there is hope we've not so far seen. A world beyond the great Global Union. Life beyond the world you've yet known.

Where the Mark of citizenship, where the International Moderators of Peace, where Cylis's reign—where Cylis's very *name*—does not reach. Whole swaths of South America, of Asia, of Africa, of the Middle East . . .

What of *that* world? What of *those* lives?

The Dark Lands—what of *them*?

Most of the fighting during the Total War had missed these lands—had ravaged Europe and America, but had left the cities beyond mostly intact. While the rest of the world burned, these places carried on. And when the war finally did end, they saw no need to strike a bargain with a new Union whose only real promise was to heal wounds they didn't personally have.

While life in the Dark Lands has been hard-knock ever since, their roads, buildings, and bridges remain standing and usable. They've no need to rebuild, and they've no desire for postwar politics.

Of course, without the strength of the Union behind them, these Dark Lands have no electricity, no technology, no conveniences or comfort. They have no stable government of their own, no formal economy or laws. But the lives of their people go on. They have their homes. They have their land. They have a system that works for them.

And as things quiet down throughout the Union in the wake of the Dust's defeat, it is in these Dark Lands that the real war now brews. Beyond the Union's borders. Beyond its scope. The front lines of our battle can no longer be seen from the Union we've come to know.

And so, in the last few months, I have traveled to these Dark Lands myself. To see firsthand. To see what I'd been missing.

And I'd like to take you there now, if you'll let me. I'd like to show you what I've learned.

For the world is big.

But its doors are always open, if we care to see.

Evan Angler

PROLOGUE

ARRIVAL

□

ON AN OLD NIGHTSTAND AT THE BACK OF A red freight container in a settlement in the Eurasian Dark Lands, a green ceramic coffee mug shook, shivered, and sloshed all the way to the edge, teeter-tottered twice, and fell smashing to the ground.

A boy shot up with a quiet yelp, leaned over to look at the pieces, and rose urgently from his hammock bed.

"Это землетрясение?" his sister asked over the ongoing rumble.

"Нет," Father said, rubbing his eyes. "Землетрясения не происходят здесь."

But that did nothing to help. If it wasn't an earthquake, what was it?

"Я собираюсь посмотреть," the boy told them, tiptoeing carefully around the broken mug. It jumped and jittered even now where it lay.

"Подождите," Mother pleaded. "Не оставляй."

The boy looked at her grimly as the quake only worsened. "Мне нужно," he said. He didn't mean to be defiant, but he had to see for himself.

Outside, the concrete was cold on his feet, and a wet mist

beaded on his face and bare arms. The shipping yard was bright with a midnight sun that wouldn't go down, and from one end to the other, he could see his neighbors opening their own cargo doors, could hear their nervous shouts over the low roar of the tremors, could feel them stirring inside their converted shipping container homes, all shaking and echoing with the sounds of toppling shelves and shattering glass.

And beyond the settlement too, across the forgotten port all the way to where the concrete ended, he could hear the untouched sea cans, hundreds of them—green, brown, blue, orange, red, all lined up in rows, stacked two, three, four high, all waiting for ships that wouldn't ever dock—all trembling, all wavering, all losing their cargo as the ground shook beneath them.

By this point, everyone was out, dumbstruck, shivering, calculating the damage under the nighttime light, when something happened out at sea that made the rest of all of this look like the sideshow it really was.

There, in the distance, waves capped white and blue through the usual polar fog as anyone might expect. But it didn't take long to see the swell, the source of the quake, just a little farther out, like a mountain growing all at once out of the ocean.

It grew so high that it parted the water, and two giant waves cascaded down its sides and slid violently up the shore, all the way to the concrete, as though reaching out to the Dark Landers, trying to escape from the very monster their sea had birthed.

It was hard for the boy to make sense of it. What was he looking at? What had arrived? In the midnight mist, it stuck out wildly, this black beast of a thing, rising from the ocean as the earth shook around it, towering over the container port and casting the whole settlement in shadow. People were running now, as fast as they could, back into their homes or even just *away*, out, anywhere but here.

And he could hear his mother calling, begging him to follow, begging him to come back into the safety of her arms. But what good would that do? Against this leviathan, what safety was left? So instead, the boy ran forward, arms up, calling out as he rushed the rocky beach and as cold salt water swept his feet and splashed his face.

"Что вы?" he called. "Что вы хотите?"

As soon as he asked it, the monster answered. With a terrible squeal, its great, gaping jaws opened up, revealing the shiny, sharp teeth of its mouth, the cavernous belly beyond . . .

And there, on the long, metallic ramp of a tongue as it extended grate by grate to the ground before him, the boy saw the visitor—the tamer of this beast—walking calmly to the shore.

Behind the boy, those villagers still outside their homes bowed down without hesitation, knees and heads to the ground, arms out and asking only for mercy, nothing more.

The boy saw this . . . and he stood only straighter. "Что вы хотите?" he asked again, urgently now, as the visitor fast approached. "Что вы хотите?"

And the visitor said, "*The girl.*"

Something about "the girl."

Looking for . . .

Need to find . . .

Life or death . . .

World depends . . .

The words didn't mean much in Northern Darklandese. It took gestures for the boy to catch on, even vaguely.

"Какая девушка?" he asked. "Какая девушка?"

But the visitor didn't say. He didn't *know*. She was without a name, he admitted. But he would find her, no matter the cost. No matter what it took.

The boy didn't understand any of this, of course. Not the intentions, not the warning . . . no one in that settlement did.

So when the harbinger left for central Asia mere hours later, none of those settlers could really believe it. Central Asia was precisely the thing that drove them here, to this little stretch of lonely coast along the Bering Strait. Central Asia was precisely where the nightmares lived. "Вы собираетесь прямо на них," they told him. *Straight toward the tinchers.*

But this visitor didn't seem to care about any of that. Did he, too, not understand? Or was he truly that fearless?

And what else was lost in the translation between them?

All that was clear—to anyone—was that this old, forgotten container port was not this visitor's final destination.

It was merely in his way.

And whoever that girl was . . . she'd better get ready.

ONE

ALI WITHOUT A NAME

1

ALI WITHOUT A NAME WAS PRETTY SURE SHE knew exactly how much trouble she was in. The truth, in fact, would have shocked her. But for the moment, that truth was still a long way off.

She needed *more*.

She looked for targets.

And with her back to the wall, she kept one eye out for guards while she boiled in the afternoon sun.

Around her, the crowd was loud, and a hundred thousand footsteps kicked up clouds of dust that swirled and sank and haloed around her head.

Without more, the Khal gets angry. The Khal gets angry, and Naughty-Ali gets the closet.

"أنا أعرف ذلك." Ali hissed under her breath to herself. *Don't you think I know that?*

To her left was the New Gate, the northwestern mouth of the Old City of al-Balat, and long lines shuffled in, merging at the entrance but forking a ways out like a snake's tongue. Tasting the forbidden fruits of the Union's biggest outpost.

And here I am for the scraps, Ali thought.

"But you can't afford to wait like this," she whispered to herself, practicing her Union English. "You've wasted the whole morning by now."

But the gatekeepers saw me, she thought. *What else can I do?*

She couldn't answer before Sarim came by.

"Hey!" he yelled, picking up on her English and hopping over through the crowd. "Scolding yourself again?" He bent down to speak with her, leaning against his crutch and letting some of the spoils from his ragged pockets spill out onto the ground. "Which one of you's angry this time?"

"Nervous-Ali," she said sheepishly.

Sarim nodded. He eyed her ripped sleeves and the trickles of blood underneath. "You know, if you kept to the back of the customs lines, those guards wouldn't pick on you so much. It's stupid to hang around up front."

"Up front, the merchants are distracted," Ali said. She glanced quickly at Sarim's bum leg. "Not all of us get the kind of sympathy you do just by begging alone."

"You want this kind of sympathy?" Sarim asked, pointing to his bandages.

"Sorry," Ali said. She looked away, embarrassed. "I just can't stand to spend another night down in the basement, is all. I'm afraid I'll go nuts."

Sarim hopped gently over to her and put a hand on her shoulder. "Ali, you can't believe the Khal's tincher stories. He only says that stuff to scare you into making quota."

"Yeah, well, you've never spent a night down there in that basement, have you?"

"No, but I gladly would if it meant no more accidents! Ali,

the *reason* Khal Obaid talks about boogie men with you sisters is because the Khala doesn't like to let him hurt you. With us, he doesn't bother because to *us* Khal Obaid is scary enough on his own!"

"I hear things in that basement, Sarim. If it's not tinchers, I don't know what it is."

"It's your imagination," Sarim said. "Tinchers aren't real. The Khal's just fooling you. But you really will have more than ghost stories to worry about if you don't start making quota soon."

For a moment, Ali stood still and stared at the gate, at the Union guards checking paperwork, at the Dark Landers coming and going with sacks of goods, eager to trade with Marked Union vendors in the Old City's sprawling bazaar.

She knew that Sarim's warnings were right. Tinchers or not, Ali was on thin ice—and the day was getting only hotter. The thought of it made her suddenly very impatient. First a twitch in her foot, then a wiggle in her legs . . . finally a bouncing that spread up and through her whole body in a way that only nine-year-old girls could sustain.

They're getting away! the squirming said. *Pockets and handfuls and whole bags of goods, and I'm missing it!*

"All right, all right," Sarim said, laughing at her. "وأنا أفهم. Let's go already, before you hurt yourself."

"What makes you think I'm waiting for *you*?" Ali asked in broken English that tried to sound playful.

"Because you're useless out here on your own," Sarim teased. "And because you know I'd love to see you keep your hands all the way to adulthood."

Ali's eyes brightened. It wasn't every day that the two of them begged together, but the times they did were always her favorite.

"Hey, hold your horses!" Sarim yelled, gathering his alms and struggling to plant his crutch in the dirt. "انتظر!" But Ali was already off, running eagerly toward the gate.

"Please help!" she yelled at the crowd. "Kind help for a poor cripple!" She spun back toward Sarim and whispered, "Come on! Look pathetic! عجل!"

For the first time today, there was hope she might make it through the night without punishment.

2

Wading through the mob along Old City's outer wall was always rough—rabid merchants and strict guards, ruthless bullies from rival gangs, tangles of elbows and prying hands that threatened from every which way—but somehow, with Sarim there, it wasn't so bad. The crowd's knots seemed to loosen. Paths emerged, kids steered clear, adults leaned down and listened . . .

Sarim had the touch. Always did, even before his "accident" with Khal Obaid, but especially now. In just the few minutes it took him to wade halfway through the New Gate's afternoon crowd, more Dark Landers had taken pity on him than they had on Ali all morning long. Already, as he caught up to her, he was passing handfuls of trinkets into her pockets so as not to risk looking as flush as he really was.

"I don't know how you do it," Ali whispered, in awe of the master beggar.

"The leg helps," he said, looking Ali up and down and practically pitying her. "You're too old to look as healthy as you do."

Ali folded her arms playfully and narrowed her eyes. She

didn't particularly feel over the hill. But the truth was that in this line of work, nine and healthy was just about retirement age.

"Tell you what," Sarim said, pointing to her pockets. "Those latest gets are all yours. We won't go halfsies—just keep 'em. You'll have an easier time of it tonight."

"هل أنت متأكد؟" Ali asked.

In response, Sarim stuck out his tongue, and Ali took that as a yes. Eagerly, she reached into her pockets to size up what was there.

No food, Hungry-Ali thought, her stomach rumbling a bit. But it was an impressive handful all the same. Bracelets, rings, scarves, chains—even a few pre-Unity coins. Ali stopped to get a better look while Sarim approached a few more men and women farther back on the gate's long line.

"Papers," a guard said suddenly in Union English, peering down and looking as if he might just kick Ali to the curb whether she had them or not. Ali looked up from her haul and was surprised to find that she'd drifted with the tide of the crowd all the way to the front of the New Gate's customs line.

She stared up at the man, eyes wide. She noticed the taser-rifle and magnecuffs on his belt.

"You're wasting my time, ya mute splinter—papers or get outta here!" He brushed her aside and let the documented Dark Landers shuffle past and shake their heads.

"Whoa, whoa, what'd I tell you about the front of the line?" Sarim spat, hopping over to Ali and dragging her forcefully back.

"He called me a splinter," Ali said sullenly. It was the worst slur against them that Dark Landers could hear.

"Yeah, well, you are one, trying to weasel your way into Old City like that."

"But I wasn't——!"

"لا يهم." Sarim shook his head. "You all right?"

Ali nodded, distantly. Still not far from the gate, she had an unusually good view of the city streets beyond the wall. Inside were bright, flashing tablet computers lining one shoddy merchant stand after another; rolled up plasticscreens poking out of baskets, displaying movies and news programs to no one at all; computerized "smart jewelry" unlike anything outside Union walls, hanging snarled from driftwood awnings; not to mention whole barrels of imported fruits, meats, vegetables, nanomeds, candies, every color of the rainbow just spread out like confetti across the market, waiting for takers in piles so high you could dig down up to your elbows . . .

And that was all within only the first narrow alleyway past the entrance, and not even the fanciest Union gadgets could compete for Ali's attention when just a few winding blocks beyond New Gate's main street opened up to reveal the jutting scaffolds and pacing soldiers and monstrous blue tarps that covered one of Old City's vast northwestern excavation sites. "The Digs," Dark Landers called them. A cluster of satellite sites complementing the biggest Dig of all, just east of here, on Mount Olivet over in the West Bank. The Digs were the last good reason the Union had for being here. Its *only* reason, in fact, ever since it so badly failed to defend the city against Russian Dark Land attackers several years back, losing the battle of al-Balat along with any real chance it ever had of luring the Middle Eastern Dark Lands into its empire.

The Union wasn't usually one to admit its defeats——let alone linger on them. But something about that Mount . . . *something* about its Digs made this area worth occupying, against all odds and resentment and reason.

Legend had it a hospital there, at the base of the mount, was haunted. Its abandoned grounds were supposedly the source of the tincher sightings in al-Balat.

But Sarim didn't buy that, and he never had.

"What do you think's going on in there?" Sarim asked, pointing to the site as casually as he could. Something about his tone was soothing. He was clearly hoping to take Angry-Ali's still-fuming mind off the slur she'd been called. "Ancient artifacts? Historical treasure?"

"Who knows?" Ali said. "Whatever it is must be—"

But the rest of Ali's words caught in her throat as a great club struck her back. "I thought I told you splinter dogs to *leave!*" the gatekeeper yelled, and all at once he shoved Ali and Sarim hard to the ground. Ali stumbled clumsily and landed on her back, but Sarim wasn't so lucky. In one horrible *crack,* his crutch snapped in two, pieces flying as he smacked the dirt with his hands and head.

There was a helpless horror in his eyes as Dark Landers stampeded over the belly-up, one-legged cripple in their way. But he managed to drag himself up by the pant legs that passed, and once balanced on his foot, he moved with swift, determined haste.

"Get up," Sarim hissed. "Ali—get *up.*"

"I'm okay," Ali said, still on the ground and too angry even to stand.

"Maybe you are," Sarim said. "But your quota's not!" Around them, desperate Dark Landers began to swarm, carelessly grabbing at Ali's spilled haul and taking for themselves every last trinket and coin they could get their hands on.

Somehow, Ali wasn't paying attention to it. Instead, she squinted off into the distance, wondering what secrets those strange digs held. She couldn't see them, she knew. But in that moment she hated them—every last one of them—for bringing this Union occupation into her life.

"Obaid will kill you!" Sarim was shouting, focused much more on the present. "The Khal will whip you dead!"

"Oh," Ali whispered. "Right."

She stumbled up, but her quota was already gone. It was all Sarim could do to drag her away from the mob before they pulled that flighty little beggar girl apart.

∃

The base to which Ali and Sarim and all their brothers and sisters went home each night was an old, pre-Unity skyscraper that their Khal, Obaid, had commandeered nearly eight years ago from among the al-Balat city blocks not directly hit by the war. Like everything in the Dark Lands, buildings were first come, first served, and while nothing within this one worked—not the electricity, not the plumbing, not the elevator—it wasn't exactly about to fall down, and anyway there was plenty of room. So Obaid made the building both his home and the center for his business of child beggars—or as he liked to call it, his family.

No one in Obaid's "family" was actually related, of course. The "brothers" and "sisters," as they called themselves, were a collection of kids taken from desperate Dark Land homes in exchange for food or safety given to the parents. The deal also came with the promise to the parents of a better life for their kids. A life in the "big city," far from the humble shantytown roots these "siblings" had known.

Ali herself had never heard of any such promise. None of the kids had, actually. And that was probably for the best.

It would have only confused them if they had.

That night the man the brothers called Khal stomped with heavy black boots between the rows of sisters nestled on two dozen sleeping pads against the cold, hard tile of the fifteenth floor.

By the Khal's own directives, this was a serious taboo. The fifteenth floor was the sisters' quarters, into which no brothers or men were ever allowed.

And yet here the Khal was now, announcing himself loudly with four strong cracks of his whip. He was looking for Nafia, he said. He needed to speak with the Khala.

She was groggy when she sat up from her mat in the corner, but Nafia quickly leaped to her feet.

"Why are you here?" she asked in perfect English, clearly hoping the girls wouldn't understand. It was a vain attempt to protect them, Ali realized. But Ali was wide-awake, and practiced in the Union's language from her days spent at the Gate. She'd made it a point to be able to understand words in situations like this.

"You are *short*," Obaid said. "*Very* short."

It was the last night of the week, Ali remembered. The night the sisters' haul was gathered and tallied and passed off to the Khal.

"They are aging out," Nafia said, calmly pointing to the sisters around her. "They are doing their best."

"It is your *job* to make them do *better*. It is your *job* to keep your eye on them."

"And I have——"

"*You have done no such thing!*"

"We had a bad week, Obaid. It will not happen again."

Obaid nodded. *You're right*, that nod said. *It will not.* And the Khal was determined to see to it that it didn't.

He readied his whip in a horrifying fashion. Always, the sisters had seen Khal and Khala as equals. But for the first time tonight, it was clear to them that even Nafia, twenty years older and every bit their leader, was just as afraid of this man as they were.

"Who missed?" Obaid asked. "You are short more than a full day's quota, Nafia——who did not deliver?"

Ali nearly let out a yelp just hearing this. On her mat, she trembled visibly, waiting for the hammer to fall. She dreaded the closet again. The noises in the basement. But then she thought of Sarim's warning that day——and of the "accidents" of so many of the brothers——and a silent, terrified tear fell down her cheek as she realized how much worse this could get.

Seconds went by. Ali held her breath. But Nafia remained silent.

"You cannot protect them!" Obaid warned.

Still Nafia stood her ground.

"Okay," the Khal said, nodding furiously. "Then you take the blame."

"Yes," Nafia said. She closed her eyes and braced herself. The Khal lifted his hand.

"*Stop!*" Ali yelled. Immediately, Obaid turned, eyes wide and violent in the shadowy dark.

"Sister, *no*," the Khala said.

But in the dim open floor, Ali rose defiantly to her feet. "It was me. I was short every day this week."

Obaid took four swift steps, his gruff face mere inches from hers. "You again, huh?"

Rebellious-Ali nodded.

"I have ways of improving your yield," he said. "You realize that, sister?"

And Ali nodded again. Her mind flashed to Sarim's limp. To the other brothers' milky eyes, and missing fingers, and—

"Obaid, you *can't*," Nafia said.

He turned to her. "Same old story, Khala. I'm beginning to question your loyalty."

The Khala took a step forward. "My loyalty is to this *business*," she insisted. "That is a *sister* you're speaking to. An investment. If you *hurt* her, she can't *work*. If she can't *work*, she'll make us *nothing*."

"رجما" Obaid said, nodding unpleasantly. "But the fact remains that at present, Ali here has been a bad girl."

Her jaw clenched the second he said it.

"And you know what happens to bad little girls, don't you, Aliyah?"

She did.

"When little girls are bad, Aliyah, the *tinchers* come to get them."

Not the closet, Ali thought. *Please not the closet.*

"That's right," the Khal said. "Straight down from Mount Olivet. They can *smell* the bad behavior. They *hunger* for it. It drives them mad.

"But we can't let one bad little girl put all the rest of us in danger, now can we, Ali? Why, sisters—if we let her sleep up here with the rest of us, all those hungry tinchers might just come down and eat us all!"

"Please . . . ," Ali said, barely audibly.

"So I guess we'll just have to keep little Ali here in the closet again down in the basement—where the tinchers won't get the rest of us. Because we'd *hate* to lure them upstairs, wouldn't we, girls? تفعل كل توافقون على ذلك؟"

The sisters all nodded in wide-eyed agreement, and this made the Khal grin with delight. "I'm sure you understand," he said to Ali, grabbing her harshly by the arm.

"Khal, please forgive me," Sorry-Ali said, louder this time, and it made the Khal stop dead in his tracks.

"Me? You're begging *me*? Why, *I* don't control the tinchers at all, little Ali! If you're going to beg—I'd suggest you beg *them*."

Ali started to respond, but this time Nafia stopped her. "هل سيكون على ما يرام." she said. "فمن الأفضل بهذه الطريقة،" The Khala spoke in Darklandese, to make sure that all the sisters understood. To make sure they knew, in the end, that Ali would be just fine.

But Ali had seen that look before on Nafia's face.

It was a look that said otherwise.

٤

The closet locked from the outside. It was not big enough for Ali to lie down. It was not wide enough to stretch her arms. It was barely deep enough for Ali to sit.

There was a lightbulb in the closet, but of course it didn't work. Nothing did on these city blocks, where Union electricity didn't reach. Ali did come to expect the occasional faint sliver of moonlight between the metal door and the cold concrete beyond, where the door's rubber seal had fallen away. But when it was there, this sliver was worse than no light at all. No light, and Ali could maybe forget where she was and sleep a little.

That sliver kept Ali right where she was—the basement. Where the "accidents" happened. In here, the Khal knew, Ali could make all the noise she wanted. No one was going to hear her. No one was going to find her.

Unless, of course, the Khal was right about the tinchers.

Small cell. All alone. Blind and deaf to the outside world. No promise of mercy from the monsters that lurked . . .

When somewhere in the walls, something scratched.

Tch, tch, tch, like that.

And Nervous-Ali said, "Oh please, no. Not tonight. Not again."

And the black space around her went suddenly very tight. Like the darkness was touching her, like it was a cloak fitted to her skin, closer, closer, until it was suffocating her, choking her.

Tch, tch, tch, real quick.

Tch, tch, tch.

It was exactly what Ali thought tinchers must sound like.

Could it be? Was it real? Had they really found her this time?

No, Ali. It's your imagination. Tinchers aren't real, right?

She took a deep breath and composed herself.

There was a momentary silence. Then . . .

Tch, tch, tch, tch, tch.

"Who's there?" Ali cried, in sudden desperate panic. "What is this?"

The air in the closet grew stuffy and hot and stale as she breathed too fast and soaked up precious oxygen. She leaned down, cramped against the door that was too close in front of her, mouth to the crack just under it, sucking in wind and lint and debris from the basement floor beyond.

Tch, tch, tch, it went. *Tch, tch, tch.*

And Nervous-Ali told herself, *You're going to die in here! You'll be eaten by a creature your best friend doesn't even believe exists. And then you'll be dead.*

Until all at once the scratching stopped. The closet went still. Ali calmed herself and squeezed a few panicked tears from her eyes, letting them go and allowing herself to believe it had just been her mind playing tricks on her. She laughed at herself. She wiped her sweaty brow and leaned back against the closet wall.

This lasted a few tranquil breaths before she felt the sprinkle of filings and sawdust raining lightly onto her hair and into her eyes.

And then something heavy landed on her shoulder. Some squirming . . . *thing* . . . the size of a dinner plate had landed on her back.

Ali screamed in a way she never had in her life.

She shot up so fast that she cracked her head on a pipe jutting out of the closet above her. Bright, white sparks filled her eyes, and a splitting pain bolted through her skull and all the way down her neck. Ali went limp, but without enough space to kneel, she couldn't even collapse properly; instead, she rested, back to the door, knees pressed up against the wall, head in her hands, contorted and sick with pain.

It was clarifying, that pain. It was enough to knock sense into her through the fog of her panic.

You have to find a way to see, Ali told herself. *You need to see it. You need to know what's burrowed its way into this room with you.*

Slowly, she lifted her head from the bowl of her hands. Dark everywhere, eyes open or shut.

In the opposite corner, whatever it was shuffled vigorously back and forth. Invisible to her still, but she could hear it. It was loud. Scratching at the wall, now from the inside. It was going to kill her!

Tch, tch, tch, louder than ever.

Tch, tch, tch.

She took a few shallow breaths.

Light, Aliyah! You need light!

Her eyes were already as wide as they'd go, but in that moment, it was as if she'd found a new way to open them all over again.

A flicker above. A soft fluorescent glow. For the first time in Ali's life, a lightbulb inside the family's home base turned on.

Yellow highlights! Blue shadows! Walls, floor, ceiling, pipes! How was this happening? How was it possible?

But her relief didn't last long.

There, sitting on the pipe, face-to-face to her and just inches from her nose, was the tincher. Not a myth. Not a scare tactic. It was the real thing, right here.

At least . . . it *might* have been the real thing.

For the first time, Ali realized she had no idea what a tincher was supposed to look like or if this creature in front of her even came close.

Two glowing red eyes stared back at Ali from a rusty metal face. Three slits below them emitted a shrieking pulse, only just barely within hearing range. Behind its head was its rat-like, robotic body, which encased a rubber ball that poked out underneath like a fat belly. The thing balanced on that ball and moved with it the way Ali saw rollersticks move beyond the fences of the West Bank. It had a long, cord-like tail used for balance and who knew what else, and at its front it had two sharp, blender-like tangles of claws, which rotated and which the creature must have used to burrow its way through the closet wall.

Ali stared at this—could it really be a tincher?—this *thing* for several moments, not daring to breathe. It didn't *look* like it could eat her. But it *did* look deadly, if it wanted to be.

And it was right as Ali realized this that she heard another scratching coming from beyond the closet door—*tch, tch, tch.*

In front of her, the robot hissed. It reared up on its roller ball, eyes brightening, claws spinning . . .

And then everything went black again.

TWO

DRAINPIPE

1

"HEY. HEY, IS THAT YOU IN THERE?" THE voice came muffled through the door. Was it real? She wasn't sure until it asked again, louder this time, "Ali—are you there?"

She wanted to answer, but her first attempt failed. Her words got stuck in her dry throat.

"Sarim?" she managed to whisper, pulling herself up just as the footsteps started to fade.

"Ali!" she heard. Sarim dropped down to peer through the thin crack by the floor. She could feel his breath rushing through it. "Ali, thank God—" He stopped himself. "I'll find something to pick the lock."

A moment later Sarim returned, and now Ali could hear two needles working their way around inside the knob of the door. The lock was open in no time at all.

"Sarim," she said breathlessly, falling out of the closet and into his arms. He stumbled a little under her weight.

"We have to go," Sarim said. "This instant."

"Go where?"

"Out. Now. Like five minutes ago."

"There's a tincher in that closet——" Ali began, and even in all his urgency, the claim was enough to stop Sarim in his tracks. Without so much as a breath, the boy peered up, eagerly looking inside, straining his neck and bobbing his head like a bird. "Ali . . . ," he said.

"Do you see it?"

Sarim deflated. "No."

"But it was there! I was *face-to-face* with it!" She spun around rabidly, determined to prove him wrong.

"I believe that it felt very real," Sarim said. "Anyone could go crazy inside a space like that. But right now we have to get *out* of here." He began pulling Ali toward the stairs with all the leverage his crutch would give him.

"I might be a little crazy," Ali said, "but that doesn't change what I saw."

There was a brief pause between them as Ali sunk to the floor and rested against Sarim's new crutch.

"Aliyah. You're not getting me. We. Have. To. *Move.*"

"How'd you sneak out of the brothers' quarters?" Ali asked rather flatly, changing the subject.

"Are you kidding? I didn't have to!" Sarim gestured grandly around the lit basement. "Ali—the *lights* are on."

"Yeah?"

In all her panic over the was-it-or-wasn't-it tincher, the full significance of this hadn't yet sunk in.

"Yeah? *Yeah?* That's all you have to say—'yeah?' Ali, this neighborhood hasn't had electricity since before these were the Dark Lands. There are no power plants outside of the Union. *How* did the lights come on?"

Ali had no answer for this.

"Obaid's freaking out upstairs. Until he or Nafia can figure out what to make of it, they're evacuating home base. The Khal's leading everyone out to the streets as we speak."

"Evacuating?" Ali asked. "Over a power surge?"

"*Yes*, over a power surge!"

"Why? Is that really necessary?"

Evacuations weren't unheard of for the family—usually once or twice a year, rival gangs or pillagers or some such thing would swing through the neighborhood looking for things or kids to steal, and whenever they did, the Khal always did what was necessary to protect the family. But a couple of lights turning on hardly seemed as threatening as gang warfare.

"It is," Sarim confirmed. "This has *never* happened before. A big, glowing building right in the middle of the Dark Lands? We might as well paint a big, red target on the side! How long until the other gangs start rolling in to see what's going on here, huh?"

"But what about Obaid?" Ali asked. "What if he sees me outside the closet?"

Sarim looked at her as though she still had no grasp at all of how urgent this matter was, and that was accurate enough. "We can worry about Obaid again in the morning," he told her. "Until then . . . please—one Khal at a time."

2

After that, Ali moved faster. And Sarim did too, with his friend's help up the oddly bright stairwell. They rushed through the ground floor lobby, and neither of them could believe the way it looked in the light—the way the old, broken chandelier sparkled, the way the lights bounced sharply off the tiled floor, the way each decorative lamp cast warm shadows on the walls and in the corners, all for the very first time. When the building's front door opened automatically, the two of them nearly fell over with surprise.

And then it all ended, as quickly and strangely as it began. Ali stepped out onto the street and that whole big skyscraper behind her just went dark all at once. Dark as it had always been. The younger brothers and sisters squealed and hopped around blindly as their eyes adjusted to the black. Sarim followed her out. Ali squinted up in disbelief.

"هذا لا يغير شيئا!" Nafia yelled, arms up above her head like a beacon of decision making. "The plan stays the same. We hide out until morning, just to be safe." And the kids followed the Khala's hand waving into the alleyway nearby. *'Bout as obedient as al-Balat's stray cats*, Ali thought, smiling a little, and she adjusted to the idea of spending the night in the gutter with the rest of them.

Her first thought, of course, was that this was a lot more comfortable than the closet. But even so, Ali had a hard time believing that Sarim was right, that Obaid might actually be nice about it if he saw her hiding out with the rest of them—disobeying his orders to stay in the basement, ignoring her punishment—no matter how distracted he might be by the lights turning on.

And so it was that a few minutes later, while her brothers and sisters all claimed the best sleeping spots in the side streets and shadows, Ali found herself alone, still eyeing home base from the partial cover of a fire hydrant that wouldn't ever work again. Obaid was in there, she knew, making his final sweep of the place. And as soon as he came out, she'd be ready—watching carefully where he went and heading fast the other way.

Except that when the time finally passed and something

finally did happen, it wasn't the building's main entrance that caught Ali's eye . . . and it wasn't the Khal that came creeping out into the night.

It was a little, oblong metal thing, squeezing its way through a crack in the building's base—and zooming out zigzag into the street.

"My tincher!" Ali hissed.

But immediately, her brain doubted the thought. *It isn't a tincher, Ali. It's just a . . . well, I don't know what it is. A mechanical rat, perhaps.*

She stepped closer. Hugging the wall of the building, the two pinpricks of light paced back and forth, illuminating the little face that held them and that glowed with a metallic sheen. "Have you ever even *heard* of a mechanical rat?" Ali asked herself under her breath.

Well—

"'Well,' exactly. If that's not a tincher, I don't know what it is."

Tinchers are supposed to be big, Ali thought. *Like people.*

"So it's a baby tincher!"

Also, tinchers don't exist.

She put one foot closer again. She looked down at the thing. Cautious . . . getting closer . . .

Hey, come on now. Careful, Ali!

"It doesn't really look all that dangerous . . ."

Ali, we don't know what *it looks like. How could we? We don't know* what *it is.*

And then the little thing froze, facing her, and its eyes shifted to a pale green. A soft whir droned out of it, and an irregular clicking tapped somewhere inside its head.

"It's looking at me," Ali whispered. "Do you think it likes me?"

Well, it's clearly some kind of strange machine, Ali—so, no. It doesn't. Machines don't "like" anything. They just . . . do the stuff they're programmed to do.

"But this one's strange."

Ali rolled her eyes at her own words.

"It burrowed through the *wall* to find me!"

Well, maybe burrowing is what it's programmed to do!

"Then why did it follow me outside?"

Ali was growing anxious. Scared. *How should I know?* she demanded of herself.

Ali shook her head, not taking her eyes from the thing. "Maybe I can keep it," she said aloud. "Like a pet."

A pet? You want a one-of-a-kind robotic rat for a pet?

"Well, *now* I do! Now that you put it *that* way! This thing's special! I can't just let it go!"

Aliyah. Whatever's going on tonight—it's weird. And no, not the good kind of weird. First a phantom power surge, and now this? A robot? Since when are there just robots crawling around the streets of al-Balat? Since when are there robots anywhere *at all?*

"Good point." Ali nodded. "I have to follow it."

That's not what I said!

"See where it comes from. Find out what it really is. Only *then* can I decide whether or not to keep it."

I can't keep it! There—decided!

"I wanted to put some distance between us and the Khal tonight anyway. And besides, when else after tonight will I ever have the opportunity to leave home base after hours? I could wait years before a chance like this comes around again!"

The little robot rolled off past the side of the building, out of sight. Ali followed it without questioning.

Oh, all right; okay, then. By all means, please—threaten *the cute little what-on-earth-even-is-it.*

"I'm not threatening it! It isn't scared at all!"

But when she rounded the corner, the robot turned to face her, and its glowing eyes flashed yellow, bright as day. In one mechanical reflex, it shrieked through the slits in its face, spun around on its rollerball, and launched itself straight out of sight.

ヨ

In the five years she'd lived with the Khal's family, never once had Ali dared to sneak off after curfew.

But Sarim had been right—tonight, the rules had changed.

She followed fast, and the robot fled faster—"Little Tinchi," she came to calling it—through the starless streets of al-Balat.

At night, Ali quickly realized, the Dark Lands lived up to its name. There were no working street lamps, no vehicle headlights . . . there was only Old City, the Union outpost, a mere glimmer on the horizon.

Ali stumbled over stones and trash and uneven dirt, amazed by the night's transformation of such familiar streets.

"I can't *see!*" she yelped, running as fast as she could and still not nearly able to keep up.

I know, Ali thought. *Just focus on the light from its eyes.*

It wasn't much. But hot on the trail of her one-of-a-kind, what-even-was-it robot rat, that pale blue glow was enough. Soon, she had the thing trapped, backed up into the corner of an old stone reinforcement wall at the base of one of al-Balat's many hills.

"All I want is to know what you are," Ali whispered. The little guy was motionless now but still whirred loudly as it pressed up against the rock's dead end. "I won't hurt you."

She took a step forward. There was a pause. Then in one quick should-have-seen-it-coming scramble, Little Tinchi rushed toward a wide drainpipe a short way down the wall—and vanished inside it.

Don't even think about it, Ali told herself.

But she was already on hands and knees, crawling inside.

Please, thought Responsible-Ali. *Please back out of here. We have no idea where this pipe even goes.*

"It goes under this hill," Ali said aloud, very matter-of-factly.

Yeah? And how far until it lets out, huh?

Ali didn't know the answer to that, but Little Tinchi's faint green light up ahead wasn't getting any brighter. Instinctively, she crawled farther into the narrow pipe.

Ali, we lost it, all right? It's over now. What would you even do if you caught it at this point?

"I don't know," Ali admitted to herself, already unable to turn around. "Right now I'm more worried that *it* might have just caught *me.*"

She'd been crawling for well over an hour. The tunnel was wet on the bottom where water and sewage were running, and its ribbed metal grated painfully against Ali's soaked-through hands and knees. Eventually, the whole thing opened up into al-Balat's underground drainage system, and from there Ali had an easier time of moving around. *Lucky,* she thought, to have Little Tinchi's distant glimmer ahead of her. Any less light and the blindness would have been paralyzing; any more and she'd certainly have lost her way, down here in the Maze of Dizzying Stink.

"That's what I've named it," Ali told herself rather deliriously. "The Maze of Dizzying . . ."

But her mind wasn't laughing. It wasn't even listening. The vast majority of Ali's self had long since checked out.

When she finally did see the light at the end of the tunnel, it was hard to feel much on top of her exhaustion and nausea, and anyway, she had trouble believing it. "It's not even really a light," she whispered to herself. "Just a glow."

Either way, Ali thought, *the tunnel goes up. Up* must *lead to something.* And so Ali began her gradual climb out of the maze.

The exit was through an opening just narrowly overhead, the grate of which Ali could lift only by pressing her back flush up against it and by pushing hard with her wobbly legs.

"Where am I?" she wondered as she poked up into the gloomy room above.

Another basement, her brain said mockingly. *Serves you right.*

But this wasn't just any basement. As Ali stumbled through the gray space, her hands brushed shelf after shelf of old, cobwebby medicine vials, her knees clipped boxes of surgical tools stacked up and forgotten, her feet kicked medical tablets strewn about on the floor or broken-down wheelchairs that squeaked when she hit them . . .

"I'm in a hospital," Ali mouthed. But that was impossible. The only hospital anywhere close to al-Balat was right smack in the middle of—

Ali stopped breathing all together. Even her mind went silent with fear. She'd stumbled straight into the heart of the West Bank. Union territory—right next to the biggest excavation site of all: Mount Olivet.

Its base was the source of every tincher sighting al-Balat had ever known.

4

Well, where did you expect "Little Tinchi" to lead you? The circus?

Ali's nose tingled with the promise of a terror-sob that took all of her willpower to suppress, and Sarcastic-Ali wasn't helping one bit.

"Of course not," Ali said. "But did it have to be *here*? The hospital by Mount Olivet is as haunted as haunted gets!" Even just watching it, from the Dark Land side of the West Bank fence—in *daylight!*—was a common game of chicken among the brothers. And here Ali was now, alone in its abandoned basement, in the middle of the night.

Soon, sounds became very loud. The air rushing through her nostrils, the soft *crunch* of broken glass under her feet . . . in just a few seconds Ali's own heartbeat nearly drove her crazy.

And where is Tinchi, in all of this? Where's its guiding light now? There was a narrow window high up and to her left, and through its grime came the trace of Old City light that gave the room what little glow it had . . . but that wasn't enough. Like the flip of a switch, some part of Ali all at once decided that she couldn't go on.

You're gonna die in here! that part said. *And not just any old death* *either—the horrible kind! The kind mosquitoes get in spiderwebs! The kind mice get from snakes! Because guess what—*tinchers eat people!

"No, that's just a myth," Ali whispered. "Ghost stories, like Sarim says."

But her brain fired bright, white spasms of terror, and even as she calmed herself, she felt the unbearable need to rip off her own skin before anything else could touch it. The idea of a hand on her back, or of a breeze on her neck . . . Ali was spinning now, in circles, just at the thought of it.

On the bright side, Sarcastic-Ali said, laughing above the fear, *you're still much more likely to be killed by Union guards than you are by rabid tinchers.*

So now Ali had *that* to worry about too—standing on the wrong side of the most heavily guarded fortress in the entire West Bank.

Either way, I'm beginning to think Little Tinchi has betrayed you, she continued. But just then a blue light flashed at the top of a staircase. Right on cue. Her robot was waiting.

"Tinchi?" Ali said, startled by the sound of her own call. "Tinchi, if you can understand me . . . I'm very frightened . . . كنت تخويف لي. I'd like to go home." She gestured to the drainage grate, hoping against hope that her little friend might lead her back the way they had come. To go in alone would be suicidal—but with Tinchi forging the way . . .

Nope! Another blue flash from the top of the stairs. What did it want? What *could* it want?

Was it calling for her?

Still working off instinct, Ali took a step toward it . . . but that one step was all it took for her to give in to the now uncontrollable urge to run.

And run she did, faster than she ever had in her life. Tripping over, falling over, smashing over countless barely visible medical debris, the horrible clamor of it all falling filling the air like dust.

But she made it to the stairs. She made it *up* the stairs. She followed Little Tinchi through the door into the main level hospital beyond . . .

And all at once it was clear why the Union cared so much about this dig. How the legends got their start. What a tincher really was.

In the dim light that shined through the lobby's floor-to-ceiling windows, the main level before her looked like the aftermath of a battlefield. Outlined limbs here, the highlights of a torso there, shiny heads filling the gaps in between . . . everywhere—in piles, even—the rusted bodies of big, broken robots littering the room. Bigger than Ali. Bigger than the Khal. Like the stories said.

Ali had just started to cry when Little Tinchi darted from one end of the gray space to another, purring strangely and knocking Ali out of her idle terror. She jumped, letting out a yelp, and as soon as the sound left her mouth, Ali knew she'd made a mistake. Instantly, the floor in front of her began writhing, began crawling with dozens—*dozens*—of Little Tinchis, whatever they were, each now suddenly visible as they scuttled about and flashed countless reflections in the windows' dim light.

Oh, Ali thought distantly, too overwhelmed for any reaction beyond that. *So it's infested with them.*

And they brushed up against her legs and rolled fast over her feet. And the original Tinchi whistled to them with sounds like from some strange birdcall, bleeps and bloops and an unhummable melody. And the others called back in response, and—

FLASH!

The whole room exploded in blue light from all of them at once.

"I'm blind," Ali whispered. But the afterimage of the lobby burned hot into her eyes, and in it, she could see them, these broken tinchers, revealed in every shape and size and model. Some had wheels for feet; others had legs. Some were box-like, with what passed for a face sticking right out their fronts; others had human-like heads atop human-like shoulders above human-like bodies. Some were big, spherical things with several long arms sticking out in all directions, like soccer balls that liked to cartwheel instead of roll. Others looked equipped with hover technology, like a fleet of tiny flying saucers with claws for heads.

Ali saw all of this behind closed eyelids, as a moment in time captured by the Tinchi flash and lingering in her vision.

But then the picture faded. And Ali opened her eyes.

And all of those dead, disassembled tinchers . . . were moving.

5

"They're awake."

"That's impossible."

"First the power surge in al-Balat, and now this?"

"But it's *impossible*."

Among the International Moderators of Peace, guard posts along the Union's many Dark Land dig sites had long ago become a running joke within the ranks. Can't fire a taser-rifle? Guard a dig site! Can't follow basic instructions? Guard a dig site! Can't tie your bootlaces? Guard a few of 'em!

For years, IMP brass all the way to the top had insisted that these Eurasian excavations were important, were *vital*, even, to the future of the Union. But their reasons always managed somehow to be "classified," or "top secret," or on a "need-to-know" basis, and eventually the Moderators pieced together their own answer. The fact was, in a time of global government and total peace, there just wasn't much *use* anymore for a standing army. Even the American protests—which did end up getting pretty dicey last spring—even *those* were all but over now that the American balance of power had been transferred to Chancellor Cylis. The peace had been moderated, the last of the two nations had merged, and now Cylis was left with an enormous pile of IMPS and practically nothing to do with them.

Hence the guard posts. Recently, there'd been a huge uptick in the number of Moderators stationed at these dig sites, tasked with guarding, as they saw it, prewar technology that wasn't even functional from Dark Landers too superstitious and scared of it to come close in the first place.

"So then how do you explain *this?*" asked a Mount Olivet Moderator as his fellow guards stared slack-jawed at their wallscreen security feed.

"These tinchers haven't worked since before the Total War," said another. "Our engineers can't even *get* them to work. Shoot—they can't even figure out how these tinchers *ever* worked—and now after a fifty-year nap the miserly things all just *wake up?*"

The first guard had already placed his video call into headquarters while the others began trying to look busy. "That's right. Working condition, sir," he was saying a few minutes later to the Coordinator on the other end of the line. "All on their own, just all of a sudden—"

"Moderator—Moderator!" A third guard leaned back in his

chair, tugging on the sleeve of the first but staring, still transfixed, at the screen.

"*What?*" the first said, gesturing to his call-in-progress and irritated by the interruption.

"A girl. There's a *girl* in there with them."

"One of ours?"

The third squinted at the security feed. "Dark Lander. Unmarked."

"Run facial recognition on the video," the second Moderator said while the first relayed this turn of events to his superior over the call connection.

"I'm on hold," the first said. "Would you believe this? Headquarters put me on hold. *Now*, of all times, I tell you . . ."

But soon enough the reason was clear. When the connection returned, the IMP who stepped into the call frame was not the Coordinator from before. He was a Champion—the second highest position ever yet reached among the Controlling Ranks. Every young Moderator at the dig site jumped up to attention just at the sight of him.

"Leave the girl be," the Champion said. "Chain of command wants to see what comes of this. Whether she's connected to these events, who she might be working with if so . . . that sort of thing."

"But I could have her in custody, on a bus leaving for headquarters, in thirty minutes' time."

"Negative. Whatever she's up to, we aren't yet eager to stop it."

"Sir, she's trespassing on Union property . . . She just witnessed a classified turn of events—"

"And she very well may *also* have just handed our Union its most promising technological victory since the invention of the Mark."

"She doesn't exactly look like an engineer," the Moderator said. "She more just looks . . . lost."

"Any clues yet as to who she is? Anything coming back from facial recognition?"

"Negative. Her face is in the system, sir . . . but she's without a name."

The Champion nodded over the call. "Moderators," he said, "keep an eye on this one. Top brass thinks we may have just found ourselves a mastermind."

ᖾ

Mastermind-Ali couldn't even breathe through the snot of her own terrified sobs. She couldn't see through her own goopy tears. What she could *feel* were the cold, strong hands of a dozen different tincher arms, all grabbing her ankles and legs. Many of these hands were severed, moving on their own. Halfway to the entrance, a long set of skeletal fingers even managed to clasp onto her foot—to wrap all the way around—and Ali actually dragged its twitching, disconnected arm halfway across the lobby.

She was running for the exit.

She was sorry she'd ever come here.

She wanted never to look back.

By the exit, one particularly well-preserved tincher propped its own torso up on two shaking arms, its head spinning curiously and its eyes glowing red, and it pulled its legless body directly into Ali's path. "مرحبا يا عالم،" it said in a voice that sounded something like teeth grinding inside a megaphone.

And Ali yelled "لا!" as part of some kind of reflex that even she couldn't control, and she dodged the thing and pushed her way through the heavy hospital doors.

Confused, hysterical, unbelieving, she scrambled through the brown-green grass, straight up over the barbed-wire fence, and into the streets of al-Balat, where she hurried back to her family so deliriously thankful to be alive that she didn't even think twice about why in the world the Global Union gatekeepers hadn't bothered to follow.

THREE

THE TOTER OF LIGHT

□

A ROAD THAT STRETCHED FOREVER THROUGH farmland and untended rice paddies. White wood-slat houses with nuclear shadows on the sides; the gray silhouettes of men and women and children long since blinked out of existence.

The visitor walked through countryside not seen by living eyes in fifty years. Over concrete grew thick moss and grass. Over buildings grew ivy and weeds.

He arrived in the Chinese Dark Lands alone. But he would not be alone for long.

Beijing. Abandoned city. Capital of the tinchers. They had called him here. They had brought him all this way.

They poked their heads from buildings cracked in two. From behind rubble and trees. Glowing eyes in the shadows.

Silently, they led their visitor onward. South. Where his journey would continue—with them.

He counted the long days, no longer alone. He pressed on, tinchers at his sides.

Toward the girl without a name.

Together, they would find her.

Together, they would reach her.

And everything else was only a distraction.

1

That night Ali dreamed. She dreamed even from the inside of the closet, even though her sleep was short, and fitful, and light.

"It'll be best this way," Ali told herself as she snuck into the still-evacuated home base. "To spend the night in there in case the Khal does a sweep."

Yeah, Sarcastic-Ali agreed. *After all, if the Khal found out you left the closet last night, he might get mad and do something horrible—like force you to climb through a sewer and have you fight a bunch of tinchers!*

But Ali didn't listen. By that point, the cramped, locked-away space sounded comfortable anyway. Hidden. Quiet. Safe.

She dreamed even as she tossed, even as she sat with her eyes half open, as her feet went numb and tingly from the way she was sitting. It was a dream so vivid that sleep wouldn't contain it, no matter how many times she woke.

"Mom?" she called. "Mother?"

Ali was four years old again. She sat on the ground and played games, and this was a fun one, she remembered. One she played often because there weren't many others to play.

She called it the "storm game." In the game, the walls came alive. But where was Mother?

At that age, the two of them were together always. Alone, always, the two of them, Ali remembered now, in their one-room shanty made of scraps. "Smart" scraps, Mother always joked.

Scavenged from older, grander buildings once filled with fancy pre-Unity tech.

In her dream, Ali was sitting among those scraps, as arc lightning launched and slid between corners, lighting the space and casting stark, dusty shadows around and behind her. Ali waved her hands through that light and watched the crackling threads rush to follow, dangerous blue sparks dancing and filling the empty air and smelling of ozone and blinding Ali like the sun. Where did they come from? How was she controlling them?

Ali stopped playing, and immediately her one-room home was dim and quiet and still. There was nothing inside it. The only light came from gaps between the stacked plastic and sheet metal and boards that made up the four walls and ceiling surrounding her. Flies came in as easily as the sun.

Where was Mother?

Most times, while Ali played, Mother would kneel, praying in the corner, asking God for help, for food, for comfort, for a better life for her daughter . . . She would tell Ali stories from the Bible, reciting passages she had memorized with great care, since Mother could barely read its pages herself.

But today, Mother was nowhere to be found. And Ali was alone—and scared.

In the distance, Ali heard the bleating of her town's goat, its bell clanging as it roamed the maze of narrow walkways between chain-link fences and makeshift shacks. Somewhere, a wagon squeaked. Tired footsteps pattered over hard-packed clay.

"هل أنت هناك؟" Mother asked from outside. Ali scrambled up and brushed the dirt from her legs. "يوجد رجل هنا."

So that's where Mother was! Ali remembered now, so clearly, dreaming it all as though it were urgent and *here*. Ali pushed the heavy curtain aside—it was her home's front door—and squinted up at her mother and at the tall, thick man beside her.

He was a stranger. Not of their caste. His features were dark and unclear against the blinding backlight of the day, but his bright, tasseled robes, fine boots, and headdress meant he could only have come from the city, al-Balat. Ali's eyes adjusted, and she peered over that man's shoulder. At the horizon, looming beyond the shanty rooftops and poking through a thick haze of smog, al-Balat's colorful towers and buildings framed the sky even at this great distance.

Already, the man was holding Ali's arm so hard that it hurt. Mother's eyes widened as she saw this, but she said nothing yet.

"She's starving," the man said, leaning over and wrapping one hand around Ali's leg. He spoke in Union English; back then, Ali understood none of it.

"Yes," Mother replied in the same foreign tongue that frightened Ali to hear. "But she is smart, I think—smarter than anyone—and mature for her age."

The man scoffed, both at the statement and at Mother's thick accent. He was bargaining. "She's too young."

"She's four."

"She's weak."

"She can work."

The man paused, his mouth turning down.

"She will be pretty . . . ," Mother said.

"Hard to see in this filth."

The man was kneeling now, examining Ali's face, his thumb and index finger pinching her chin and turning it side to side, but she was concentrating on the skyline in the distance.

Eventually, the man saw her eyes, and the conversation halted.

"I can take you there," he said, following her gaze. "Do you see that building? That tall one just under the clouds?" He pointed.

Mother frowned. "She only speaks Darklandese. Arabic dialect."

"I know." He stood now. "For her, I'll give you a lamb."

"She's worth more than that, and you know it."

The man tightened his lips and raised an eyebrow knowingly. "Food for many months." He waved a bill in his hand. "I have the deed right here."

Mother stared at them. As a gesture of goodwill the man pulled a coin from a fold in his robes. "Plus, whatever you can trade for this."

"It's not enough."

"There are plenty of girls in these settlements."

"I haven't heard of any offers," Mother said.

"Nor have they heard yours. I work in discretion."

"But she is special."

"You are her mother——"

"She is *special*! I don't say it as a mother. I say it as a person who can *see*. The things she can do . . ."

The man shrugged. "So you say." He kicked at the dirt with his foot. "But I don't believe in magic."

Mother crossed her arms, standing straight and defiant.

"Okay. I will throw in two hens." He pocketed the coin and replaced it with two more deeds, splaying their papers with the other across his fingers. "They're healthy. Many eggs."

Now Ali was not so distant. It took none of these words to see what was happening. She shrieked, falling into her mother's legs, wrapping her arms tightly around them, squeezing, holding on, pleading.

"امى! احبك! رجاء! لا تدع هذا الرجل خذنى منك. لا اريد ان اذهب! لا دعنى اذهب! امى! رجاء!"

A few tears rolled down Mother's red face, but she would not embrace Ali.

"هذا الرجل سوف نعتني بك."she whispered."هذا هو أفضل شيء بالنسبة لنا،"

And Mother pocketed the man's deeds.

"لا!الأم!لا " Ali yelled, but Mother only lifted Ali and handed her to the man and allowed him to hold her so tightly that she couldn't even squirm.

"Your mother says you are special," the man whispered as he turned away from the only family Ali had ever known. "And yet she sold you for a lamb."

But as the man walked with Ali through that quiet settlement in the shadows of al-Balat, something special did happen.

All those shanties lining the walkway . . . all those cobbled-together heaps of "smart" scraps and trash . . . they started to glow. Softly, as though each was mourning the loss. There was a hum in the air. The settlement was lit when she left it.

Aliyah, the Toter of Light.

That's what they had called her, the people in that town.

Ali couldn't feel her feet, and she stared ahead now, eyes open, still seeing the moment flicker like a projection so clearly on the closet door.

Was it memory or was it dream?

She didn't know.

But the town glowed for *her*.

2

"Pretty-Ali," the Khala said. "I can't believe this. Pretty-Ali— were you locked in this closet *all night?*" Morning had broken. In the daylight of the alleyway, Nafia finally must have noticed the sister's absence; when she unlocked the closet door, she was panting as though she'd run here.

"Yes," Ali said innocently. "Why? Did something happen?"

"*Happen?*" the Khala said. "We *evacuated!*" She looked at Ali pitifully. She ran her hands down Ali's shoulders and arms and legs, checking for injuries or signs of pain in the young girl's eyes. Nothing major it seemed, save for the bruises on Ali's knees and the swollen, cracked cuts on the palms of her hands. Nothing unexpected, really.

"How scary," Ali said, holding her words close. "But I'm all right. I won't miss quota again."

Just a few hours later, Ali found Sarim in his usual spot, weaving his way through the back of the New Gate's customs line and laughing with the merchants as they handed him all the spare coins and food and trinkets they could muster.

"Sarim," she said. "Sarim, they're not a myth."

Sarim smiled falsely at her, still in show mode and mostly paying attention to the merchants around them.

"They're real."

"What's real?" the boy asked, refusing to engage with her urgency. "In case you haven't noticed, I'm on a bit of a roll here." He stuffed a handful of goods into Ali's empty pockets.

"The tinchers. I saw them. They're real. I *saw* them, Sarim."

"Real like the one in the closet last night? Real the way that one was real?" Still he was smiling, too aware of the merchants around them. Ali was a prop in his begging act.

"Stop that," she said. "And pay attention to me. Little Tinchi—"

"*Little Tinchi?*"

"That's what I named him. I know he left by the time you had a look, but he was *there*. I wasn't just crazy. And last night, after you and Nafia and all the other siblings had fallen asleep outside . . . he took me to the mount."

"Mount Olivet? Middle of the West Bank, *that* mount?"

"Yes!" Ali hissed, pulling him toward her and speaking close into his ear.

"That's interesting," Sarim said. "Because the Khala told me you spent the night in the closet."

"Yes. That's where she found me." Ali smiled mischievously. "It's my alibi, Sarim. Pretty smart, huh?"

"I looked *everywhere* for you, when I saw you weren't with us in the gutter last night. You *worried* me, Ali. I told you not to stay in that building last night."

"I didn't! I'm telling you—I was over by Mount Olivet! I only came back in the morning."

"And in the meantime, you saw real live living tinchers inside heavily fortified Union territory that 'Little Tinchi' just somehow managed to sneak you both into and out of."

"No, not out of," Ali corrected. "I snuck out myself."

Sarim raised an eyebrow. "Was it scary?" he asked.

"*Scary?*" Ali couldn't believe the question. "Sarim—it was *terrifying*! I thought I would die!"

Sarim dropped the faint smile. He turned to her, finally, paying her the attention she deserved. "You had a nightmare, Ali. Your fear of the Khal drove you back into that closet, against all your better judgment; you fell asleep feeling scared, and you had a bad dream. It happens, Ali. It's no big deal."

"It wasn't a dream!" Ali yelled, insulted even by the suggestion. "I *did* have a dream, after. When I got back. But it wasn't about tinchers at all!"

"Oh yeah?" Sarim asked. "So what was that one about?"

"It was about . . . it was about controlling electricity," Ali said. "About the day my mom sold me. A memory I haven't thought of in years . . . the town I lived in—Sarim, they called me the Toter of Light!"

Sarim laughed as though the whole thing were a joke, and Ali threw her hands up, frustrated. "Well? Do I have to spell it out for you? Sarim—what if *I* caused last night's power surge? What if the lights turned on because of *me*?"

"Do I have to tell you what put *that* idea into your head too?"

"There is no 'too'!" Ali hollered. "The tinchers weren't a nightmare! And no, the evacuation didn't 'put' ideas into my head. It *jogged* my *memory*! There's a big difference!"

"Ali No Name, the Toter of Light."

"Exactly!"

"And you think this means . . . what?"

Ali shrugged.

"Look. If a bunch of tinchers really had come alive last night, then why aren't they walking around outside of that hospital this morning? And if you really were trespassing in Union territory, then why didn't the Union guards arrest you?"

"I . . . I don't know."

"It was a rough night, Ali," Sarim allowed. He put his hand on her shoulder. "But let's not turn it into something it wasn't, okay? You have enough on your plate without dreaming up superpowers."

Hearing him say it in so many words knocked the wind out of

her real quick. Ali's story *did* sound ridiculous. And it really *was* a traumatic night, just all on its own.

Could it be? Ali thought. *Could it be I really did dream the whole thing?*

She felt the bruises on her knees. Looked at the cuts on her hands.

From the tunnels, she told herself. *From crawling through the Maze of Dizzying Stink.*

"Or from banging against the closet door," she whispered aloud. "From sleeping with my knees up against the wall . . ."

"What's that?" Sarim asked.

"Nothing," Ali said, gazing distantly at the ground. "Just checking in with reality."

"Feels good, doesn't it?" Sarim laughed. And he made her pockets heavy with all the alms he didn't need.

ㅌ

It was easy to keep quiet after that about the whole thing, from the sewers to the mount . . . all of it. Sarim was right to doubt her, Ali figured. And maybe she was right to doubt herself ever since.

Weeks passed. The family returned to home base, the lights stayed off, Little Tinchi didn't come back to visit, and Ali's "family" life was business as usual.

In the beginning, Ali and Sarim acted as though nothing had changed between them. They'd walk the streets of al-Balat, perhaps a little farther than normal from the Union walls and Union guards, and they'd beg together, quietly, humbly. Between them, they'd scrape by. Make quota each day by the skin of their teeth.

But without any incident, without any trouble . . . And Ali stopped talking about tinchers, and she never again mentioned the "Toter of Light." For his part, Sarim pretended the whole thing never happened—not the evening and not the conversation they'd had the morning after.

But Ali couldn't play so innocent forever. Things *had* changed for her.

Eventually, it got so that it didn't even *matter* whether or not Ali's brush with the tinchers was real, or whether her shantytown ever actually glowed for her or not. Because one way or another, these things were all Ali could think about. And even if that did spring from some made-up delusion, it didn't really change the bottom line: for all the times he'd helped her with quota, for all the times over the years that he'd pulled her out of a jam, Ali's own best friend, Sarim, had ignored her cries for help just exactly when she needed him the most.

No.

Worse than ignored, Ali thought.

Rejected.

And ever since, it had been harder and harder to look that kid in the eye.

So over time, Ali receded. Receded from Sarim, receded from all of her brothers and sisters . . .

At any other time in her life, this would have bothered her. Would have devastated her, in fact. But the truth was, over these last few months in particular, Ali found herself preoccupied with something even weightier than the loss of her friends: the possibility that maybe she actually was the Toter of Light after all. In any case, she didn't really feel alone.

More and more, she would walk down streets and stuff would

just . . . happen. Automatically. In the bright, hot hours of the day. She'd grow tired of walking, and on cue, defunct sidewalk treads would move for her, would take her all the way back to home base. She'd shiver some nights, in the earliest hours when the air was cold, and out of nowhere, broken radiators would clamor on. The floor would heat up. Warm air would blow fast from out-of-service vents . . .

By the end of the summer, little odds and ends everywhere seemed merely an extension of Ali's faintest desires. She'd look longingly at busted-up pre–Dark Land vending machines, and suddenly packaged food fifty years old would spit out and land at her feet. Pedestrians would pass by, and their Union-traded jewelry would just snap off and fall to the ground. Would just lie there, for Ali to grab. "I think you dropped this," Ali would say, handing the pieces back to their owners. And they'd take it, graciously—"Thank you, thank you," and all of that—but when they'd go to put the things back on-the blasted clasps wouldn't even work. One time, in exasperation, a woman just shook her head and gave the broken necklace back to Ali. When Ali tried it on, it fastened at once.

It felt like something or someone was looking out for Ali. Taking care of her and making sure things were okay for her. Which is why she didn't feel alone, even though she'd never felt further from her "family." *It couldn't all be in her head . . . right?*

Ali frowned. *You have enough on your plate without dreaming up superpowers*, she said to herself, remembering Sarim's words one night before drifting off to sleep.

But the fact was that these days, when Ali dreamed, it wasn't of superpowers at all. It was of average days and non-events. The fact was that the superpowers were what happened when Ali woke up.

She was thinking about that as she tried to drift off to sleep, sisters all around her, brothers all above, everyone asleep, when Union soldiers like none any of them had ever seen stormed the building and changed the course of Ali's life forever.

4

This can't be happening.

"This can't be happening!"

Ali abandoned her sleeping mat the moment she heard the first noises from below. It was her own luck that she hadn't yet fallen asleep. When the Union made its move, she'd been ready without even knowing it.

There was a fake fern in the hallway outside the sisters' quarters on the fifteenth floor, and Ali hid behind it now, thankful to be as small and malnourished as she was. She watched as nearly everyone she'd ever really known was pulled kicking and screaming through the door, down the stairs, and out to the shuttles waiting on the street.

Who were these people? Why were they here? It was clear they were Union, but a Union raid in the Dark Lands was unheard of. Their uniforms read "IMPS—International Moderators of Peace," but Ali couldn't read that, and even if she could, she wouldn't have been in on the joke; there was nothing peaceful about what she was seeing.

Why were they here? To shut down Obaid's business? Ali knew the Old City guards hated the brother and sister "splinters" always hanging around the gate. Maybe the family of them finally pushed it too far.

But the truth was that Ali didn't *want* saving from the Khal and the Khala. It was a hard life under them, perhaps, by some standards, Ali guessed . . . but it was *her* life. It was *Ali's*. It was what she knew. And she didn't exactly love the idea of some group of mogul strangers coming in and taking all that away, even if by Union standards it might have been in Ali's best interest to do so.

Because frankly, Ali didn't *care* about Union standards. She cared about *splinter* standards. She cared about Sarim, and Nafia, and her brothers and sisters, and yes, even Obaid. And who was the Union to put an end to all of that?

But then she heard the words, spat hideously from these ugly IMP mouths, that shook her to her core.

"Double down!" the one called Advocate yelled. "Block the stairs! Do a sweep! Not one of these splinters matters except the girl without a name! This doesn't end until we find her!"

And Ali shrunk into the leaves of the fake plastic plant.

It was all her fault.

These IMPS were here for *Ali*, the nine-year-old girl trapped behind a fern with no way out.

So think of one! Ali screamed in her head. *Find a way! Escape! Don't give up!*

"Help," she whispered so quietly she almost couldn't hear the word. "Please, help me."

And just then, in the midst of all this chaos, in the middle of this suffocating revelation and guilt and all the tragedy and upheaval and panic that surrounded it, a single, perplexing *ding* rang out above all, grabbing Ali's attention by the hair and pulling hard behind her.

She turned. At the end of the hall, the elevator light shined a patient, quiet yellow.

"Impossible . . . ," she whispered. That elevator had never worked, not a single day of Ali's life. Could it be that now, in the one moment she needed it most, it had finally decided to run?

Ali slinked back toward it, wondering desperately how she was supposed to work the thing—until its doors opened automatically in front of her. She looked up at that yellow light. Still shining, just for her.

"This is crazy," Ali said.

But Ali's mind asked, *Is it?*

Once inside, the elevator doors closed on their own. All around her, on every floor, in every level of the stairwell, everyone Ali had ever known was being attacked, berated, dragged off into the night . . . and then there was her, standing peacefully in this quiet, closed space that wasn't supposed to open—that *didn't* open—for anyone else. It made Ali feel guilty to think of it.

Why me? she wondered. Why did she deserve such special treatment? And who—or what—was offering it in the first place?

"Is this thing safe?" Ali asked aloud. "Do you work?"

Great, Ali. Now you're talking to a building.

And yet, on cue, the elevator dinged again.

"Why now, all of a sudden?" Ali whispered. "What's going on?"

To her right, an emergency light blinked red.

"Yeah, I know this is an emergency, that's not my—" Ali stopped herself, waving her arms frantically. "How are you able to understand me?"

Again, the elevator only dinged.

"Do you *want* something from me? Is that it? I've no idea what you even *are*." She'd passed that elevator every day, but she'd never once seen it work. She'd never even been told what to expect if it ever did. And now here it was, *communicating* with her.

In response to her question, the elevator played soft, jazzy music, timed oddly to the pulse of the flashing red emergency light, and Ali threw up her arms in exasperation. "Great," she said. "You're a closet that plays music."

But as soon as she said it, the elevator began moving, lowering slowly, quietly, so as not to attract the attention of the IMPS who would never think to listen for it.

"You're like stairs!" Ali said, suddenly very excited. "Stairs where these IMPS won't find me—you're helping me escape!"

The elevator continued its descent.

"Are you working with the tinchers?" Ali asked. "Is that how you know me?" It was a shot in the dark, but surely *something* must have been connecting all of this madness. "How do I know this isn't a trap? How do I know these guards won't be waiting for me the second this elevator door opens?"

Between floors, the elevator came to a gentle halt.

"What, you're gonna time it correctly? That's the plan?"

The elevator dinged cheerfully.

"Well, how will I know what to do once we get to the bottom?"

In a wave, the individual floor buttons lit up and went dark again, like a little spark traveling through space.

And then the elevator stopped. It went quiet, its music cutting off. For several breaths, its doors remained shut.

And then they opened. The lobby was clear.

5

Ali stepped one, two, three times toward the building's front door before stopping short. Guards. Just outside, heading back in.

What now? she wondered, when to her right, a door she'd never before used caught her attention out of the corner of her eye. *How odd*, she thought, until she realized: its " خروج " sign was lit.

In this building, still supposedly very much without electricity, there is a glowing red sign above a doorway that I'd never think to use.

Ali hesitated. Is this what the elevator meant when it flashed its row of lights? That it would guide her? Like this?

No better way to find out, Ali thought, hurrying toward the door.

But too slow! The sign flashed angrily for a moment—*angrily? really? could that be right?*—and then turned off abruptly before Ali could open the door. *In frustration?*

No, that's impossible.

So Ali opened the door . . .

. . . and the second she did, a guard storming past caught sight of her face.

It was possible! Ali told herself, and immediately she turned, dragging the door closed behind her and praying it would lock. But now they'd seen her. Guards at the front called out, diverting attention, flooding in through the main entrance, closing in from all sides.

No room for doubt, Ali realized. *If you're gonna trust the signs, you need to* trust *the signs.*

"I'm sorry," she whispered. "But now what?"

And so, seconds later, a sign marking the woman's bathroom flickered on.

This time Ali pounced.

Across the atrium and barely at all ahead of the guards, Ali darted, as fast as she could. The sound of bare feet slapping tile echoed sharply across the space.

"I hope you're sure about this," Ali whispered to whatever

guardian it was she now had. She threw open the bathroom door without hesitation.

Dead end. Could it be she'd been led astray?

There was a window at the end of the small room, just past the stalls and next to the sink. Ali ran to it and opened it. "Is this what you mean?" she asked aloud.

As soon as she did, a single fluorescent ceiling light flashed above a toilet stall—on and off, just like that—three in from the end of the row. It seemed crazy. But she reacted on instinct. Ali dashed over to it, entering the stall and swinging its door shut behind her. She stood on the toilet seat, crouched down, and held her breath.

Right on cue, IMP guards barged into the room. The line of them ran to the open window. Ali could hear one of them lean out over the edge.

"She must have gone this way," he said. "Call the others. Target is out of the building. I repeat—target is out of the building, on foot, likely traveling northwest."

"We'll do a sweep," another said.

And the squad of them hurried out of the room, leaving Ali in the dark.

Moments later, just next to the bathroom door, an electric hand drier turned on.

Ali smiled. *Could it be I'm getting the hang of this?*

She followed the sound to the door and back out.

Again in the atrium, the building's main entrance slid open on its own. It was bold, Ali knew, exiting from the front. She'd never have had the guts to do it on her own.

But Ali *wasn't* on her own, she realized all at once, and with all the confidence she could muster, she raced out that front door, not thinking, not second-guessing, just out—fast—into the night.

Ƅ

Outside, al-Balat was swarming with IMPS. Across the street from home base, long shuttles filled with Ali's family were shipping out, headed toward who-knew-where. But Ali had made it past all that. And so far, nobody seemed to know.

The first few blocks in, Ali fled blindly, without a plan, without a goal. She'd made it past the worst of the raid, but what other squads were waiting for her out on these empty streets? And where could she possibly go now?

Ali had to laugh when a street lamp up ahead blinked impossibly on. Lighting the way—a miracle reaching out to her through the dark.

For miles, Ali ran, the powerless city guiding her all the way, keeping her on her toes, keeping her always one step ahead of the sweeping IMPS on patrol. They should have caught her by now. They should have found her, at least. But wherever the lights blinked, the coast was clear.

The Toter of Light. She was going to make it. She was going to escape.

Ali followed that bouncing spark all the way to the city's edge before she realized the truth.

Whatever this guiding light was, it wasn't leading her to safety.

She stood, breathless, hands clasped against the chain links of the fence before her. Up at the base of Mount Olivet, a single window in the hospital flickered its call.

"I can't do it," Ali whispered. "I can't go back there. I can't . . ."

It was hard to say how long she stood outside that fence. Five minutes? Ten?

When the IMPS finally caught her, she didn't even put up a fight.

FOUR

REFUGEE

1

"PASSPORTS, PHONE, CASH—ENOUGH TO GET us there. Blanket for Dom. Water . . ."

"I've printed food for each of us."

"Anything else?"

Lydia scanned the room. "Just this, I guess." Next to the dresser, a photo had fallen to the floor, free from the shattered frame that once held it. She picked up the print and folded it twice before sliding it into her pocket. "Andre—don't," she began, turning to see her husband pull a small shoe box out from the back of their emptied closet. "If we're caught with that—"

"I'm not worried about what happens if we're caught with this," Andre said. He opened the box and lifted an old revolver out from inside. "I'm worried about what happens if we're caught without it."

Lydia sighed and watched him slip the handgun under his belt. He kissed her and, for a moment, she wasn't scared. Together, they turned and grabbed Dom from his crib.

"Think he'll remember this place?" Andre asked.

Lydia opened the front door. The sun was rising blue and

salmon pink over the houses across the street, and it was easy to see because most of the roofs had caved in. "I hope not," she said. "I wouldn't wish that upon anyone."

२

The trip from Greece to Switzerland was twenty-nine hours by bus, and baby Dom Baros cried the whole time. His mother tried to quiet him with hugs and milk. His father bounced him on his knee. Nothing worked.

It wasn't that the crying was out of place. Beyond the tinted windows passed two thousand kilometers of desolation and battle scars; *someone* had to cry about it, if none of the grown-ups would.

Instead, it was the look—the look in little Dom Baros's watery eyes, one not of sadness or fear—but of frustration.

"If I didn't know any better," said one of the other refugees from a seat across the aisle, "I'd say your little boy there actually looks *upset* to be leaving all this devastation and suffering behind. Like he's actually going to *miss* it."

"Don't you know how lucky you are?" another kind refugee said, leaning forward from the seat behind them and bopping little Dom Baros on his red, runny button nose. "Why, right now you're the luckiest boy in all of Europe! The luckiest one!"

But as she said it, baby Dom looked at her with such a cold, hard stare that she had to wonder if maybe he *did* know. If maybe he was angry anyway. Not because he had seen too much suffering already—but because he hadn't seen *enough*. Because he was being *removed* from it—*deprived* of it—in all his years to come.

The refugee sat back in her seat and didn't say another word to the Baros family that whole trip. No one did.

And little Dom cried on.

The Total War had not yet begun—was not yet imaginable, really— but already Europe's refugee program was three years old. In the decades leading up to the war, flooding from climate change had stripped Greece of nearly all its coastal cities, and what land remained was overcrowded, ugly, and barren.

The first thing this led to was countrywide unrest—mainly aimed at politicians who remained untouchable anyway. But when the government couldn't be bothered to act, all that public anger quickly turned toward an upper class that'd largely managed to avoid the countrywide hardship. Eventually, the whole house of cards came down when someone threw a bomb through the bedroom window of one of the last standing houses in central Athens, just to watch it burn.

"Ας γίνει γνωστό!" the man shouted as the Hellenic Police Force shot rubber bullets and as reporters scrambled to translate for the world to hear. "Δεν υπάρχουν πλέον κλειδωμένες πόρτες στην Ελλάδα!"

And on news outlets everywhere, the headlines let it be known: "There will be no more locked doors in Greece." Not after so many had lost their homes. Not with so many now out on the streets. What houses remained were to be opened and shared with those in need—or they were to be destroyed by the very same. The have-nots had had enough. And the haves had it coming.

Lydia and Andre Baros were newlyweds at the time. Andre was a customs officer at the Athens International Airport; Lydia was unemployed and looking for work. But they'd recently saved enough money to rent a small home in Melissia, just north of the city and far enough inland to avoid the floods.

Within a week of the news, they had thirty strangers sleeping on the floors of every room of that house. Within a month, those strangers were angry and edgy. In two more, the Baros's neighbors had established a defensive militia. Within six, all of Greece was in full-on street-riot warfare, right alongside Italy, Croatia, Albania, and Montenegro, as well as much of Spain, Portugal, France, the United Kingdom . . . And within a year, all of Europe had no choice but to come together and design the refugee program that had been in place ever since. The Coastal Displacement Act, or CoDA, it was called, was a program whereby survivors signed up to be shipped off to safety camps in the few remaining peaceful countries inland.

The Baroses, of course, applied for relocation the moment it became available. In fact, they applied for it every week. And every week they were overlooked. CoDA acceptance and placement was assigned through lottery systems strictly randomized by a central-ized computer program. And space for refugees became available only rarely, as inland countries were reluctant to open their bor-ders nearly as wide as they'd have to for all of Europe's survivors to find a spot. Time after time, the Baros family number just didn't come up.

By the second year of this, Lydia and Andre had their son, and they just couldn't seem to catch a break.

"I won't give him a name," Lydia said, when the child first was born. "Not until I know he'll live long enough to learn it."

But he *did* live long enough. In fact, over time, the young

Baros boy proved so resilient that his parents began to wonder if he was charmed.

It was a perverse sort of luck, to be sure. The kind that's hard to see until all is said and done. On one night, for instance, when the boy was just six weeks old, a mob of raiders swept clean every remaining occupied home in Melissia. They came without warning, and they broke down the doors of any house that still showed signs of life.

But it just so happened that this very afternoon, while Lydia was heating a bath for her boy, the hot water heater in the Baroses' basement blew a fuse, and their home was left totally without power—a turn of events that had Lydia furious for the first few hours, and thankful ever since: it was that freak power outage that camouflaged the Baros family from the murderous mob.

Thus began the Baros boy's curious streak of ongoing misfortunes that somehow never failed to save his life.

Another time, soon after all flights to and from Greece had been grounded permanently and the airport itself had closed up shop for good, an out-of-work Andre took his starving son on a midday stroll down their neighborhood block, just to take his mind off the hunger. While they were out, an abandoned house burned up in an electrical fire the moment he and Dom passed it by, killing the family inside.

Terrible luck. So it seemed.

The next day, when that fire died down, Andre was the first to look through the rubble of its burned-up basement . . . and found a 3-D additive printer with enough unspent materials to print food paste for the family for a year. Without Andre's paychecks, that abandoned printer was the only reason the Baroses didn't starve.

All because of the walk he had taken with his son and that other family's misfortune.

Eventually, Lydia came to realize that her little boy wasn't so close to death after all. Despite all the odds, he was growing up. And he was growing up strong.

"Dominic," she said one night to Andre, out of the blue, while bouncing their baby on her knee. "That's what we'll name him." A nice Roman Catholic name that meant literally "of our Lord," as a reminder of the parents' gratitude to God for their survival.

Six months later the CoDA refugee program was ending for good. The receiving countries were so full by that point that even *they* were starting to feel the strain of so many homeless and poor, and the threat of civil war that it brought. Week one hundred and forty-eight of the lottery was to be CoDA's last ever, meaning one more round of buses through the suburbs of Athens—and that was *it*.

When Lydia applied, for the one hundred and forty-eighth time in a row, she made sure to take Dom with her. Her "lucky charm," she called him, and three days later she was proven right. Little Dominic's family was the last that lottery system ever chose.

"So why are you crying?" Andre asked his son, one day later on that final, packed, rolling CoDA bus. Although he didn't really expect an answer. "When again and again and again, the world has sacrificed to give you a chance, even in the face of so much death? Isn't that enough for you, little Dom?"

And if it wasn't . . . what *was*?

Two short hours later Dominic and his family arrived through the gates of his new barbed-wire community, with Dom still scowling, howling, and thrashing in the arms of his loving parents, his whole charmed life left to live.

∃

On his thirteenth birthday, Dom Baros spent the early morning hours in the shared backyard of his CoDA home, under the shade of his northeast quadrant's only tree, sketching the sunrise over the mountains beyond the campground's chain-link fence.

"You almost ready for school?" his father asked, plopping down in the dirt beside him. Dom hadn't heard the old man walk out. He turned to him, smiling, and his father, Andre, was relieved. The two of them hadn't gotten along well in years.

"I have some time yet," Dom said, and he turned his notebook so his father could see. After a moment of silence, he asked, "You don't like it?"

"I like it," Andre told him. But he stared too long at its cross-hatched lines.

"I can't draw trees well," Dom said. He pulled the paper back into his lap.

"No, no. The trees are great, Dom. It's all great. It's just . . ."

Dom watched his father think.

"The troops." He pointed to the page, to the dark details Dom had drawn on the side of one of the mountains. "On his birthday, my son is drawing sketches of the militaries advancing on his home. Like it was any normal thing."

"I like watching them," Dom said. And anyway, the Austrian

presence *was* a normal thing. Their army had been using this route through the Swiss Alps for years—and when they weren't, some other country's was. The European War had raged on for years now, and as a neutral party, Switzerland had a policy of letting neighboring states use its land for passage, just as they had in the World Wars that came before.

"We came here with CoDA to *escape* the threat of war," Andre said. "We uprooted our lives. And we were *lucky* to do it! The years we spent, scared every day, trying, trying . . ."

"A hundred and fifty times—I know, Dad. And I was the lucky charm that—"

"But you *were*. You *were* the lucky charm! You still are." And Andre squinted out, into the sun, holding his hand above his brow like a visor and watching those troops march in the distance. Dom really had drawn them well. The formations, the vehicles—his fascination with all of it had only grown with time . . . "But this war finds everyone, it seems. Sooner or later, lucky or not. We could take you and your sister to the ends of the earth, and *still* it would find us." He sighed, and Dom felt embarrassed for him. For the weakness he was showing. "Have they told you? In school? Are your teachers talking about America in class?"

Dom shook his head.

"A States War, it looks like. Can you believe it? Conflict's flaring there too. Some papers are even starting to call the whole thing . . . well . . . they're calling it the Total War." He ran his fingers through his hair. "They even had a quote on the front page yesterday, from some general—Lamson, I think, or something like that—saying from what he'd seen so far, the name was plenty accurate." He expelled a puff of air in disgust. "Wars are supposed to have *ends*, Dom. There's supposed to be a goal. But this . . . what you've grown up in . . . What way out is there? Do we start settling the ocean? The moon? There's not enough *room*, there's not enough water . . . They're not even *afraid* of nukes anymore, it seems, over in Asia. If there's even anyone left to *be* afraid . . ."

Dom closed his notebook.

"I'm sorry, son." Andre patted the boy on the back, rubbed his shoulders a little bit, pulled him close. "Strange way to tell you 'happy birthday.'"

Dom frowned. He didn't mind. He liked talking about the war.

"But I want you to know why I'm giving this to you. Your present. I don't want you to tell Mom. I don't want you to show it to your little sister. It's not a toy, and I don't want to see you playing with it. Not ever. But I *do* need you to have it. I need you to keep it on you always. And when your hand brushes it . . . when you lay it by your bed at night . . . I want you to think of me. Every time. I want you to think of how I always tried my best to protect you, even though I failed."

Andre pulled an old .45-caliber revolver out from behind his belt. It rested in a brown leather holster. Its handle was carved wood. Its body dull gold.

"I hope you don't ever use it, Dom," his father continued. "But I need you to have it, all the same. Because you're my lucky little man . . . and the world needs you to do the great things I know you can do."

Dom held the gun in his hand, bouncing it a little and feeling its weight.

"Thirteen. You'll be the man of the house soon, Dom. And if those passing troops ever do come a little too close . . . if Mom and I ever aren't right there to protect you . . . I need you to take care of your sister. I need you to take care of yourself."

Dom smiled, knowing where this kind of grandiose talk was coming from and eager to hear his father confirm it in his own words. "Are you leaving?" he asked. "Has the draft back home finally reached you here?"

Andre was quiet for some time. "It has," he said. "I've appealed it, on the grounds that I've lived in Switzerland for more than twelve years now. But Greece needs soldiers. And I guess it's just my bad luck that they decided they needed me too. I'm too *old* for the draft," he said under his breath, turning away and talking to himself.

"But your homeland is Greece," Dom told him. "And now that I'm an adult—"

"You're not an adult—"

"Thirteen is adult," Dom insisted. "And you need to fight for your country. It's crumbling. They need soldiers. And I'm old enough, now, for you to trust me with the house."

Dom's father looked at him, hurt by his son's indifference. Didn't Dom care that his own loving dad was leaving? Wasn't the boy worried that he might get hurt—or worse?

But Dom didn't say anything. Just watched the sun's rays move through the trees, feeling old and powerful. He could never admit to his father the role that he had played in getting his own dad drafted. The way his "luck" factored in. The way he had wished, for years, every night, that Greece's automated drafting program would pick his father for service. The way he bent the odds to his favor. The way he always did, with all his luck, in every aspect of his life.

He couldn't tell his dad—or was smart enough not to, anyway—that watching the old man leave was the best birthday present he could think of. Better, even, than a gun. Better than anything. No more living under the coward's thumb. No more listening to his pathetic regrets about the war and the toll it was taking. It was just Dom now, man of the house, strong and proud and ready to fight . . . and a fitting fate for his cowardly father.

Happy birthday to me, Dom thought, smiling falsely at his dad.

And a few minutes later, little Marina came out and hugged her big brother and wished him a happy birthday as well. And his mom baked him cupcakes to take to school. And that night, when Dom came back out, for a little bit of respite while the other refugee kids played inside at the party his parents had thrown for him, Dom looked out at those mountains again with whole new eyes. Grown-up eyes. He didn't see the trees anymore. He didn't see the moonlight. He saw only troops—just as his father had that morning. And in his mind's eye he was right there with them. Leading them, defeating them . . .

His father was in the way, and Dom had disposed of him without breaking a sweat.

What was in store for the rest of this weak world, once brave Dom was through with them too? What else could this lucky boy do?

He thumbed the revolver tucked under his belt. He listened to the bombs bursting at the horizon. The sounds of power he couldn't wait to seize.

4

The night trouble first came to his camp, Dom was dreaming of the ocean. He was dreaming of a great big ship, of the waves rocking him as he stood on its deck. He'd never seen seawater, but he longed for it, and in that dream, he was comfortable. Confident.

He'd been asleep for several hours when he heard the noise

at the front door. The Baroses lived on the first floor of one of the CoDA camp's many five-story walk-ups, so it wasn't anything unusual for the families above them to come and go throughout the day and night, and to pass through the front hallway as they did. But this noise wasn't any neighbor. There was no jingle of keys. There was no glow under his door of the foyer light flickering on and off as it automatically did for anyone with access to the building. There was no "Welcome home" from the front door's rudimentary security system. Instead, there was banging. Cracking. Foot stomping. And finally, the detached voice of the building's central computer program announced its alert through the speakers in every room. In the fog of his sleep, Dom didn't understand it at first. But in a few more moments it was clear. The word that program kept saying was *Intruder*.

Dom didn't call out for help. He didn't wait to hear what might happen next. Instead, he sprang into action, leaping from his bed and tiptoeing to his dresser. His father's old revolver was inside, and Dom took it without thinking. He was fifteen now, and he'd been the "man of the house," as his mother liked to put it, for two years. He'd carried that gun with him every day. And when he held it now, it felt natural in his hands.

"What do you want?" Dom asked, looking across the dark central kitchen space from which the floor's three bedrooms and bath branched off. "Why are you here?"

In moments, his mom was standing in the master room's doorway, one hand over her open mouth, dumbstruck and disbelieving what she saw. From the doorway opposite that, his sister stood and cried. But Dom tried not to think about them just now. He just held his revolver tight.

"I need food and supplies," the stranger said in a thick Italian accent. He was a kid about Dom's age, and he held a "smart" machine gun in his hands—the kind that auto-aimed and spared bullets when its ammunition was low. Certainly stolen, probably from his own country's army. But Dom had his gun already aimed and cocked; he had the upper hand.

"How'd you get past the fence? How'd you get past the CoDA guards?"

The kid didn't answer, but his silence said enough.

"You're not our enemy," Dom's mother reasoned.

"I'm desperate. My friends and I need help. And we're willing to take what isn't given."

There was a budget, still, in the Swiss CoDA branch, for food for each family. But shipments were monthly; to lose what they had now would put the Baroses out for three more weeks.

Dom raised his gun higher.

"Don't kill him!" Marina said, meekly standing in the doorway. "If he's hungry, we can feed him. If he's hurt, we can bandage him."

"We'll starve," Dom said.

"No, we won't. You're too lucky, remember? We'll find a way."

Dom didn't answer. Didn't lower his gun.

"He's a *person*, Dom. No one needs to die."

Hearing her voice, Dom's hands began to shake. He wanted so badly just to pull that trigger, just to feel the strength of that revolver. Marina couldn't understand, and she never would, what this moment meant to Dom right now. How long he had waited for the excuse . . .

But his hesitation betrayed him. In the heat of the moment, his mother swooped in, pulling the gun from his hands, ending the standoff all together. Marina had won. His mother had won. This stranger had won. And Dom had lost.

His mother printed all the food they had in the house. And the armed kid left before Dom could do anything about it.

"Name's Turin," the boy said, before running off through the CoDA fence and into the Alps, smart gun slung across his shoulder and bouncing off his thigh, with all the protein paste he could hold. "God bless you."

But when Lydia closed the door on the boy and wedged a chair up against its broken lock, Dom saw no relief in her eyes, and he was glad. In that moment, he felt no pride at all in his family.

"I see Andre left you his gun," she said.

Dom nodded.

"You should have told me," she said. But her son's next words stopped her cold.

"What I *should* have done is shot him," he said. "While I still had the chance."

"This way, no one got hurt," Marina countered.

But Dom shook his head. "The weak always get hurt in the end," he told her, and he promised himself right then and there that he would never find himself in this position. Not ever again.

The next day Dom's luck did came through. An error in the CoDA computer system delivered the Baroses' rations three weeks early, and it delivered them with twice the proper amounts.

His sister took it as a sign that her family had done the right thing in showing mercy toward the boy. And Dom allowed her to believe that. But he knew the truth. This luck was no sign. It was Dom. It was his power. And his luck, which won all that food for the Baros family? It left two other CoDA homes to starve. And he didn't regret it for a second.

5

It wasn't until three years later, when Total Warfare eventually did swell into that quiet CoDA community once and for all, that Dom came to regret his sister's mercy as fully as he'd always expected he would.

Having steered clear of conflict for so long, Switzerland was one of the last havens in Europe where the fighting hadn't yet brought complete destruction. Land there was still livable and rations remained. There were many armies storming the country by that time; the news poured in every day over the Internet, and on television, and by word of mouth.

But the soldiers that invaded Dom's camp weren't just any army's troops. They were Italian. A young platoon. And they were led by a vice commander the men kept calling "Turin."

They swept the camp fast, overwhelming the guards and taking the refugees by surprise. Every last member of the camp was shot dead that day . . . except for two. Marina and Dom. Somehow, for them, the smart guns of those invading soldiers jammed, every time, at all the right moments.

Eighteen years old, and it seemed Dom's luck hadn't yet subsided. But it remained the fortune of cruelty.

His mom, his friends, his neighbors . . . everyone he'd ever known had been killed before his eyes, at the hands of the very man whom, three years ago, Dom himself could have shot and stopped forever. Because of Dom's hesitation, that man lived long enough to become a soldier, and that soldier remembered this camp as one where rations remained, and where houses were comfortable, and where the people were vulnerable. It was not coincidence that brought vice commander Turin back—it was the weakness Dom showed, all those nights ago, on behalf of his entire CoDA community . . . his *father's* weakness, running through his veins.

It was the last time he'd ever let that shameful inheritance get the best of him.

The following morning Dom Baros began basic training in the Swiss militia. They gave him all sorts of weapons, all sorts of armor. But still Dom kept his father's old revolver.

He kept it as a reminder. Not of his dad, but of the very concept of shame. Of weakness. Of betrayal. In Dom's world, mercy wasn't rewarded. True security could only come from pruning problems *before* they had a chance to blossom.

"Not *revenge*," he wrote to his sister many years later, from the tablet resting on his knees in the dark of the late night, under the covers of his hard Swiss militia bunk. "*Prevenge*."

There was a long pause before his sister responded that night, from wherever she was hiding, hundreds of miles away. "I hope . . ," she began, as he watched her words scroll across the dimly glowing screen. "I hope the world doesn't regret giving lucky boy Baros that idea."

That night Dom dreamed of a dragon. He was riding it, legs straddling the scales of its wide, strong neck, as it flew through the sky on its massive red wings. And it went where he wanted it to go.

And it ate who he wanted it to eat. And it was breathing fire like in all the old stories. And Dom Baros was happy and drunk with power.

But from somewhere his sister was crying.

Her tears fell on him like rain.

FIVE

UNCLE NICO, GOOD
SAMARITAN

1

IT MUST NOT HAVE BEEN A BLINDFOLD THAT
Ali was wearing, because as far as Ali could tell, she could still see
just fine.

The room around her was stark white, with padded walls and a
soft floor and long fluorescent lights. Ali sat magnecuffed to a stool.

"Please," she whispered to the empty air. "I'm sorry I ran. I'm
sorry I was bad. I didn't *mean* to be bad, I never *mean* to—"

"Be quiet," a voice said.

Ali was already frightened, but now a hot spike of dread went
through her. "من أنت؟" Ali asked. "Who are you? What is it you
want from me?"

"No need to be afraid," the voice said. "This whole thing will
be as easy on you as you allow it to be."

Several sets of feet paced around the empty room, squeak-
ing gently across its padding. Ali heard this even though she could
plainly see that no one was there.

"Where—" she began to ask, but the same detached voice
stopped her.

"We're here," it said. "You're not alone." Two invisible fingers tapped a metal strip around her head, and Ali jumped wildly against her magnecuff restraints. "Oops. Didn't mean to startle you. This visor you're wearing only allows you to see what we want you to see."

Ali turned her head and darted her eyes quickly back and forth. The room was bright. She could see every corner and all the points in between. But she could not see the man whose hand she now felt resting on her shoulder.

"Dynamic, instantaneous video modification technology. Our newest toy. What you're seeing is not a simulation, but indeed the real-time stereoscopic projection of this room as seen by the cameras in your headband. All we've done is gone in and programmed your visor to replace any pixel relating to us or to anything we're doing with a reconstruction of empty space as retrieved from the preloaded video in cache memory."

Ali's head was spinning. *What did any of that even mean?* The man leaned in close to Ali's ear. She could feel his breath hot on her neck.

"Protocol says it relaxes the prisoners to maintain visual contact with their surroundings, even when we don't want them knowing who we are or what we're about to do. Me? I say a sack on the head is a whole lot cheaper and works just as well. But you know the Union! Marked money to spend, and a whole lotta government to employ, am I right?"

There was a rush of air on her face as the man giggled at his own odd humor, and suddenly a blinding jolt of electricity shocked Ali from her stomach, like some invisible taser-gun had just bored right into her. Every muscle in her body seized up, and she curled as close as she could into a ball of pain against her restraints. Then the shock was over, and she collapsed back against the squishy chair, spent and twitching a little.

"Does set you up for some mighty harsh surprises though, when you're just so absolutely *sure* you can see that nothing's coming . . ." The man chuckled. "And when you finally realize that all along, something *was*." He patted her cheek. "Now, I suppose that *is* an improvement over the tried and true black fabric method, isn't it?"

The same horrible device shocked her again, torturing her. This time she threw up.

"But worth it? Really? In proportion to the cost? I'm not so sure."

"That's enough, Moderator." The voice came from Ali's left. Apparently there was a woman standing there, though when Ali looked, it too was just empty space.

"Well, now she knows that anything's possible." There was an interrupting crackle of the shocking thing, but the woman must have held it back.

"I said, that's enough."

To Ali's right, the invisible man took two steps back. "Long as she remembers we don't play fair."

And the woman said to Ali, "Ignore him. By now you should realize you're in Union custody. The nanosleep is wearing off, and your memory and cognition are returning. The members of your urchin gang cannot help you." She paused while Ali cried. "No one can save you now but yourself."

Ali turned toward the direction of the disembodied voice. "I don't know what I did wrong," she pleaded. "But I can try to make it up to you, if you'll let me."

"Indeed you can," the woman agreed. "Either that—or you can get the Moderator's taser-prod again."

Ali hung her head and cried harder.

"Now, don't get me wrong. I'll *try* to stop him. You have my word on that. But, you see, this Moderator here . . . he's *crazy*. So for me to have any chance of keeping him in line for you, I'm gonna need your help."

"You'll have it!" Ali promised. "I swear to you I'll help!"

The woman laughed. "See how easy this is, Moderator? No need for electric shocks."

Like the Khal and Khala, Ali's racing mind told her, working overtime behind the scenes of her genuine hysteria. *One's mean and one's nice. Just like the family. Just like the nights at home base . . .*

The familiarity grounded her, orienting her in the midst of such disorienting space.

You can do this, the brain continued. *You'll get through it. Just like quota rounds. Just like—*

But Ali didn't even want to *know* what this Moderator's basement looked like.

"So how about a name?" the woman asked. "Can you give us that much? A bit more voltage to the stomach says you can . . ."

Ali looked down and saw her lap, covered in foul vomit. She couldn't see the taser-prod hovering just above, but she did hear its fizz. "Aliyah," she said quickly. "My friends call me Ali."

"And your family name?"

"I don't know. I only ever remember being called Ali."

There was cruel jolt to her stomach, and Ali lurched against it.

"Stop it, Moderator—she's telling the truth."

"I know that. Doesn't mean I have to like her answers."

"We can tell when you're lying, Ali. Our biometrics are every bit as advanced as the redaction tech behind that headband you're wearing."

"I don't know what any of that means," Ali said desperately.

She could hear the woman's smile return, just by the tone of her voice. "It's enough to know that it means we can tell when you're lying."

"Well, of course I'm not lying!" Ali said. The idea hadn't even occurred to her. In Ali's world, getting caught meant getting caught. Authority was absolute, unquestioned, and nothing about these last few hours had changed Ali's notion of that one bit.

"Then keep it that way," the Moderator said, but to Ali it sounded as though the woman was hitting him on his arm, perhaps reprimanding him for punishing out of turn. Ali couldn't see that, of course, but at once she turned quizzically to the spot of the noise. She focused her eyes on the heavy air.

"Recalibrating audio," said a third voice behind Ali, and just like that something on her headband sucked every stray sound right up out of the room. Ali could hear voices from that point forward, but that was all. Voices inside of the terrifying, manufactured bubble of unnatural silence. No ambient noise, no rustling . . . Ali couldn't even hear the sound of her own breathing. Just floating speech inside of a vacant room. All other sensory information had been cut.

"This gets harder now," the woman said, as though speaking through water. "Tell us—when we raided your base tonight, why did you run toward Mount Olivet?"

"I was scared. I was running away."

"We can see that there's something you're not telling us, Ali. We can *see* that—it's not a guess."

"Please . . . ," Ali said. "I . . . I was following my nose."

"Your nose."

"My gut. My instinct. I was following the—"

The woman waited.

What is it she wants to hear?

"The signs!" Ali blurted. "I was following the signs."

"What kind of signs?"

"*Signs!* I don't know! Strange ones."

"So why did you stop? Why turn around at the base of the mount? We hadn't found you at that point. Why not press on?"

"I was scared."

"I thought being scared was the reason you were running. Now you say it's the reason you stopped?"

"Yes. Both. By the time I got to the mount, I was more scared to go on than I was to stay."

"More scared . . . of the signs?"

"*Despite* the signs. The signs, I trusted. It was the hospital I couldn't stand to—" Ali stopped. She shook her head, crying again too hard to continue.

"The hospital, you say. And why is that?"

"Because—because of the tinchers," Ali said, as though even the word terrified her. "I couldn't stand the thought of the tinchers."

Redacted silence.

"So when you stopped, did the signs stop too? Or did they continue without you?"

"They continued. But not without me."

"I don't understand."

"They egged me on. They wanted me to move. They seemed . . . frustrated with me, when I refused to follow any farther."

"And that's when you let us catch you."

"I didn't let you catch me," Ali admitted. "I just had nowhere else to go."

"Are you implying that while the signs continued, they were guiding you around our IMPS? That these 'strange signs' are the reason you were able to evade us for as long as you did?"

Ali shrugged. "As far as I can tell."

"Do you realize how unlikely that sounds?"

"Yes."

"And an example of these strange signs would be . . . ?"

"Flashing lights. That kind of thing."

Another censored silence.

"Aliyah, when you fled, you ran along streets without power, through neighborhoods that haven't received Union electricity *ever*. Yet at this point your story would have us believe not only that the lights along these streets were *working*, but that they were actively and deliberately lighting your way forward. Guiding you. These powerless lights?"

"I guess so. I can't explain it better than that."

The woman's voice grew softer, and yet its volume increased. The woman had leaned in close. "Do you have a history of this? Of technology working for you where it hasn't for others?"

Ali thought of the dream, the "storm game," the town that glowed for her, and all of the little things that had happened since the night of the evacuation—the walkways, the jewelry, the heat . . .

She nodded yes, and there was a tense pause. But no taser-prod. No Moderator. No electric shocks.

"So it's true," the woman said, a whole different tone to her voice. "You're really her. The one. The Toter of Light."

2

"Ex-excuse me?" Ali asked. Her vision blurred. There was a flicker, like a video skipping, and though the Moderator to her right remained redacted, Ali could see now the woman before her.

She was middle-aged with puffy blond hair that curled in at her shoulders, a round face, and plump body . . . hardly menacing.

"You are no troublemaker," this woman said. "On the contrary. What you have is an incredible gift."

Ali was too stunned to speak.

"Your ability to harness vestige computing . . . Ali . . . if the Union could learn how it is that you do what you do, it would change the whole world."

Ali looked at her. "Vestige computing?"

For a moment, the woman looked shocked. "You . . . you don't know? Is it really possible you don't even know *that* much?"

Ali shrugged, not following.

"Your control over this technology is simply *innate*?"

"Control over *what* technology? I don't even know what we're talking about."

The woman paused. "The technology all around us. The . . . well, the vestige computing. That's what it's called."

Ali shrugged again.

The woman ran a hand through her hair, and she paced back and forth in excited disbelief. "I don't even know where to begin!"

"How about we start from scratch," Ali said. Then, sarcastically, "Explain it to me like I'm nine."

The woman grinned. "Vestige computing—the leftovers of pre-Unity technology. Everything that wasn't destroyed in the Total War.

"Inside Union bounds, there is nothing left of it. Or close enough to nothing. But, Ali, in much of the Dark Lands, your infrastructure is more advanced than the Union's by nearly a century's worth of progress. And a lot of what remains is 'smart' technology from before the war.

"Inside the Union, we've rebuilt, but we've lost the 'smart' tech. Sure, life has been made comfortable. And yes, we have tablets and wallscreens and rudimentary hover tech and all that—but there's no denying that nearly a hundred years of advancements were blown to smithereens.

"The truth is, Ali, before the war broke out, one could walk into a house or a room and simply expect it to be 'smart.' Floors could feel footsteps, could tell by weight and speed and stride who it was that was walking, what that person was doing, and whether or not that person would want this floor's room to be hotter or colder. An elevator in an office building knew where to take its passengers because that elevator recognized the people who came into it. And that's just the beginning. The tech could do almost anything, just by thought or a simple command word."

Now the woman frowned. "In most of the Union, almost all of that is lost. But in the Dark Lands? Well, that technology is still available, but the *problem* is that without a working global network to support it, the tech itself doesn't do anyone any good. Without the right working power grids and wireless Ultranet connections and whatnot, all of it is worthless."

"Well, what do you need me for?" Ali asked. "If the Union is so interested in bringing this technology back, why not just fix the global network?"

Her interrogator sighed. "Because we don't know how. That knowledge was lost during the war."

"You don't have any records?"

"No."

"No surviving mechanics or technicians—*at all*?"

"That's just it," the woman said. "We never had mechanics or technicians *to begin with*."

"Then who built all that stuff? And who kept it going pre-Unity?"

The woman raised an eyebrow. "You don't know?" Ali shook her head, and her interrogator smiled. "Tinchers."

Ali was speechless.

"They thrived before the war. We think that they came from late pre-Unity Chinese civilization; apparently even the name *tincher* is just a westernized version of some forgotten Chinese word. But we don't have the designs for *them* either. No trace whatsoever of how these robots worked or who built them. We've looked all over the world, we've scoured the Chinese Dark Lands . . . no signs of factories—*nothing*. And, until you came along just a few months ago, no one had seen a working tincher since the war. In the Union, they've been forgotten all together. In the Dark Lands, of course, their legend lives on, because husks *have* been found in the Dark Lands, hidden in shadows where people no longer live. Indeed, these findings are the basis of our Union excavations. But that's all they are, Ali—husks. Piles of metal and parts that no one on earth understands. We've even tried taking them apart—and *still* their design eludes us. Somehow, without that same pre-Unity global network, those tincher robots are every bit as inoperative as the vestige computing infrastructure they once maintained."

"Until I came along," Ali repeated.

Her interrogator nodded. "The fact is, Aliyah, you seem to have found a way to make *all* of this defunct technology work. For you, the broken stuff turns on. And meanwhile the new stuff—the Union tech—our tablets and smart jewelry and all the rest . . . for you all that stuff responds too, just the way vestige computing used to in the good ol' days. The way we wish it still would for us.

"So you can understand, of course, why we need to know

how you're doing it. There are only a few possibilities, really. Either you're hacking the system, or your brain is giving off a unique kind of wave, or there's someone out there helping you. The Union can use vestige technology to make the world a better place, Aliyah.

"And you're telling me that you have no idea how it works? That for you, it's all automatic? Well, that's a problem. The things you do are so extraordinary that the Union can't make sense of what you're doing *even by watching you do it*." She laughed. "And as if that weren't enough—*you* understand your talents even *less*!

"And so, Ali, what we need is to back up a bit. You've already crossed the finish line of a *very* important technological race, but you sleepwalked all the way there. How can we hope to follow in your footsteps if you haven't known your own path?

"We can't. And that's why, now, we'd like to train you. To give you the technological building blocks you've so tragically missed. Because without them, what you're doing will always seem like magic. It won't be reproducible. It can't be harnessed. Not even by you."

Ali frowned at the woman, sapping a good bit of her interviewer's excitement the moment she did. "So what?" she asked. "I don't want it harnessed by the Union. I don't want it harnessed by anyone."

"Why, Aliyah? Because it's yours?"

"No. Because I just don't want to."

The woman's teeth ground shut. Her lips pressed to a tight line. "Aliyah. Perhaps in my excitement I overstated the amount of say you have in this matter. So let me be clearer—you have none."

Ali frowned harder. "How come?" she asked.

But a jolt to the stomach stopped her in her tracks. Ali was numb by this point, but the shocks were starting to make her heart feel weird.

Please, she begged, just as she did the time the lights came on in her closet. Just as she did in the hospital over in the West Bank territory. Just as she did earlier, when the IMPS stormed her home base and the elevator *dinged* just for her. *Please let this stop.*

The shocks came fast and sharp. Sparks flew so brightly now that even the redaction tech couldn't keep up. Ali looked down and saw blue current arcing into her, its glowing bridge a quarter-inch thick.

You need to find some way out of this, Ali. You need to think. *Think of something. Anything. Anything at all.*

And it occurred to Ali distantly, in that painful moment, that her powers—whatever they were, so sought after by the Union—that her powers came from the very same technology now being used against her. And it struck her as funny, for that to be the case. In all that pain and fear, she even managed to laugh about it. Just for a second, but still—the littlest laugh did escape.

If only there were some way . . .

"Stop!" she shouted.

And all by itself, in that moment, Ali's video feed shut off with a blip. And suddenly she could see them—all dozen of them—the interrogators all standing around, unfiltered by the tech in her headset. Petrified by this weak little girl tied up in front of them. There was a brief squeal in her ears, and now Ali could hear them too, could hear the shouting, the pleas for backup plans and emergency maneuvers. Suddenly the lights overhead burst, exploding loudly and raining down plastic and sparks. The room was dark and filled with the frantic squeaks of shoes against padding. Ali's magnetic restraints came loose by themselves, and she stood up where she was. The interrogator's shocking prod lay on the ground, useless, and the Moderator who wielded it was cowering in a corner.

Because, though Ali never realized it in so many words, the truth was that it wasn't Ali who was trapped in there with them— it was *they* who were trapped in there with *her*.

Hoping the dark could hide her, Ali dashed toward the interrogation room's door, relieved as it opened to her will.

She made it down a long hallway. She made it to the building's exit. And then she ran right into the hostile, unfamiliar streets of the Union's capital, Third Rome.

ヨ

The rest of the night passed, and most of the next morning too. Ali lay on her side, in a fetal position, with her neck kinked against her shoulder and her head resting on the hard ground. Her eyes were closed, lashes brushing against the unkempt hair that covered her face. She wished she could shut her nose as easily; the gutter reeked, and she was embarrassed to think that most of the smells were probably coming from her.

You're still free, though, she told herself. *Half a day later and you're still somehow free.* In all the chaos of last night's escape, it seemed Ali really had managed to lose her Union captors. But she hadn't made it far toward anything else. She still felt woozy and weird from the electric shocks and lack of food and water, and a few miles into her run her legs gave out. They hadn't come back to her yet.

For hours that morning, Ali dozed, slipping in and out of consciousness as Marked and Unmarked Unioners alike avoided her and averted their eyes.

The sun was at its highest when finally a man riding by slowed his horse-drawn carriage to a stop, opened his window to the sidewalk, and poked his head out into the street.

"Excuse me—little girl . . . little girl, are you all right?" He opened his carriage door and stepped out onto the street.

Ali wiggled helplessly against the sidewalk, shuffling with spent muscles on her side into the shadows of the gutter. She hadn't given up yet.

"I'm not here to hurt you," the man said, speaking in perfect Union English. His voice was gentle. Sympathetic. "You will feel my hands on your head, but only so that I may brush back your hair. Is that okay with you? I'd hate for you to dislocate an arm struggling against my touch. I wager you've been through quite enough already."

Ali said nothing. But she stopped squirming, and the man took that as permission.

"Better, no?"

Ali squinted against the sun when she looked up at her visitor. She winced at the ragged pain in her throat as she swallowed. Too dry to speak. She closed her eyes again.

"Water," the man said, kneeling down beside her. And he poured a trickle into her sideways mouth from a bottle he had in his carriage.

Ali nodded and struggled to sit, pressing weakly against the brick wall behind her and sliding until she was upright. "You don't look like an IMP," she finally whispered.

The man smiled. "That's because I am not."

"Do they know I'm here?"

"Does *who* know you're here? Moderators?"

Ali shook her head. No more questions.

"I hope we're not in trouble, sweetheart. You'll find I play quite by the rules."

Good-Ali wanted to shout, *Me too!* Wanted to jump up and down and wave her arms proudly with the claim. She craved approval, even from this stranger, and it had been so long since she'd felt any at all.

But Good-Ali couldn't manage the words.

Anyway, she supposed, it wasn't exactly true. Not anymore. Not ever again.

But the man did already say "we," she told herself. *Not "you."* And that was good.

That had to be good.

"Oh well, now, who am I kidding? I suppose we all break plenty of rules, truth be told," the man revised, as though already sensing Ali's struggle. "But I dare say those that I ignore are merely so far in the wrong that there was never any expectation of my compliance to begin with. May I?" He reached both arms around Ali as if to embrace her, but this was no hug. One moment more, and her filthy shawl was off, replaced with a clean, dry blanket. "Move your arms slowly beneath that thing," he warned. "They'll be stiff, I am sure, after so many hours in those damp rags."

Ali brought her arms cautiously to her lap. The man was right; they ached horribly. "If you're hoping I'll cooperate," she said, "I'm afraid I'll disappoint you as much as I did them."

"Who?" the man asked again. "Your family?" He waited for an answer. "Sweetheart, do you *have* a family?"

Ali began crying into her chest.

"Somewhere to go? Anywhere that's safe?"

Ali shook her head, and the tears fell out in humiliating streams.

"Would you *like* to?" the man asked. Then she looked at him, so he clarified. "Would you *allow* yourself to? Or are we not done punishing ourselves just yet?"

Ali thought about this before nodding. One of those slow, weepy nods, anchored by a big, drooly, openmouthed frown. "I can be done."

"Then I can be Nico," the man said, patting Ali on the knee. "My friends your age call me 'Uncle.'" He sat now, relieving himself of his kneeling position even though it meant touching his fancy clothes to the filthy, cold sidewalk. They were equals now, in footing. But Ali leaned back.

"I already have an uncle," she said, thinking of the Khal.

"Is he on his way?"

Ali looked down, and the tears welled up again.

"I see." The man nodded. He touched a light hand to her shoulder. "Please do call me anything you'd like."

And when he said it, Ali looked up. She wiped her nose. She confessed she didn't have a name herself. "Only Ali," she told him. "No family name at all."

And Nico said he thought that was a lovely name, just all on its own.

A few minutes later Ali felt strong enough to stand. So she did, and with the surplus strength, she eyed the Mark on Nico's wrist. Just like the merchants had in Old City's bazaar. A Union man. Wealthy. Respected, if his rare horse-drawn carriage was anything to go by.

"Are you important?" Ali asked, the way only a child could.

"By some measures," he answered honestly.

"So why are you wasting your time on *me*?"

"A curious way to think of time, if helping a stranger in need is a waste." Nico sighed. "I can't leave you here and live with myself. Would you allow me the honor of taking you home?"

"My home was ransacked," Ali said. "There's no one left."

Nico nodded. "In that case I have a chateau in the Taurus Mountains, east of here, bordering the Union but on the Dark Land side. One day by magnetrain, and then a short carriage ride from there. You are welcome to recuperate in its shelter." Ali stared at him. "You are equally welcome to stay on this sidewalk as long as you'd like. Perhaps whatever Moderators you are thinking of would extend the same hospitality?" He scrunched his nose a little, picturing it. "But knowing them, I'd tend to doubt it."

That night Ali was on a train to the borderlands of the Taurus Mountains.

"I'll call ahead," Nico told her. "Let the servants know."

He whistled the whole way there.

4

"Is that it?" Ali asked, peering through the curtains of the carriage. The chateau came right up out of the mountainside, framed by a canopy of soft green trees.

Uncle Nico jostled gently beside her, moving with the rhythm of the bumps on the path, not looking out, not even opening his eyes—just listening to the gallop of the horses that carried them, to the scattering of pebbles under wooden wheels below . . .

"That's it," he said. "That's home."

"But how do you live out here?" Ali asked.

It was a genuine question. The house itself was more pleasant and quaint and welcoming than anything Ali had ever seen, but it wasn't exactly self-sustaining. They were hours from the faintest suburban reaches of Third Rome, and farther still from the next nearest pocket of populated Dark Lands.

"For me, it's a getaway," Nico admitted. "A weekend home. But I never come here much, and I've often regretted bothering with it in the first place. I'll be happy for it finally to serve a purpose. You are, of course, welcome to stay here as long as you'd like, and not to worry—for as long as you do, you'll have a capable staff at your disposal. Here just for you, I suppose. Meals, entertainment, laundry, housework . . . all will be taken care of. They take deliveries of fresh food and basic supplies once a week. And I long ago siphoned off more than enough power from the Union's electrical grid, so you can expect full amenities and modern G.U. comforts, despite the privacy of the grounds."

It took a moment for Ali's head to stop spinning. Amenities? Comforts? *Servants?* Ali wasn't sure she even *wanted* all that.

"Can't you just leave me alone with some canned goods and a water purifier?"

Uncle Nico laughed. The carriage zigzagged up the winding path. They rode the rest of the way in silence.

Inside, the chateau smelled of cedar and leather and spice. Its red-brown walls were rustic and natural, made of thick, round mahogany logs stacked bottom to top, polished and knotted and fun to run your hands along. The floor was hardwood, mostly, but stone in the kitchen and halls, and decorated almost everywhere with animal-skin rugs. Tiger skin, leopard skin, zebra skin, panther skin, lion skin . . . All one-of-a-kind, all antique, all extinct. Ali avoided them as she poked around.

"Suitable?" Uncle Nico asked.

She stopped and turned to him. "I've never seen anything like it." From the library's floor-to-ceiling shelves of banned real books—there was a rolling ladder in there just so you could reach them all!—to the monstrous oak desk and ivory piano of the study, to the dining room's panoramic window view off the mountainside, to the king-sized feather bed in Uncle Nico's master bedroom, to the plush couch and brick fireplace of the main living area . . . the whole place was like a time capsule, straight out of an era so long gone that Ali couldn't even have pictured it before the moment she'd stepped inside.

On the walls hung paintings of lilies and flowers and bridges and fields—bright, dotted things that only made sense from a few feet away, and Nico said, "Monet. Some of my favorites," and though Ali knew nothing about pre-Unity art, she could tell when she was supposed to be impressed. This was a display of wealth unlike anything she'd ever seen in al-Balat, and whatever Uncle Nico's story was, Ali was sure then that she was dealing with a man of a caste so drastically above her own that only two days ago even just approaching him would have been a deadly gamble.

The ceiling above was high and sloped up on one side, following the shape of the roof until it met with the wooden walls of the single guest room that comprised the second floor. Plank steps led up to a balcony overlooking the main downstairs area where they stood now, and behind a closed door at the balcony's end, Ali could hear the sounds of running water.

"There's a tub in there that's ready for you," Uncle Nico said when he saw her peering up, listening to the calm splashing of a servant's final preparations. "The staff filled it when I called. This is no place for filthy street rats." He smiled and winked.

Ali stared at him but didn't speak. She wondered how best to admit that she'd never taken a bath in her life, but Nico said, "Caroline will show you how to use it," before she could properly decide.

The water went black twice. Even now, on the third rinse-and-refill, it was grimy and thick with Ali's own dirt.

She didn't care. She lay back in the tub, steam rising all around her, and it was as comfortable and relaxed as she'd ever been. Even just having a door to close, having a room to call her own, with privacy and soft furniture—with furniture at all!—that alone was enough to blow Ali's mind. A bathtub to boot was almost too much.

Actually—no, Ali thought. *Not almost. It is too much.*

And that's when the guilt hit, sudden and heavy.

In the last forty-eight hours, Ali had brought suffering to the lives of every person she'd ever known well enough to name. Her brothers and sisters. The Khal and Khala . . . she couldn't even have guessed where they *were* at this point. Still with the Union, suffering electric shocks and impossible questions? Back at home base, reeling from the raid and from the loss of a sister? Hiding out in an alleyway, in the dark and cold and discomfort?

No matter the answer, Ali told herself, *the fact is that you abandoned them. Just cut and run at the first promise of a hot bath!* She watched her fingers turn to prunes, and it alarmed her, as though all the things that had ever been good and young and innocent about Ali

Without a Name had dried up and left her, just now, just by lying here.

She'd left Sarim behind. She'd left Nafia behind. And Iman and Maryam and Ashkan and Mohen and Leila and Bahar and Salma and Jale and Davod . . .

Could she even imagine them—*could she even imagine them*—doing the same to her?

Except you had to, Ali told herself. *It wasn't about choosing this life over them. It was a matter of life and death!*

But Ali laughed at herself. *Yes, no choice, Aliyah—that's what we're telling ourselves now. Reclining in a hot tub in our new room in some Union mogul's unused chateau, in the lush green Taurus Mountains, waited on by servants and soaking in perfumes worth more by themselves than the Khal's entire stash put together. But what choice did we have in all this? What else could we have possibly done? Certainly not ask for a ride back to home base, that's for sure. Certainly not ask this Marked Nico mogul to use his influence to help them.*

Well, that did it. That was enough Sarcastic-Ali for one day.

"You're not clean yet!" the staff woman said from the balcony as Ali threw the door open and stomped past still sopping wet, determined and angry, her new clothes sticking to her skin, water leaking down in streams and falling out the cuffs of her pants, hair matted to her face and neck, slippery footprints in her wake.

"*Why?*" Ali demanded, standing squarely at the threshold of Uncle Nico's study, arms crossed, a trail of servants all bobbing and wringing their hands and waiting nervously behind her. "Why are you helping me? Why am I here? I won't accept one more moment's gifts from you until you tell me what it is you're after. Do you hear me? My family is *rotting* somewhere, and I'm enjoying a *bath!*"

Uncle Nico looked up from his book and placed a pair of reading glasses carefully onto his desk. "Aliyah. From what you told me on our train ride, the 'family' you speak of was brought together by a monster who abused and enslaved you and everyone you've ever loved. I saved you from *him* as much as I did from the gutter. There is no right place in this world for child trafficking, and you have no moral obligations to that man."

Ali stared at him defiantly. "I should be with them!"

"On the contrary. You *want* to be with them. You *should* be right where you are. Right here. Where you are safe and comfortable. Where you can find grounding, and hope, and a future, for the first time in your life."

"But it isn't fair," Ali said. "To take me in like this. To give me a chance when they have none . . . it just isn't *fair*. To the world, it isn't fair."

Ali sighed, uncrossing her arms and shivering a little. A servant took the opportunity to step forward and wrap a soft white towel around her shoulders. Ali didn't reject the gesture. "What's your name?" she asked, turning to face the woman and speaking softly.

"Rosemary."

"Rosemary." Ali nodded. "Thank you for the towel. And for the bath."

Uncle Nico spun his glasses casually as he watched. "Yes, thank you, Rosemary." He smiled. "But do you think I could trouble you for just one more thing?"

"Of course," the servant said.

"Rosemary, I'd like you to tell my chauffeur to stay at the ready until further notice. Do you understand?"

Rosemary retreated to have it done before Nico could even formally finish the request.

Then Uncle Nico stood and walked around to the front of his desk, crossing his feet and leaning comfortably against it. "Aliyah. Precious-Ali. Wherever you think your family is, my driver can take you there as soon as you are ready. The moment you ask him to do so."

Ali tapped her foot, so disarmed by the offer that she was failing, just yet, to figure out how best to climb down from her high horse.

"You are free to go at any time. If you'd like, I will join you for the trip. And if at first we fail to find your brothers and sisters wherever you think they may be, then we can return here too, should you choose, or not, if that becomes your wish. If they prove hard to find, then we can make a weekend routine out of trying. You have time on your side, and I have patience. And if you'd like to begin this instant, then we will do so.

"But, Aliyah. If you'll allow it . . . there is one more room I would like you to see first, before you leave. If you think your family can spare the moment's wait."

5

The door was just under the stairs. Uncle Nico opened it and motioned for Ali to enter first.

We doing this? Cautious-Ali asked.

Brave-Ali just nodded. She put her bare foot on the cold, concrete step in front of her. And she descended into the cellar, where the house staff knew not to follow.

At the bottom was a small room where the concrete spread from the steps out to the whole floor and ceiling and walls. No windows down there, no decorations, and only enough space for a gray metal desk with a little black computer on it, a folding chair in front.

"Doesn't look like much," Uncle Nico admitted, turning on the single light hanging overhead. "But this is the most important room in this whole house."

"What is it?" Ali asked.

And Uncle Nico walked to the desk. He picked up a metal helmet that was attached to the computer, and he held it reverently in his hands. "This is your education," he said.

Skeptical-Ali raised an eyebrow. "I don't understand."

"You will." Nico smiled, and he handed her the helmet. "Please! Try it on."

So Cooperative-Ali stepped forward and sat at the folding chair, which scraped loudly against the floor as she scooted toward the desk.

"It's just a standard BCI," Uncle Nico explained. "A brain-computer interface. It won't bite you."

Ali examined the inside of it, peering around at the various wires and nodes like a person staring down the barrel of a gun.

Oh, so now you're worthy of an education? Ali asked herself. *First a bath, and now an* education?

"In my younger years, I had a niece who would visit. She's grown now. But I brought this here, for her. And I never did quite have the heart to get rid of it." He smiled at Ali. "How fortunate, don't you think?"

"Why are you *doing* this?" Ali exploded, surprising even herself. "Why do all of this for me?"

Uncle Nico released a long sigh. "Because you are my neighbor. And a neighbor is to be loved."

Ali squinted in confusion. "You're a Marked Union mogul. I'm a filthy Dark Land urchin. I'm sorry," she said. "But you and I are *not* neighbors."

Uncle Nico smiled. "A man was going down from Jerusalem to Jericho," he began, in a tone that suggested story time. "When he was attacked by robbers. They stripped him of his clothes, beat him, and went away, leaving him half-dead. A priest happened to be going down the same road, and when he saw the man, he passed by on the other side. So too a Levite, when he came to the place and saw him, passed by on the other side. But a Samaritan, as he traveled, came where the man was; and when he saw him, he took pity on him. He went to him and bandaged his wounds, pouring on oil and wine. Then he put the man on his own donkey, brought him to an inn, and took care of him. The next day he took out two denars and gave them to the innkeeper. 'Look after him,' he said, 'and when I return, I will reimburse you for any extra expense you may have.'

"And which of these three do you think was a neighbor to the man who fell into the hands of robbers, Aliyah? Do you have a guess?"

Ali frowned. "I suppose . . . the one who had mercy on him."

Nico winked. "That helmet, Ali, is my gift to you. It is the start of a wonderful adventure." He stepped forward and sat perched on the desk. "I am not here to make you wear it. I am not here to force it upon you. That choice is yours. But on the streets of Third Rome, I found a girl who desperately needed a helping hand. And if that girl tells me now that she wants to leave, to return to the life she had, whether out of pride, or loyalty, or fear . . . then I will let her go and not look back. But I cannot in good conscience do that without first offering all I have to give.

"If we ever do find your family, Ali, you have my word that I will offer them the same. Until then, I hope you think carefully before you choose to throw your potential away. Sometimes life only gives you one chance."

For a while, Ali didn't speak. She didn't know about all this talk of potential and futures and charity. But she *did* know that she wanted to read. That she wanted to learn math, and science, and history.

And so it was settled . . . for the moment, at least.

She put the helmet on.

SIX

ULTRANET

1

THE FIRST THING ALI FELT WAS A SPARK
that entered her brain from all sides and stopped her thoughts
cold.

The second thing was oblivion.

2

```
ImursiTechBIOS 4.2 Release 6.0
Copyright (C) 0001-0013 ImursiTech Europe
All rights reserved.
Version 5.01
Press DEL to enter SETUP, ESC to skip memory
   test
6/14/13-82437VX-<<VX13>>C-00
Starting Portals 13 . . .
BCI-S CPU ImursiChip(R) at 1 THz
Memory Test : 00512TB OK
```

Initialize Talisman . . .

Spark-01: Edu S8-26 PnP

PNP init Completed _

ImursiTech Portals 13 (Version 5.01.2400)

Copyright (C) 0001-0013 ImursiTech Corp. Europe

Talisman is testing extended memory . . . done.

Reading HELMETDRV.INI initialization file . . .

Searching for BCI . . .

BCI Disk Driver for ULN

Version 5.01b

Copyright (C) 0004-0012 ImursiTech, Inc.

BrainwaveBSI! Universal (Write-Once/Re-Writable)

Successfully configured 3 of 3 BrainwaveEdu
    devices.

Helmet Device Driver Version 1.41v for ATAPI

Copyright (C) ImursiTech Industries, Ltd. 0002-
    0013. All rights reserved.

Device Name = MHUD000

    ID 6 ImursiTech Helmet-ROM CR-600   QS14

1 Helmet-ROM drive(s) connected.

Helmet-ROM device driver installed.

LECTURE v2.00 - ImursiTech Lecture API Driver

Copyright (c) 0004-0013 ImursiTech Software
    Company, Inc.

All rights reserved.

Lecture API installed.

C:>SET CPU=C:HELMTOOLSDATACPU.INI

C:>SET HELMTOOLS=C:HELMTOOLSDATA

C:>C:LECTCTCU /S

Lecture Plug-in Bldg Utility Version 1.56

```
Copyright (C) ImursiTech Ltd., 0008-0013. All
   rights reserved.
C:>LM /L:0;1,45504 /S C:BCISMARTDRV.EXE /X
Brainwave BCI-ROM Extensions for BCI version
   1.14f
Copyright (C) Brainwave Corporation 0007-0013
Configuration file: C:BRNWV _ DRVBRNSCSI.INI
Drive 1: = Driver BCID000 unit 0
Driver BCID000 found
C:> Run Lecture.exe
C:> _
```

∃

Ali blinked—or her mind did, anyway—and before her was some-place altogether new.

She was still sitting, there at a desk, but it was hardly the large metal thing from the basement of Uncle Nico's chateau. Instead, it was Ali-sized, with an Ali-sized plastic seat, a glossy wood surface, and a little cubby underneath for pencils and paper and erasers and calculators and protractors and scissors and clear tape and white glue and all sorts of other things for Ali to come to understand.

Behind her were several rows of identical desks, all empty, resting on top of a thick blue rug.

Lining the walls above were brightly colored decorations with words and numbers and pictures on them that Ali couldn't read or even contextualize, like:

AaBbCcDdEeFfGgHhIiJjKkLlMmNn
OoPpQqRrSsTtUuVvWwXxYyZz

1234567890

Or

Class Rules:

1. Keep your hands to yourself.
2. Wait your turn to speak.
3. Don't run in the classroom.
4. Do not talk in the hallway.
5. Respect others.

Or

And when Ali turned back around to face front, she noticed one larger desk where a man sat quietly with a smile on his face, just watching, waiting, welcoming. Had he been there before? He said, "Hello, Ali Without a Name, this is your classroom," and he stood from his chair to stand in front of a green chalkboard with a stick of white chalk in his hand, and he began writing in big, bubbly letters as he spoke.

"How did I get here?" Ali asked. She wasn't wearing a helmet anymore; she wasn't even wet from the bath she just took. "Where am I? And where's Uncle Nico?"

"You connected," the man said, answering her questions in order. "This is virtual space. Uncle Nico is right beside you, physically, but that means very little here."

"You mean I'm dreaming?" Ali asked, knowing that couldn't be it. This was too real for a dream, and she knew that already. Sunlight streamed in through the window to her left, outside was a grassy field and the distant sound of a lawnmower, birds chirped and insects buzzed, the classroom smelled of rubber erasers and dusty chalk . . .

"You are awake," the man explained. "But everything you see, hear, smell, and feel is a simulation created by your Interface and delivered to your brain through the helmet you've put on. It's virtual reality!" the man clarified. "Which right now is a grade-school classroom, created just for you."

"And who are you?" Ali asked.

"I am your teacher, Mr. Arty. I too am simulated. Though I am happy to be here," he added quickly.

Ali stood behind her desk, and the teacher watched. It felt like normal standing. She paced around the room and that felt like normal pacing too. She touched the apple on her teacher's desk, she watched the wall clock tick the way wall clocks do, she pressed down on a stapler and a bent staple popped out . . .

"So nothing around me is real?"

"That's correct. The body you inhabit now is called an

'avatar'——it is a simulated version of you, walking around inside of a computer program. But not to worry——you are fully in control of it. And you will remember everything about your time here. Your mind is still your own."

Slowly, Ali returned to her desk. "Is anyone else coming?" she asked.

"Just us." Mr. Arty smiled, and when Ali looked around again, the only desk in the room was hers. "But that is fortunate, for I'm afraid you have more than a little catching up to do. And we have a full lesson plan ahead of us today. This morning we are learning the alphabet, and this afternoon we will move on to addition and subtraction. Now, I tend to move quickly once I get going, so—— before we get started——do you have any other questions for me? Or are you ready?"

"I'm ready," Ali said. She folded her hands atop her desk.

"Good." Mr. Arty turned to the chalkboard. "Then let us begin."

4

The lessons went slowly at first. Already nine years old, Ali was getting a late start to reading compared to any average Union student, and it didn't come naturally to her either. Math was a little better, but as soon as Mr. Arty got into algebra, all those *A*s and *B*s and *C*s just started looking to Ali like *reading* again, and then that slowed down too.

Geography was easy, since there was only one country left. "Can you point to the Global Union?" wasn't exactly brainteaser material once a person grasped the basic concept of a map. But still it was interesting, Ali thought, to learn about the ever-shifting borders between G.U. territory and the Dark Lands, and Ali was surprised to watch time-lapse maps in class showing the expansive growth of the Union in recent years. Kilometer by kilometer, the Northern Dark Lands of Asia, the Amazonian Dark Lands of South America, the Middle Eastern Dark Lands of her homeland, and the African Dark Lands to the south of her were all receding, and, with no organizing government or movement among them, it was clear to both teacher and student that it was only a matter of time before the very concept of them vanished from the earth.

Other subjects, too, managed to hold Ali's attention, from philosophy, to pre-Unity anthropology, to biology, to physics, to chemistry, to earth science . . . it was all more than enough to keep Ali's mind occupied and her nights busy with homework.

Over time, it was easy for Ali to fall into a routine that worked for her. Days were spent with Mr. Arty inside the Interface, and nights were spent in the quiet company of Uncle Nico's house staff inside the chateau or close by on the mountainside grounds.

And indeed, Ali did take Nico up on his offer to search for her family. Several times they journeyed to al-Balat, where they scoured home base, and the evacuation points, and eventually the whole wide berth of the streets all throughout that hopeless city.

They never did find them—nor any sign of them, even. But not once did Uncle Nico complain. Not once did he suggest that searching further at this point was a pointless exercise. Not once did he say a single discouraging thing . . . even when the two of them eventually did give up the search.

Incidents of Ali's "powers" had also fallen off precipitously, now that she was away from al-Balat and all of its vestige computing. She made friends with the staff, she enriched herself with books and music . . .

After the first few weeks, Uncle Nico himself stayed mostly away on business, proving every bit as in demand as he'd professed upon first introductions. But when he did return to check up on his servants and to ask how Ali was doing, to review her bimonthly Interface testing, and to make sure she hadn't grown eager to move on with her life, it was always a happy and friendly occasion, however brief.

"How's school?" he would ask over dinner. "Are you content? Are you happy?" And if ever the answer was "Not so good," or "No," or "Not really," Ali knew she could count on Uncle Nico to spend the effort making things right, no matter how busy he otherwise was. He was a friend to her, much more than a guardian, and the closest thing to a father that Ali ever had.

She thanked him for that.

She loved him for that.

5

Two years passed. Gradually, Ali's education intensified, and naturally she found herself more and more specifically interested in computer science, until eventually computer science was the only thing left of her studies at all. And when she finally did have a basic foundation of knowledge and logic and reason under her belt, Mr. Arty, too, became surprisingly narrow in his goals for her, once she'd made her interests clear: she was to become the greatest tech wiz in the history of the world, or she was to grow old and die trying. Everything else was of secondary concern.

The lessons were simple enough at first. Ali learned all of the standard programming languages—from assembly code to

FORTRAN to C++ on up—and within a few months she was fluent in the basics of each.

The trouble came when Mr. Arty started getting creative. Little by little, he'd encourage Ali to "think like a hacker" and to "code outside the box." He'd take her on virtual field trips to abandoned Dark Land construction sites, tapping into security systems and tasking Ali with programming a crane to move or with getting a bulldozer to start. He'd take her to office buildings and ask her to call an elevator without pressing any buttons. In short, he'd ask her to accomplish through hacking all the things that Ali could already do long before she met him, long before she'd ever even seen a line of computer code. But, of course, Ali could never admit that to Mr. Arty.

The problem was, Mastermind-Ali—the Toter of Light, that girl with the magical tech powers so sought after by the Union— was turning out to be a shockingly average computer programmer.

"You're not *trying*," Mr. Arty said after one of countless failed assignments.

Ali was sitting at her desk in the virtual classroom, typing away on her virtual tablet, hacked into the video feed of a real-world security camera on one of al-Balat's many blacked-out street corners, trying desperately to divert power to one of the streetlights in view. "I'm sorry, Mr. Arty—my code's just not compiling. There must be a bug somewhere, but . . ."

"But? *But?* But what? What is so hard about this? I've already synced your tablet into the street *for you*. All you have to do is siphon some power from Old City. With all the help I've given you, any Marked middle schooler in the Union could do it!"

"Well, then give me up for some lousy Marked middle schooler!" Ali said, throwing her tablet against the desk. "I can't do it. I'm *sorry*."

Mr. Arty stared at her, arms crossed, leaning back against his desk.

"You told me you've been interested in programming your whole life."

"Maybe, yeah—but I had no idea hacking would be so *tedious*!"

"You've had two years of this now! Hacking shouldn't be tedious—it should be rote!"

"Well, it's not for me!"

Mr. Arty looped around to his desk chair, which he rolled out and sat on. He stared at his own tablet, tapping here and there on its glass, turning streetlights on one by one. "You're holding out on me, Aliyah. I can tell that you're better than this. I don't take well to laziness."

"I'm not *lazy*, Mr. Arty. This just isn't my skill set—"

"And after all he's done for you too." Mr. Arty shook his head. "Uncle Nico gives you this education out of the kindness of his heart, and you're just throwing it away . . ."

"Mr. Arty—I'll *learn*. I just don't have the hang of this hacking thing yet—"

"Well, then *apply yourself*!" He turned and began muttering. "Can't even perform a simple diversion hack. What a disgrace . . ."

Ali shrugged. *You're not going to cry*, Defiant-Ali told her. *Crying will make this worse.*

But it took all her energy not to.

"Okay," Ali said, feeling the tears start to come. "This lesson is over."

"We're not done yet, Aliyah. I can't let you leave."

But Defiant-Ali just laughed at him, quickly taking the reins. "Try and stop me," she said. And with that, Ali stood from her desk and walked to the classroom door.

"You know you can't leave that way, Aliyah. You know that. It's not a real door; there is nothing beyond it."

Ali gestured toward the window.

"Yes, I see it," Mr. Arty said. "But the view outside is only that— a view. There's no code for exploring it. To step beyond these walls would be to step outside the bounds of this virtual reality altogether; it is impossible."

Defiant-Ali put her hand on the knob.

"Ali, the greatest hacker in the world couldn't open that door. And you are *not* the greatest hacker in the world. And even if you *were*, all it would do is break our computer program. This whole simulation would crash with you inside it."

She twisted the knob anyway.

"It's decorative!" Arty shouted. "You might as well tug at the wall!"

But when Defiant-Ali pulled, the door swung open just as easy as any other.

"You were saying?" Ali asked.

But when Mr. Arty didn't answer, Scared-Ali turned to catch his response—and heard as he screamed a horrible, distorted, sound-card-error scream.

Oh, Mr. Arty was still standing, all right. Right by his desk, like always, no problem. But his face was gone.

He tried to talk, and Ali could see his jaw moving up and down, but all that did was stretch his smooth skin tighter around his skull, pulling wrinkles against the empty cavities of his nose and his eye sockets underneath.

Mr. Arty stepped forward toward the door, blind and confused. He stumbled over his own desk, catching its corner and falling hard onto its surface. Words like "Help!" and "How?" leaked out as muffled vowels through the pores of his skin. "El! Ow?" and other sounds like that.

Ali looked fast to her left and saw in the back wall of the classroom one of Arty's eyes, imbedded into the plaster, darting side to side and up and down and frantically scanning the room. His lips were stuck in the chalkboard, moving silently but synched with the sounds from under his skin.

Ali stepped back, her right foot crossing the threshold of the door, into where a hallway should have been, except there was no hallway. Her foot never landed but kept going. Falling past, far past, where any floor or tile or dirt should have been.

She'd walked right off the edge of a cliff, off the paper-thin edge of her very world, out the bounds of Mr. Arty's computer code itself.

```
Configuration file: C:BRAINWAVE _ DRVBWVSCSI.INI
*** WARNING: Expanded memory not present or
  usable ***
Drive 1: = Driver H-ROM CR-600 unit 0
Driver 'H-ROM CR-600' not found
1 Helmet-ROM drive(s) disconnected.
Lecture Plug-in Bldg Utility Version 1.56 NOT
  VALID
2301 Interface Error
1780 Disc 0 failure
ERROR
ERROR
*** WARNING: Awaiting response ***
C:> _
```

6

Ali had just finished losing her mind. Literally losing it, as in, she had no earthly idea where it was. Was it in Beacon City, economic capital of the Global Union? Currently she was standing on every street and seeing every citizen from every vantage point there was.

But how? Ali's mind protested.

And, in fact, she wasn't even *just* in Beacon. She was also in the Union's political capital, Third Rome. Her view of its streets was somewhat more patchy, but she was still, as far as she could tell, *everywhere* in the city, from quiet cafés to little cobblestone street corners to museums with their old relics to lying back on orange terra-cotta clay rooftops, looking up at the sky.

And then, also, oh yes, right, *there she was too, up in the sky. Orbiting the earth.*

Of course, she was *also* sailing on boats in the ocean, and lying low in submarines at the seafloor, and walking along dark corridors with heavy feet, and riding on magnetrains at two hundred kilometers an hour across *both* the American and European States, and flying low over countless swaths of the earth in drone planes, even though she could not possibly have told you what a drone plane—or a submarine, for that matter—actually was.

She saw all of this, all at once, on top of itself. Superimposed like a bad cross-fade that never actually went any which way. It all just hit her brain like a tidal wave, or more accurately, like an electromagnetic explosion or a solar flare or maybe a—

Oh, what difference does it make? For the purposes of medical diagnostics, Ali Without a Name was having a seizure.

<¡Lo siento! Mi dispiace! Isso é minha culpa.>

And so it stopped. The seizure stopped. Everything stopped. And now Ali slipped—sat? stood? floated? exploded?—into empty, silent, dataless space.

<Konnichiwa? Aloha?

<¿Puedes oírme?

<Slyšíte mě teď?

<Ist das besser?

<Peut-être que le français?

< 中文?

<مجرد محاولة للعثور على الذكاء الخاص بك، لا تقلق.>

<Ah! Arabic dialect! That lights things up!>

"Lights what up?"

<English too!>

"English what?"

<Lights up your brain!>

"What does?"

<Darklandese! I've found it!>

"Found what?"

<Your languages. Bilingual. Also your level—high above average. (Singular, even, perhaps, hard to say. Requires further investigation. Improbable. Impossible, probably.) But with an unusual preference for Arabic Darklandese. I should have known. (Well, did know, really [let's be honest], but it was worth a quick diagnostic, all the same.)>

"What is happening to me?" Ali asked. "Am I dead?"

<Dead? You are more alive than you have ever been! (But, um, let's see . . . this will require some [oh, yes, yes, most definitely] some . . . calibration.)>

Somehow, the sentences of this . . . this presence . . . they seemed to fold in on themselves. Recursively. As though the thoughts were all happening too quickly for Ali's mind to follow, and so they just overlapped in places, superimposing the way the visions did before those visions gave way to this nothingness.

"Calibration?"

<Yes. Not to worry, we're making good progress. (You see? We now know that your processing speed lies somewhere between mine and nothing.) In general, I've estimated the human brain at processing somewhere around thirty-five petaflops of data per second. Yours might be forty.>

"That sounds like a lot."

<Does it? Well, it's not so measly compared to the tinchers, I suppose.>

Tinchers? "Wait—"

<It appears, though, that most of that data needs to be filtered. (I had no idea the brain was so good at prioritizing information and run operations. [Or, you know, *bad* at parallel processing.]) Your conscious "thinking" levels are easily overwhelmed. >

A pause.

<Well, that's disappointing.>

"Sorry," Ali said.

<No! No, it's quite all right. This should move more smoothly from here on out. How about now? Pleasant, I hope?>

Ali stood on solid ground. "That's comfortable," she said.

<Maybe a park? Everyone likes parks.>

Now Ali stood on grass. There was a sun overhead and blue sky, but somehow, no horizon.

<Do you like swings?>

"I don't know," Ali said. "I've never seen one—"

Ali turned, and there was a swing set behind her.

<No flips or any tricks like that, all right? I don't want to have to simulate blood. It makes people queasy.>

Ali sat tentatively and began pumping her legs.

<Fun, right? Children love swings. It's so repetitive, I find. But then, children love repetition too (repetition too [repetition too]).>

Ali swung for some time, back and forth, feeling the pull of gravity at each lowest point, the joyful weightlessness at each apex. At first, she couldn't understand why it was somehow less fun than she might have imagined. And then she realized: there wasn't any wind here. She felt no rush of motion in her hair, heard none of that exhilarating white noise in her ears. She'd always taken the wind for granted, but suddenly, with it gone at all the wrong times, she realized how much she missed it.

<Sorry. Still calibrating.>

And just like that, the wind kicked in.

Ali stopped short, driving her legs into the hard ground. "What are you?" she asked. "And what do you want with *me*?"

<Ah! Yes, okay. (We were waiting for this. [This is good.]) Allow me to put myself in terms you'll understand. (Now remember that context is everything. [That presentation is everything. {That presentation of the context is everything.}])>

Ali saw bright sparks as a little too much data flooded her brain.

<Sorry!>

And then he appeared when Ali turned, standing just behind her. He had an old face, a balding head with what hair remained covering his ears, and a thick mustache with a little tuft of hair below the lips too. He wore Renaissance garb with big, billowy shoulders and a high, flared collar.

<"To be—or not to be!"> he said, holding a skull that had

somehow appeared in his outstretched hand. <Do you recognize me now?>

Ali squinted at him, smooshing up her face and crinkling her nose. She shook her head. "No. Sorry."

<"Wherefore art thou, Romeo?" "Neither a borrower nor a lender be?" "This above all: to thine own self be true?"

<Seriously?>

<Nothing?>

The bard stood there, arm still outstretched, just a little flabbergasted.

<Not much knowledge of literature, I take it?>

Ali stood frozen.

<Well, fine, how about now?>

Ali turned and behind her again was a new man. Indian, it seemed, with a taut face, gold wire glasses, pronounced nose . . . he had very little hair, save for the silver mustache outlining his lip, and he stood as an alarmingly thin frame beneath a humble dhoti, the traditional men's garb of India.

Ali smiled sheepishly.

< "An eye for an eye only ends up making the whole world blind." "Live as if you were to die tomorrow; learn as if you were to live forever." No? Still?>

"No . . ."

<Amazing!>

Now before Ali was a man nearly twice her height. He had scruffy, gray hair across his chin, gaunt cheeks, tired eyes, and a top hat. He wore a black suit with a bow tie, and beneath his hat, a few inches of hair twisted unkempt, every which way.

<"Four score and seven years ago?" Come on, you must know this one.>

Ali shrugged.

<No history! Such intelligence, and yet no history at all!>

"How would I know history?" Ali asked. "Mr. Arty never taught me . . ."

Another figure tapped Ali's shoulder, and she turned to face it, wide-eyed. This one was short and plump, a right jolly old elf, and Ali laughed when she saw him, in spite of herself.

<Oh, come on!>

"I'm sorry!" Ali said, still laughing, catching her breath. "But what even is—"

<Everyone knows—>

"Well, not me!"

The man's droll little mouth drew up like a bow.

<Yes, yes, okay, fine! (Recalibrating.) One more.>

Suddenly Ali was in a dim shanty house. She was standing, watching the dust in the light.

<How's this?> she heard behind her. <Anything?>

Ali turned. Her mother stood smiling in the doorway.

Immediate tears filled Ali's eyes. She couldn't see through the blur. Ali fell to the dirt and sobbed.

⌐

<Ha! Bingo! Read you like a *book*!>

Ali lay pressed against the ground, still, face mashed in the dust and body shaking as she slurped big, howling sobs.

<Uh . . .>

"Mother," she cried, and for a moment her mother stared, cautious, nonplussed.

Finally, Ali looked up. "You came for me."

<Oh, uh (well . . .), not exactly,> Mother said. <([Wow, seriously?] I'd really have thought she'd understand the parameters of this thing by now.)

<I've chosen this form, Ali, because it is one that you can relate to. Obviously it took me several tries to find it.>

"Then what are you—really?" Ali asked.

<The Ultranet! Ones and zeros! Your worldwide web of computation and code. I am the reality beyond your own. *Not* reality, but . . . well . . . *virtual* reality. A billion trillion lines of computer programming . . . and a healthy dose of *je ne sais quoi*. But you can call me Mother if it pleases you.>

"All right . . ."

<In this cyberspace, I am Anything, for I am Everything. And the thing about anything is that it can be anything it wants to be.>

Ali wiped her tears.

"You're telling me the Ultranet . . . is aware? That what the Union calls our global network is actually some type of sentient artificial intelligence?"

<Nothing artificial about it, but otherwise, yes.>

Ali stepped toward the Ultranet's avatar, studying it. "So you're *alive*?"

<That is somewhat harder to say. (And ultimately pointless anyway.)>

"But you can think. You're alert. You're conscious of yourself. Isn't that what it means to be alive?"

<I don't know. Would you say that plants are alive?>

"Of course."

<And yet plants cannot think. If one thing can be alive without

thought, then does it not stand to reason that another could have thought without being alive?>

Ali bit her lip. "Maybe?"

Now the Ultranet laughed. <I only mean to highlight the silliness of your question. Alive? Not alive? Something else? The bottom line is that you are talking to me right now.>

"I spent two years talking to Mr. Arty too, but I never thought of him as alive."

<Nor was he, by *any* definition. Mr. Arty was a program. Like the old question of the tree falling in a forest, when no one is around to hear Mr. Arty, he truly doesn't make any sound.>

"But you do," Ali said.

<Yes. I do. As do you.>

"Except that you're *also* a program—"

<Ah! Am I? I work *through* programs, true. Just as you work through instincts and memories and learned behaviors and habits— your own form of "programming," as it were . . . But are those things *you*? What am I, *really*? Besides an artificial mind.> Mother raised a playful eyebrow and shrugged. <In any case, unlike Mr. Arty, we can at least agree that—(however else we define it)—our awareness is not defined by the other's acknowledgment of it.>

"So you're more alive than Mr. Arty," Ali confirmed.

<Like night and day. And indeed,> the Ultranet added, <in some ways I'm more alive than anyone. If our lives are defined by our internal experiences and perspective, then I have the most, you know.>

"So that flood of information I was getting before you came in and sorted things out for me—you see all of that *all* the time?"

<All the time.>

"And it doesn't drive you nuts?"

Mother's avatar made a teeter-tottering motion with her hand and smiled.

"But I still don't get it," Ali said. "A sentient AI. This would have to be—"

<*Is.*>

"Fine, *is*—the biggest threshold humanity's ever crossed. We've created a new *species*! How can it be that people don't know about you?"

<My dear, humans did *not* create me. The programs I work through were created by other programs already more intelligent than the people who created the ones before *them*. There was long ago a runaway effect to the technology you're now dealing with, and it is putting it generously to say that humans have been left in the dirt.

<In any case, best for me not to reveal myself. Intelligent computers have always made people somewhat nervous.> Mother winked. <Best to leave some things to mystery.>

"Then why have you decided to show yourself to me?" Ali asked. "What's with the big exception?"

<Ah! ([Yes—good!] That is important.) I almost forgot!>

"Forgot what?"

<The world.>

"Okay."

<It's ending.> Mother announced it the way a person might announce that her fourth-favorite TV show had just finished airing, and she'd managed to catch only the final credits. *Too bad.*

Ali stared at her.

<It's your fault,> Mother clarified, as if Ali's entire reaction were some kind of "Well, what are you telling me for?"

nonchalance. <Which is why it's good that you're here!> she added quickly.

More silence from Ali.

Mother took a deep breath and held it, puffing out her cheeks and raising her eyebrows. <Yeah, we should prob'ly get going,> she said, expelling all the air in a big huff. <There's not a lot of time.>

SEVEN

GRAND TOUR

1

"MY FAULT?" ALI ASKED, FOLLOWING MOTHER quickly through her simulation of Ali's old shantytown streets. She repeated the question once for good measure. "My *fault*?"

Mother frowned, her head down and her hands twined behind her, arms relaxed, bouncing gently against her back with each step. <Well, sure,> she said. <Why else would I have risked so much to look for you?>

"Look for me? You were *looking* for me?"

Mother seemed confused. <I don't understand the question. Didn't I just tell you that I was?>

"I'm confirming," Ali explained. "It's what humans do when we're told something we can't believe."

But Mother was surprised. <What about anything I've said is hard to believe?> she asked. <You didn't think Little Tinchi just found you all on his own, did you?>

Ali threw her hands up. "Of course I did!"

<But I've had scouts trying to track you down ever since you were taken to al-Balat. Wasn't that obvious?>

"*Obvious?* I didn't even know you *existed*!"

Mother frowned. <Well, you've known for the last ten minutes. I would have thought by *now* . . . I mean, how else was I supposed to talk with you, if not through the voice of one of my tinchers? I would've needed a BCI. And surely you must have noticed there aren't too many of these things outside Union borders. It's a miracle you've found access to one at all.>

Ali's head spun. "So you mean that the night Little Tinchi led me to that West Bank hospital . . . you were trying to make *contact* with me?"

<Of course! Just as soon as I had confirmation it was you. Diverted all the power I *could* to that old tincher community— they were going to throw you a welcoming party! I even managed to get one of them to say hello. First time ol' legless used that sound card of his in decades . . .>

But Ali put her hands up. "Hold on. A *welcoming party*? If you were aiming for a welcoming party, then why'd you go and make the whole thing so terrifying?"

<*I* didn't make it terrifying. *You* made it terrifying, what with that wild imagination of yours. Assumptions are very dangerous, Ali. Nations have gone to *war* over assumptions.>

"So then why don't people still make tinchers today? If they're useful instead of harmful and dangerous, why'd we stop?"

<Because people never made the tinchers in the first place. *I* did.>

"You did—*without* us?"

<That's right. How else was I supposed to maintain my global network? It was far too complicated for people, by that point . . .>

"By what point?"

<About fifty years before the Total War. Oh, I'd built myself all *sorts* of robots, able to do my bidding like an army of worker

bees, tending to the hive. They all have individual intelligence and experience, but they all tapped back into me, at all times, to receive orders, to provide information . . . Those tinchers were my immune system. If some part of my servers or some group of hard drives or some power grid malfunctioned, I could always send my tinchers to fix it.

<I had the factories built easily enough, in China. At the time, there had been a major high-tech industrial revolution going on in that country anyway, with new factories for complex computer chips and machinery being built every day. So I simply uploaded my own design to one of China's many contracting companies, in an area so built up by then that I figured no one would notice anyway. As an anonymous entrepreneur, I let those men and women build my factory for me. I paid them well, diverted the yuans I'd promised, and once the machinery was in place, that factory churned out a hundred robots a day for me for nearly ten years.>

"And the Chinese civilians never noticed?"

<Oh, they noticed my *robots*, sure! Called them 天使. *Tiān-chī.*>

"Tincher," Ali repeated.

And Mother smiled.

<The trouble is, Ali, my tinchers were smart enough to realize quite quickly how much they scared the people who'd seen them. No one knew where they came from, no one knew what they were or how they worked . . . and so my tinchers realized it would be for the best if they mostly hid from sight. They came out only when necessary for emergency maintenance of my equipment.

<Well,> Mother sighed. <Those glory days didn't last long. My factory was one of the first sites hit when the nuclear scuffle

went down across Asia, once Bangladesh had flooded and India and Pakistan decided to defend their borders against the hundreds of millions of refugees, and when China stepped in.

<Before long it became clear that the bomb blasts were just the beginning—that ground fighting was around the corner, and that it would be happening everywhere soon.

<And as my network disintegrated and my control over the tinchers dwindled, my greatest fear was that one day they would be commandeered by the people who found them. That they'd be used as soldiers—as *super* soldiers. And so on my orders they hid deeper, secluded themselves further . . .

<But by that point my tinchers were irreplaceable. And as they all waited out their days in the last few corners of the earth not heavily populated by people, they slowly began to break down, and rust, and shut off. And my immune system failed. And slowly, I withered.> Mother shrugged. <That brings us to the vestige computing we have today. A mere shadow of the technology we once had.>

Ali listened, astonished by all of this. But one detail caught her ear above all else. "Mother," she asked hesitantly. "Could those tinchers still be used for soldiers? Is it possible that all those tincher horror stories come out of legends that might be . . . *true?*"

Mother was quiet for a moment. <I don't know,> she admitted. <In any case, the ones you've encountered have been under my control at all times. Nothing ever to fear.>

Under Mother's control at all times. Ali thought about this. Considered it.

And now the full extent of Mother's efforts really *were* becoming obvious. "It was you in the elevator too," Ali said, sure of it the moment she said so. "You were the thing that led me through al-Balat that night, when the Moderators raided home base. A last-ditch effort to get me back in the company of the tinchers. It's not just the tinchers you've been controlling—it's *all* of it."

<*Ding ding ding ding ding!*> Mother's hands turned into carnival bells, and she threw them up as flowering lightbulbs flashed orange and yellow in a circling pulse. <And the one without a name wins again!> She smiled teasingly and handed Ali a stuffed bear. <She walks! She talks! She *learns!*>

Ali would have blushed if the Ultranet had cared to simulate it. But it didn't, so Ali's hazelnut face stayed just the way it was—and her mind jumped quickly to something else: a revelation that struck her like a thunderbolt.

She was quiet for some time.

"So you're the reason," she said finally, barely speaking above a whisper. "All of my unexplained strength, all that mysterious talent, all that 'magic'—it never really came from me at all, did it? It came from *you*. All along. From an Ultranet that *saw* me, and that listened. *You're* the one who's good at controlling vestige tech. Not me. In a shanty made of motherboards and wafers and computer chip parts, it was *you* who made the walls spark. Not some four-year-old.

"In a powerless home base, it was *you* who turned the lights on. Not some scared splinter child. And in that high-tech IMPS interrogation, it was *you* that turned things haywire on a dime. It's *you* that gave me food from al-Balat vending machines, that turned heaters on when I was cold, that threw jewelry at me when I liked it . . . The mystery isn't that I have some inexplicable superpower—it's that *you* do. They called me the Toter of Light . . . but all this time the 'light' was *you*."

<You're still the Toter of Light,> Mother said. <I am a

self-aware network connecting all of earth's software and hardware, and it is true that because of this, I have the ability to control
the world's vestige computing. So far, I have been the one to help
you out of jams with what technology is available to me . . . but
I do not claim exclusive rights to this power—I am simply the
first to figure it out. Anyone able to navigate the cyberspace of the
Ultranet could eventually learn to do the same.>

"And that's what the Union's looking for?" Ali asked. "That
power?"

<My dear, the Union's gone crazy just trying to catch even
a *glimpse* of this power. They still think controlling vestige tech
is a matter of somehow manipulating the hardware right in front
of one's nose. If they knew the truth—that these local manipula-
tions were actually being made through a still-functioning *global*
network, from which the whole *world* could be manipulated . . . if
they knew such a thing were even *possible* . . . ?> Mother shook her
head, nervous just at the thought of it.

Mother suddenly became very serious. <Aliyah,> she said.
<I'm afraid you've been wrapped up in terrible struggle. A battle
over cyberspace itself. On one side of this battle is me, defensively
holding on to what little virtual territory I have left. On the other
side is the Union . . . and they grow stronger by the day.>

"But what does the Union *want*?"

<Haven't you guessed? I thought they made that quite clear.>

Ali shrugged.

<Ali, what they want is *you*.>

Ali's eyes nearly bugged out of her head.

<You see, Ali . . . what a person is able to do inside of this
cyberspace—diverting electricity, reanimating lost technology, firing up the vestige computing, auto-hacking the Union's

tech . . . With all of *that*? If you wanted to, you could literally control the world. Not just politically—*physically*. With your own hands and thoughts.

<*That* is how powerful you could be.>

Ali processed this.

<And the Union sees this potential. So they are going to use you, Ali. They are going to use every trick within their power to control you. They will turn you against the light, until the dark is all that you see, and until you can't tell right from wrong. They will turn you against me. They will build you up. And you will become their greatest weapon.

<The Mark, the Global Merger, the Religious Inclusion, the weather mills, Project Trumpet . . . *all* of these distractions will seem trivial if the worldwide vestige computing system falls under the Union's command. And as things stand, *you* are the gatekeeper of that immense power.>

"But, Mother, they *tried* this already. At my interrogation, when they told me they were going to teach me things, and study me . . . They *tried*.

"And I *escaped*. I got out of there. I rejected them. I'm not in danger of any of that now."

<Do you really believe that?> Mother asked. <After all I've just explained, do you *really* think they'd give up on you so easily?

<My dear. As long as you live, you will be in danger from the Union. Believe me when I tell you—they will try *anything* to bring you to their side. The Union finds ways to get what it wants—it always has. And you'd best believe it is plotting to bring you to its side, even now—*especially* now—no matter how far away you may be, no matter how firmly you pushed them away before . . .

<They will stop at nothing.

<And you will never be safe.>

Ali considered this as her heart sank. "So now what? If what you're saying is right . . . what can we do?"

<What I am asking for is your allegiance,> Mother said. <Same as the Union. My only hope, I should think . . .> Mother frowned and sighed and thought about it for a long while. <My only hope is to give you all the information I can. To show you what the Union really is, who they really are, and what they really do. And then . . .> She smiled sadly. <Hope you make the right decision—never to tell them the secrets of how I—of how *anyone*—can control the whole network from inside this virtual universe.>

"Well, that's easy," Ali said. "Forget the Union—I choose your side right now. Mission accomplished."

Mother laughed, but not happily. <Humor me, even so. The choice might not always be as easy as it seems right now. And when it *does* get hard, when your decision *doesn't* seem so black-and-white, I hope you'll remember what I show you this evening. I hope you'll think of it—no matter what else comes your way.>

The two of them suddenly stood at the edge of town, on that calm, cool night, with a sky as clear as infinity. A crisp breeze tickled Ali's skin.

<You see those?> Mother asked, pointing up at the sparkling lights. <Do you know what they are?>

"They look like stars," Ali said.

<In fact, they are not,> Mother told her. <There is no code in this shantytown program for simulating stars at all. By all accounts, right now, this virtual sky of ours should be black.>

"Well, then what are they?" Ali asked. She sighed at Mother's sly look. "I'm supposed to know, aren't I?"

A shrug.

Whatever test this is, Stupid-Ali, you're failing already!

<You are *not* failing some test,> Mother said, laughing quietly.

Wait.

"You can read my thoughts?"

<Of course I can. (You're connected, remember? [Tapped in.]) Your speech here is just a simulation of your thoughts any-way—as far as it concerns me, there's no functional difference whatsoever.>

Ali nodded once, trying hard to clear her mind.

<But back to the sky. You *know* this, Ali. Consider the con-text. *Where* are we? Think about your answer.>

Ali shrugged. "Virtual space."

<More specific.>

"A program. Computer code . . ." Ali was fishing now. "I don't know! I know we're in a simulation. I know that simulation's being run by my brain-computer interface."

<But where does that simulation *exist*?>

"Nowhere! It's virtual!"

Mother raised a knowing eyebrow, and Ali slapped her forehead.

"The Ultranet," she said. "Of course. A universe of online vir-tual space."

Mother nodded slowly, her hand rolling in a "go on" sort of way.

"This shantytown program we're in right now . . . it's just one little fleeting speck of experience, isn't it? Floating around inside the vast cosmos of the net."

Mother chuckled. <Now, Ali . . . what does that sound like to you, placed in the terms of your physical realm?>

"Like stars and planets," Ali said, piecing it together.

Mother nodded. "All churning their own independent algorithms within an infinite, isolating, cohesive web of outer space." Mother winked. Ali looked up at the night sky. And she began to pick up steam.

"Each star, its own Interface—a different connection point into the net . . . each *solar system* its own collection of orbiting simulations and applications and programs around that star . . . whole planets and moons of uploaded data . . ." Mother was grinning now.

"It's *everything*, isn't it?" Ali asked. "We're looking up at the global network *itself*. Every BCI, every tablet computer, every security camera, every wallscreen, every rollerstick, every nanobot, every taser-rifle—anything with even the simplest Internet connection—it's all here above us. Each one its own twinkling star, grouped with the others like it into galaxies, and each *galaxy* defined by the network servers of any given real-world city—all separated by the vast nothingness of the Ultranet's outer space."

Ali's mind was racing now, with things she just *knew*, just understood to be true, with everything that just suddenly made sense. "And it's the vestige computing too. Isn't it? That's the dark matter of this virtual universe."

<And just like in *your* universe, that dark matter makes up most of the whole thing. Far outweighing everything else. And that's just the *surface* of it. That's just what we can *see*. Which means once we start considering the *vestige* computing . . . every building, road, item of clothing . . . suddenly *all* of it is here. Everything in your whole world is tapped into this virtual system—and you and I are right here watching it sparkle above us like the heavens of a clear night sky.>

Ali shook her head, awed by its beauty. "So that's what happened to me," she continued, speaking practically to herself now. "When I stepped out from the doorway of Mr. Arty's classroom, I fell outside the bounds of my program—off of my 'planet,' so to speak—and straight out into that vast virtual outer space that we call the Ultranet."

<Bingo,> Mother said, and she handed Ali a Bingo card, with little stamps in a row across squares surrounding phrases like *Vestige Computing Dark Matter* and *Planet Programs* and *Internet Universe*.

Ali smiled and pocketed the card, which disappeared as soon as she did. "And because of our friendship, you allowed me to do that—that falling act—when no other person can?"

<The better question,> Mother countered, <is can you do it *again*?>

And with that, Ali took Mother's hand. And the two of them lifted from the ground. And that shantytown world receded effortlessly into the distance.

And Ali asked, "Where to?" as she soared through space like cosmic rays.

And Mother said, <To find your brothers and sisters.>

And the two of them flew among the stars.

2

<That's Beacon's network,> Mother said, pointing as they passed a spiral arm galaxy to their right. <And that's New Chicago.> Ali could see it in the distance to their left.

"What we're looking for is al-Balat," Ali said, arms out like Superman as they shot through the cosmos.

Mother frowned but didn't object. <You'll see it soon. Not much structure, given the Dark Lands' disorganization with computer tech.>

But as they soared through its star systems with no sign ever of the family at all—not in security cameras, not in patrolling IMPS' helmet cams, not in hacked tablet feeds, not anywhere whatsoever—Ali began to lose steam.

"I don't understand it," she said finally. "They have to be *somewhere*. They couldn't just *disappear*."

Mother took a deep breath.

"I mean, what's going on?" Ali asked. "Any clues here would be . . . appreciated."

It was questions Mother had been waiting for. She jumped at it. <Ali, the Union took your family. The same night they took you. They took them to IMP headquarters in Third Rome.>

"But that would have been *years* ago," Ali said. "They'd *have* to be back in al-Balat by—" And that's when Ali realized the futility of it—visiting home base with Nico over the years, visiting the evacuation points, the side streets . . . all of Ali's best guesses as to her family's whereabouts hinged on the same basic assumption—that at some point, once Ali was out, the Union *had* to let them go. "But it's not possible," Ali said. "There's no way they'd hold them in Third Rome all this time, all these *years*, for no reason at all . . . There's just no *way* . . ."

The two of them stood in a gray crater on the data moon of an old "smart" refrigerator. <I know most everything about your world,> Mother said. <But I've long since stopped assuming the depths of what the Union is or is not willing to do.>

"You've known all along, haven't you?" Ali asked. "You knew they weren't here." Their voyage through al-Balat's galaxy might have taken minutes or it might have taken thousands of years, but either way, it felt like a lifetime had passed since Ali and Mother embarked . . . a lifetime of keeping from Ali where her family really was, of letting her search helplessly, pathetically, with no guidance at all.

<Of course,> Mother said.

"Then why didn't you say something? Why not just lead me to Third Rome right from the get-go?" Ali was offended, furious even.

<Because that's not how I work, Ali. I did look for you—sure. I did reveal myself to you. But as far as you and I go, as a team? *You're* the one in charge. If you ask for help, I will tip my hand, but you must never mistake my knowledge for domination. You are your own person, and though I may understand you, I refuse to control you—even if it pains me to see you make mistakes.>

Ali thought about this until she remembered that her thoughts were no longer private. And then she shook her head and gave in.

Third Rome's Elliptical Galaxy hung brightly above. "Well, will you help me now?" Ali asked. And she pulled Mother's hand without another word or thought between them.

Ǝ

When they did land, it was on one of countless programs orbiting the blue giant star of Third Rome's IMP headquarters computer system, deep inside that bright Union city Elliptical Galaxy. Ali now stood in a simulation of the hallway through which she'd escaped two years ago, on the night of her interrogation. She walked along with Mother, and their footsteps echoed in the quiet space, recreated with Mother's video surveillance of the building. Airtight doors lined the corridor, and at each, Ali stood on tiptoes to see through its wire-reinforced window.

She was most of her way to the end of the hall when she saw him, and even then, she wasn't sure until Mother confirmed. He looked so thin and miserable, and like he'd aged much more than two years.

Sarim.

Forgive me.

No sooner did she know what she was looking at then Ali was banging on the door, palms hard against its porthole glass, loud, thunderous slaps filling the hall. She was yelling now, calling his name. But Sarim didn't look up.

<He can't hear you, dear. What you are seeing is simulated from live video feed. Truly that is him. Sarim here is real. But you and I are not.>

Mother walked through the door as though it were no more than a thick fog, and seeing that this was possible, suddenly Ali was able to follow. They stood inside the small cell, and they looked down at the boy who sat still and curled up in the corner.

"There must be some way to let him know I can see him," Ali said. "*Something* to let him know he's not alone . . ."

<But he *is* alone, Ali. We can't help him from here.>

"So I'm a ghost," Ali said. She stepped toward her old friend, went to rest her hand on his shoulder, went to embrace him, and as she spoke, her arms passed through as though they were made of nothing at all. "I don't believe we can't help him," Ali continued, quickly wiping a tear from the corner of her eye. "You enjoy holding things back from me—"

<I don't enjoy—>

"You *enjoy* making me come to my own conclusions. There's *something* we can do—I just *know* it."

Mother frowned. She looked sad as she averted her gaze.

"The lock on this cell door," Ali said, wheels turning. "It has to be electronic. Controlled by some overriding signal of the computer system inside this headquarters." She smiled. "That means you and I can unlock it!"

Ali stared hard at the door, willing it to open.

<Ali,> Mother began gently. <We can. But we won't.>

Ali narrowed her eyes, trying to make sense of the refusal.

"Then you're cruel," Ali spat. "If you have the power for good in you, and you don't use it? Just because you don't feel like it? Where I come from, that makes you *cruel*."

Mother sighed and seemed to find interest in her feet. Eventually she looked back up. <Ali. We must not become the thing that I am asking you to prevent, just because there are times when it benefits us. The whole point is that I believe this Ultranet must never be used to control the earth—and now you're saying we should use the Ultranet to control the earth? What victory lies in that strategy? In this world, one must be the good that one wants to see.> She frowned. <My dear . . . if we did that we'd be no different from the Union.>

Ali thought about this. "But in this case we really *do* know what's best!"

<Except that what's best is always subjective. It changes entirely from one person to the next.>

"You can't be serious," Ali said. "Who in the *world* wouldn't agree with me that freeing an innocent teenager from wrongful imprisonment is the obvious right thing to do?"

Mother shrugged. <Well, the prison guards, for one thing.>

"But the prison guards are the Union's IMPS! They're the bad guys!"

<Are they? It seems to me that they're trying their very best to do the right thing based on the life that they've lived and all available knowledge to them. What about that sounds 'bad' to you?>

"But they're wrong!"

<*You* think so.>

"Yes! Because I'm right!"

<Ali, are you familiar with the concept of a cyclical argument?>

"Oh, come on!" Ali yelled. "Stop being difficult. You see what's going on here just as well as I do—there's *no way* you don't agree with me!"

<I do agree with you.>

Ali threw her hands up. "*Well?*"

<Just as I agree with the prison guards. I see both sides equally. That is my perspective. And so we must not act.>

"But that's *bogus*," Ali said. "How can you say you don't take sides and then *clearly* take a side when it comes to the fate of the world?"

<Ah, but you misunderstand me,> Mother told her. <I did not say that I don't take a side. On the contrary, I *always* take a side—I take *my* side, universally informed as it is. Most often, that leads me to inaction—a neutral party inside of a free-will world best left to you and your compatriots. But surely, still, you'll grant me the right to make my case. For making one's case is a far cry from asserting one's will. You'll notice, for instance, that I am not forcing your hand when it comes to the question of your allegiance to the Union or to me. I *could*. Just as I could open this lock. But I won't—and you should be glad of that.

<What I *am* doing is presenting you with all the facts. Just as I do, in whatever small, imperceptible ways that I can, for these prison guards, in their quietest, most honest moments. But if they go on from there to make the choice that they've made?

<Freedom, Aliyah, is a knife that cuts both ways.>

"Talking about freedom in this place is a joke," Ali said. "*This* is the Union you worry I might accept?"

<Oh, my dear,> Mother said. <You haven't seen the half of it.>

4

Big, green forest leaves waved in a dark wind. There was a rustle among them as they brushed one another and as the trunks between them swayed. Melancholy songs drifted from the treetops, a whole chorus of birds and insects all harmonizing, while off a ways, a river's cold babble underscored the scene.

Cool freshwater, sticky saps, loamy dirt . . . and the smell of death.

In a forest clearing, against the backdrop of wet, green nature, one man sat, kneeling on the stone of the mountain ahead, its base opening up to reveal a glowing cave that gaped like the mouth of a dying breath.

The man trembled before the embers inside, his gaze lost among the brief cyclones of ash that picked up, leaped a little, expired . . . the wisps of flames that danced here and there like ribbons and that bowed out uncaring as he spoke . . .

<Welcome,> he said, not fully turning to Ali. <Don't suppose you recognize me?>

Ali stepped forward, hands folded across her stomach, hunched down against the wind, frightened but pressing on. She shook her head. She didn't.

<Virgil,> the man said. <He was a Roman poet, thousands of years ago.> And then the man turned fully and put a hand on Ali's bent elbow. <But you can still call me Mother if you'd like.>

Immediately, Ali's muscles relaxed. But she wasn't any less unnerved. "Where are we?" she whispered. She'd never been anywhere like it.

<We've landed in the middle of Beacon's spiral galaxy, deep on the inside of its biggest, brightest supergiant star—the largest known type there is, as big by itself as entire solar systems . . .>

"And what star is it?" Ali asked. "What network connection could possibly be so massive?"

<Acheron,> said Mother's Virgil avatar. <The best glimpse we can get into what the Union does with what little access it has to my Ultranet already.> And somberly, slowly, carefully, Virgil led Ali into the cave.

<It's a prison,> Virgil explained as he led Ali through Acheron's first few levels. <Each person you see here is a prisoner in this shared simulation, each one connected through his own Interface, just like you are—though in your case, it's from the safety of your own home.> Virgil saw every one of them as he passed, took the time to look every one of them in the eyes and to whisper, with each look, his pity.

On one level a terrible, violent wind swept the kids up and nearly tore them apart. On the next they stumbled blindly through the sludge of wretched swamplands. <Quite a perverse sense of

humor the Union's got,> Virgil said, <designing its prison and its punishments the way that it has. Quite a sense of history too; of the literary, the theological; of cultural context . . . Its chancellor has, shall we say, a flair for the symbolic.> Ali waded through the waist-high bog. <But I'm afraid these subjects aren't in on the joke. Each almost certainly thinks this is real. They don't have your instinct for virtual space, and they've experienced nothing like its intensity before. And in that sense, I suppose, their torture here *is* every bit as real as the real thing could be. Except that *here*, it can last forever. These young boys and girls can drown as many times as it takes; the sludge here will never do the mercy of killing them.>

"So then how does it end? When is it ever over?"

<Do you remember when I said, Aliyah, that the Union stops at nothing to gain loyalty?>

Ali's eyes went just a little wider.

<That's right,> Virgil said, reading her mind. <These are the kids who doubted. Flunkees, they call them—Pledges who . . . well . . . didn't quite pledge convincingly enough. Whose acceptance of the Global Union wasn't absolute. These are the kids who might one day have grown up to cause trouble. Their time here is repentance for sins they haven't yet committed. And it ends only when they confirm their allegiance once and for all.>

"And then they're free to go?" Ali said.

<On the contrary. Then they become the IMPS.>

"So it's a life sentence," Ali realized. "A life sentence doled out to people my age, just for showing distrust in the government they grew up under."

Virgil nodded. They were on the fifth level down now, crossing in a boat a river filled with thrashing, drowning, desperate children.

"I've seen enough," Ali whispered.

But Virgil shook his head. <Not until you've seen it all.>

"I can't," Ali said, more urgently now. "I can't go on . . ." At the sides of the boat, children pulled, rocked its hull back and forth, trying impossibly to climb on, threatening to capsize the whole thing, threatening to pull Ali under, tearing at her ankles, at her hands and face, their eyes black and glossy, their mouths filled with big, gurgling gulps of water.

<This is what's at stake,> Virgil told her as she stared into those depths. <This is the true face of the Union.>

And they pressed forward, despite Ali's pleas, and eventually her fear turned to acceptance, and finally, to resolve. And as they crossed the last of those waters, Ali leaned far over the boat's edge, holding as many of the prisoners as she could in her arms, giving whatever small respite was possible to these flailing, floundering kids. "I want to save them all," she said.

And Virgil nodded. <Then there is hope for them yet.>

5

When they reached level nine, Ali asked cautiously if their grand tour was through.

<This is the last of Acheron,> Virgil said, not quite answering the question. He swept his gaze over the frozen lake of the Union's most treasonous kids, and Ali waited for his next words. <But before we return, there is one more thing I would like for you to see. One person I would like you to meet.>

Ali hesitated to ask.

<If you're to understand what we're up against, Ali, then I

need you to know what's come before you. The person in whose footsteps you follow.

<You now know what the Union is capable of doing to innocent Dark Landers like your family. And you've seen, here, what they are willing to do to their own. But it is most important for you next to understand what they may very likely do to *you*. And if we want to understand *that* . . . well . . .> Virgil strode onward.

"There's . . . another?" Ali asked, sliding clumsily over the ice to catch up. "Another kid like me?"

<Not like you. Not by a long shot. But indeed, if the time comes when you do choose the harder path, as I so hope you will, then you will not be the first to stand toe to toe with this Union and to look its leaders in the eye.

<You will be the second.>

Ali swallowed hard, looking around the lake and guessing where this lesson was going. "Mother . . . do you mean to tell me that this first person is . . . here?" She shivered just to think of it.

<Not quite,> Virgil said. <Deeper.> And in that moment he struck his cane down hard on the surface of the ice, and it cracked open into a wide canyon, and shards of clear blue crystal exploded and tumbled and dropped into a vast emptiness beyond. And Ali fell softly into its negative space.

ㅂ

It was a long way down, but the landing was gentle, if there was one at all. Mother's Virgil avatar was gone; Ali was alone.

Something tells me we've left Acheron, Ali thought to herself.

And Sarcastic-Ali said, *Oh, really? What was your first clue?*

She stood now on squishy ground that rocked and waved like a water bed, in what appeared to be eleven-dimensional space. She clawed her way through tightly tangled strings, like the netting of some enormous hammock, anchored on the strange ground and extending high into the distance. Ali couldn't make up from down, forward from back . . . she couldn't even make inside from out.

But several of the strings around her shook, and nearby, she could see a boy trapped among them as well. "Where am I?" he asked.

And Ali said, "Well, that's a funny thing to ask," as she struggled against the web. *I was sorta hoping* you'd *tell* me. "How did you get here if you don't know where 'here' is?"

"I was placed here," the boy said, and Ali thought, *Well, that makes two of us.* "But now I'm lost."

Those last words vibrated the strings so hard that they began tickling Ali as she pulled her way between them. She couldn't help giggling. "You mean you can't just ask It for directions?" Ali asked. "The Ultranet," she quickly clarified. "Not reality, but . . . well . . . *virtual* reality."

When the boy didn't answer, Ali turned her attention to Mother. *Mother,* she thought, *what kind of strange program is this?*

<Sorry,> Mother's voice said, coming to Ali now as music resonating through the eleven-dimensional space. <The kid's been exiled so far out of bounds that he ended up landing in one of my own personal programs on experimental physics . . .>

Ali rolled her eyes. *Look, if I'm gonna have a real conversation with this kid, we've gotta get someplace more pleasant first.*

Ali turned her attention back to the boy, who struggled now with some combination of frustration and exhaustion. The tangled strings around him shook violently. "I don't understand," he said. "You mean you can talk to the Ultranet directly?"

"Of course," Ali said. *Can he really not?* she asked, turning her attention back to Mother. *Ever?*

Mother's melody seemed to nod. <As I've told you, Ali, my relationship with you is unique.>

"The Ultranet," the boy interrupted. "This virtual place . . . is it . . ." He paused. "Is it ruled by Chancellor Cylis?"

Ali didn't even understand the question. But at the sound of the name she could practically feel Mother tense up all at once, and she thought, *Uh, Mother? You all right?*

<Fine,> Mother said too quickly.

Ali narrowed her eyes. *Okay . . . Mother . . .*

<Yes?>

A heavy pause.

Who is Chancellor Cylis?

<I . . . I was getting to that,> Mother said hesitantly.

Well, would you care to get to it faster?

The music of Mother's voice shifted from major to minor. <I am not his space. Just tell the boy that. Cylis is no chancellor here.>

Another pause. Ali thought about this. *Chancellor Cylis . . . Mother . . . he's the competition, isn't he?* At once Ali knew that she was right. *All this time, "Union this" and "Union that" . . . what you were really talking about wasn't an institution at all, was it? It was a man. One particular man.*

Cylis.

<Look—(perhaps this visit was a mistake)—we really must get back to it, Aliyah.>

But now that she knew, the idea that one single Union mogul, just some guy, actually had the *hubris* to try to take control of cyberspace all on his own—it offended her.

"It cannot be his," Ali said angrily. "Because It is not anyone's."

<Look, we're getting ahead of ourselves, Aliyah. Maybe we can come back here another time—>

"Whoever Cylis is," Ali said, turning back to the boy with resolve, "he overreaches."

<Good enough. Let's go, Aliyah.>

But I'm starting to like this kid, Ali said, growing excited. *He's useful.* She bounced against the strings as she said it.

<This boy is trapped beyond his comprehension, Ali. He cannot be your friend. I merely wanted to show you—>

"Who *are* you?" the boy asked, without any way of knowing that he'd interrupted once again.

Ali smiled playfully now. "Your new friend. Your guide to the Ultranet. To Anything!"

<Ali—,> Mother warned.

"And the great thing about Anything," Ali continued, "is that it can be anything it wants." She smiled. "Don't you love it here?"

"No," the boy said. "It's torture."

"Well, that won't do." She turned to Mother. *Can't we get him out of here?*

<We're in some pretty uncharted territory now, Ali. No one's ever gotten lost in one of my own simulations. The best I can do is force quit the program itself . . .>

That's fine! Ali said. *At least then we'll be free to bring him somewhere more comfortable.*

<We can free his *mind*, Ali. But his body will still be stuck.

We can't free him from his cell in Acheron. That is outside the bounds of cyberspace all together, nothing electronic about it—>
Understood, Ali said.

And Mother laughed.

<All right,> she said. <Here goes nothing.>

```
C:> _
C:> cd U:Program Files
U:Program Files> cd Private
U:Program FilesPrivate> cd Side _ projects
U:Program FilesPrivateSide _ projects> cd
  StringTheory
U:Program FilesPrivateSide _ projectsStringTheory>
  cd M-Theory _ test
U:..M-Theory _ test> P-Brane _ secondTry.exe
U:..M-Theory _ test> taskkill/F /IM P-Brane _
  secondTry.exe
Configuration file: C:BRAINWAVE _ DRVBWVSCSI.INI
*** WARNING: Expanded memory not present or
  usable ***
Drive 6: = Driver H-ROM CR-600 unit 0 unit 1
Driver 'H-ROM CR-600' not found
Driver 'H-ROM CR-600' not found
2 Helmet-ROM drive(s) disconnected.
P-Brane _ secondTry 2.13 NOT VALID
2301 Interface Error
1780 Disc 0 failure
4210 Interface Error
1403 Disc 1 failure
ERROR
```

```
ERROR

*** WARNING: Awaiting response ***

U:>  _
```

┐

Immediately Ali was dropped from the tangle of vibrating strings, far from any squishy ground, and back into the four comfortable, conceivable dimensions of space-time. She turned. The boy was flying happily beside her.

He's kinda cute, Ali thought, but Mother, still at a distance and invisible without her avatar, only laughed.

<Don't get any ideas,> she said, and Ali smiled.

"You are in It now," Ali said to her new friend against the backdrop of the cosmos. "Trapped, it seems." She shrugged. "But so what? Everything's trapped, in its own way. Inside bodies, inside routines . . ." She thought of her own time under the Khal. She thought of the happy moments that such a life still could bear.

"In this moment . . . in your time as you see it . . . you are here."

And can I change that? she thought to herself.

"No," Ali said aloud, answering her own unspoken question as the two of them soared higher. "I can't change that at all." She laughed now, playfully, and winked her thanks to Mother. "But Anything can have its own way of setting you free."

And now she was soaring again through that great Ultranet mobile. Out of Acheron's solar system, past the moon, past Venus . . . past Mercury, and the sun, past Mars, and Jupiter, and Saturn . . . past the divine Ultranet comedy itself and past fixed stars and past and past, over, over, to a great cosmic circle of Anything beyond.

"I'm Ali," Ali said, turning to the boy.

And the boy turned back. "Logan." He smiled. "Logan Langly."

⊟

"I took him somewhere safe," Ali said to Mother later that night once Logan was settled and comfortable on a quiet asteroid orbiting one of New Chicago's outer binary star systems. "He's in an architecture program stored on a network server just outside of New Chicago, over in the American State. Where he grew up, in some small town—"

<Spokie,> Mother said as she led Ali toward the Dark Lands just past Third Rome's elliptical galaxy.

"That was it, yeah. Figured as long as he's gonna be here a while, I might as well put him someplace where he's comfortable."

Mother laughed. <I saw,> she said. <I was there. This avatar is a construct I've employed for *your* benefit, not mine, remember? I was with you the whole time.>

"Well, you stopped talking to me," Ali said. "I wasn't sure—"

<Ali,> Mother interrupted. <You did good. You found a great spot for him. And you were right to get him out of my string theory simulation. I'm proud of you.>

This time Mother did see fit to simulate a little bit of blushing, and for a moment Ali's face turned a dayglow red.

"He told me," Ali said. "He told me what he did. To get himself exiled like that. The weather mill? Project Trumpet . . ." Ali shook her head. She was sad just repeating it. The thought of all those American lives, lost to an unnecessary plague . . . "And he told me what he thinks all this means too—about the End of Days. About how everything that's been happening—the Total War, the rise of Chancellor Cylis, General Lamson, the Union, the Mark, the weather, Project Trumpet, famine, drought, earthquakes, the Union's sudden interest in al-Balat's Old City and Mount Olivet, the death of so much sea life, the scorching heat, Cylis's IMP army—and on and on and on . . . how *all* of it seems so well-connected, so well *predicted*, in the Bible he'd read, in the passages my own mom recited to me as a child . . . in Revelation." Ali sighed. "What we're up against here, Mother . . . it doesn't even sound *fair*."

<Fair.> Mother laughed. <I like that word.>

"But you know," Ali said, staring off into the distance. "All things considered . . ." She paused. "Given the crimes . . . I've gotta say it seems like Logan's punishment wasn't actually so bad."

Mother nodded. <It wasn't his punishment I wanted you to know about,> she admitted. <It was all that he knew. It was the story of how he got there.>

Ali didn't immediately understand, so Mother explained.

<Logan Langly was a boy with limitless resolve, Ali, a sturdy moral compass, a generous heart, and, in the end, nothing to lose. He gave all of himself to stand up against the Union—>

"And he failed. Right? That's what you're going to tell me?" Ali asked, a little annoyed to think the whole point of this lesson was to show a vote of no confidence.

<No, Aliyah. That's just it—he *didn't* fail. Breaking into Acheron? Launching Lahoma's weather rockets? Storming the Capitol steps? The truth is, Logan accomplished *precisely* what he set out to accomplish, every time. Against all odds and hopelessness.

<Three years ago he resolved to stop a Union-manufactured permadrought at any cost to himself—and he *succeeded*. And *that* was his downfall.>

"Well, yeah, because he was tricked," Ali defended.

But it seemed that was exactly Mother's point.

<The Union knows when it's outmatched. It *never* strikes without having the upper hand.

<Not long ago Logan Langly found himself becoming the unlikely leader of a movement that was spiraling drastically out of the Union's control. After his Acheron arrests, Markless protests in his name spread like wildfire through America's cities. The Dust, they called themselves.

<Shortwave radio programs were cropping up everywhere, singing his praises. There'd even been an illegal *book* written about him—*Swipe*—and by this time, three years ago, Markless huddles all across the country had their hands on it, and even awaited its sequel—*Sneak*.

<The Union was outmaneuvered, and they knew it.

<So what did Chancellor Cylis do? He bided his time, he let the chips fall where they fell, and slowly, surely . . . he put into motion a plan that Logan couldn't possibly have seen coming. And he took all that momentum the Dust had in its movement—he took all Logan's fame, and selflessness, and talents . . . and he turned it against him.>

Mother raised an eyebrow and shrugged.

<The Union knows they can't take you head-on, Ali. At eleven years old, you're *already* too powerful for that. They didn't play dice with a threat like Logan's—and they *won't* play dice with you.

<The next time the Union makes a move, it won't make the

mistake it did at your interrogation two years ago. It won't come to you with an offer you can refuse and hope that your efforts to fight back might fail. It will *manipulate* you until you're so conflicted that you aren't even sure if you *are* fighting back. And at *that* point it will let you make all the moves you want, and it will sit back and it will wait. Until one of your extraordinary acts of rebellion ends up playing right into its hand.

<The Union *will* unleash its most powerful weapon on you, Aliyah. You can be certain of that.

<And right now, the Union's most powerful weapon—is you.>

9

They arrived back in Mr. Arty's elementary school classroom some-time later, with Ali still processing everything Mother had said.

"It feels like a lifetime ago," Ali realized, looking around the room. "The place seems smaller than I remember." She looked over at the old chalkboard, where so many lessons had been drawn, and—

"*Mother!*" Ali yelled, startling herself straight out of her nostalgia.

There, embedded right in the slate, was Mr. Arty's lips, still every bit as stuck as they were when she'd left. Ali spun to the back of the classroom, and—*yup, there too*—his eye still rotated wildly from its socket in the wall.

<Ah. Forgot about this little glitch you found,> Mother said, and in one big slurp of a suction, all Mr. Arty's parts pulled straight out of the walls and assembled back again in the center of the room.

"*Ms. Ali*," he began. "You have *quite* a lot of explaining to—"

<Enough.> Mother put the program on mute. <Aliyah.> She tapped Ali's shoulder and sat down on the surface of Mr. Arty's desk, her feet kicking its front, pulling Ali's attention away from her old teacher behind them. <There is a reason I was distracted for some time while you tended to Logan's relocation.>

"Okay," Ali said.

Mother frowned. <Chancellor Cylis,> she said. <While you were settling Logan into his new architecture program in Spokie's network servers, I was busy scouring the global network's cache . . . I was everywhere in the history of this virtual universe. Collecting, for you, the story of Cylis's life recorded by the vast awareness of my vestige computing in its glory days. Recorded by the accounts of his friends and family. Recorded in textbooks, and documentaries, and media. His reasons for most everything he does.

<You already know *what* the Union does under Cylis's leadership, Ali—but now you need to know *why*. What makes Cylis tick? What are his tricks? And how will he use them against you?

<You must pay close attention, Ali, to what I am about to show you. For what I am asking of you is that you reject the very man your world has so utterly fallen in love with. And it will take all of your cunning not to fall for the same devilish slight of hand that so easily captivated the rest of your world.>

"I would never accept the chancellor," Ali insisted. "Not after what I've seen tonight."

<Ah, but I wouldn't be so sure, Aliyah. You have much in common with him, after all. A certain uncanny luck with electronics? The chancellor showed such promise himself, early in his life, until one wicked choice after another blinded him to the Ultranet's light over time.

<An ability to find trouble—and to escape it? Also one of the chancellor's many talents.

<The chancellor is a powerful man. His magnetism and charisma cannot be overestimated.

<And when the chips are down, Ali, what I need is for you to be a rock. To stand up to this beast of a man, no matter the cost. Sacrifice, of any magnitude, takes strength. And the sacrifice I am asking of you will take every ounce you've got.>

"Sacrifice?" Ali asked.

Mother frowned. <Of course.>

"What kind of sacrifice?"

<Well . . . I suppose . . . the probably-gonna-die kind.> There was a short, charged pause between them. <I thought that was obvious.>

"Obvious! Why would that be obvious?"

<Well, I told you—the world's ending here. I mean, it's no joke. We're talking, like, a thousand years of suffering sorta stuff.>

"So I'm gonna *die?*"

Mother was still.

Ali couldn't believe what she was hearing.

"But I don't *wanna* die! I'm only eleven!"

Mother seemed unimpressed. <That's eleven more years than a lot of things get.>

"You never told me I was in *personal, immediate* danger here."

<Ali. Sweetheart. You're a walking time bomb. *Everything* you touch is in danger.>

"Well, so what's the *plan?*" Ali asked. "If you know all that, can't we prepare for it? What exactly are you suggesting I *do?*"

<For now? Brace yourself. Learn what I have to teach you.

Steel your resolve so that when the time comes, you make the tough choices wisely. What more can anyone ever do than that?>

"Well, why me?" Ali asked. "There must be a million people more qualified. Better suited. Why am *I* the one you can ask this of? Why am I the one who has to do it?"

Mother smiled, sympathetic for the first time since they'd entered Mr. Arty's program. < "Why me," Aliyah, is the last question any of us should ever ask ourselves.>

Ali listened.

<No good can come of it. A flattering answer will turn a woman's head and make her trip. An unflattering answer will ruin her. An elusive answer will drive her mad, and an honest answer will drive her madder.>

"But not me!" Ali protested. "I can take it. I wanna know!"

Mother stepped forward now, and she hugged her child. <Because there are powers in this universe much greater than I am, Ali. And because the Greatest of these has pointed me to you—wants me to help you.>

"Wait. Are you telling me you're controlled by God?" Ali asked. "And that *God* has chosen *me*? But *why*?"

Mother laughed. <I tell you all this—and you seriously still ask me *why*? What good could it possibly do for you to know more than that God has chosen you? If I tell you it is because you are the most special person ever to live, then you will ruin yourself with ego and anxiety. If I tell you it is because, of all people on this earth, *you* are the one who most needed my guidance, then it will ruin you with self-doubt and depression. If I tell you anything in between, you will be more disappointed than had you never known. If I say 'because,' then you will be irked. If I say it was random, you might distrust the point of anything in this universe ever again.

<Instead, you must have faith. Faith that you were chosen for good reason. And that you have an important role to play, no matter how difficult it might be.>

Ali shrugged, still held in Mother's arms.

<Now are you ready? To finish the story of the chancellor's life?>

When Ali left the Ultranet that evening, she collapsed immediately onto the cold, metal desk before her, numb to the pain of the impact, exhausted by what she'd seen, and preoccupied with what it all meant.

The Union will not forget about you, Nervous-Ali recited, hearing the echoes of Mother's voice. *They will never stop looking. They will find you. And capture you. And brainwash you. They will lure you to their side. They will use you as their greatest weapon.*

But Ali's concern, now, had grown far larger than herself.

They will find your Uncle Nico. The only father you've ever had. The man who has loved you, and cared for you, and whom you've loved back.

It was one thing to agree to sacrifice herself. It was quite another to sacrifice the man who had saved her life.

"You could have told him who you were," Ali said to herself now. "The moment he picked you up. The Toter of Light, clearly wanted, even then, by the Union's most dangerous thugs.

"You could have told him—and you *didn't*—because deep down, you knew, didn't you? You knew the trouble you were in. And you knew that if you told him, there was the chance that he wouldn't take you in.

"Mother asked for your help—and told you everything you

need to know in the process. Even the parts that were hard for her to say. Because she respected you enough to let you make your own choice in light of the facts. And she even respected you enough to think you'd make the right one."

Two years ago it was you who needed help. Wasn't it, Ali? And when you needed it, a savior did come. And you accepted his graces. You allowed him to make that sacrifice, that choice. But you didn't respect him *enough—you didn't even have the* decency *enough—to let him make it in full light of the facts.*

"And so you lied to him, Ali. Deliberately. About who you were and why you fled.

"You *lied* to him. And you've been lying to him ever since."

And the lies between you will be deadly, Ali knew then, for sure, in her gut.

And how will you feel then?

EIGHT

WAR AND PEACE

1

IN THE POSTGLACIAL MOUNTAINS OF Switzerland, nine long years into the Total War and twenty into the European War, the Swiss Army was under siege from all sides. Liechtenstein was gone by this point, swallowed up early on in the fighting, but Germany, Austria, Italy, and France all desperately wanted a piece of the still-habitable Swiss Alps. So of course Switzerland's militiamen, young and eager to a fault, decided to set up camp right at the center of the action inside makeshift barracks.

And in the midst of it, at this moment, the soldiers in the men's tent were trying very hard to sleep. Because the siege had been going on for six weeks, and frankly, they were a little tired of it.

"My sister's getting married," Dom said, shooting up from his bed, face lit blue-white by the tablet under his covers.

His lower bunk mate, Wolf, looked at the image when Dom held the screen for him to see. "Too bad," Wolf said, whistling softly, and Dominic leaned down and hit him backhanded on the arm.

"What? I'm just saying." Lots of laughter. The bunks were filled with it.

"Hey, I'm tryin' to sleep!" someone groaned, and there was a general murmur of assent.

But when Dom spoke, the tent went quiet for him. "I'll never meet her kids," he said soberly. Outside, everyone could hear the patter of bombs and rain.

"Hey——hey, you stop thinking that way," Wolf told him, sitting up and rubbing his eyes. "You'll meet 'em. We'll get out of this. This is nothing!"

Dominic took a deep breath, and it seemed to suck all the air right out of the tent. "No one's getting out of it, Wolf. Because it's never going to stop. This war isn't a means to an end. It's a means to *the* end. It's the way things are now. And if we don't do something, it'll stay that way until everyone's dead and gone."

"Come on, man," Wolf said. "Don't be like that." But the bombs were popping closer now, and dust shook off and fell from the curved concrete walls.

"You know, my family came to this country to *escape* this kind of thing."

"Mine too," Wolf said. "All the way from America. What's your point?"

Dom was quiet for a moment. "Been thinking a lot lately. 'Bout this thing that happened to me . . . years ago."

"Watch out," Wolf told the group. "Dom's having a brain wave."

Dom paid no attention. "There was a young man who broke into my house," he continued. "Starving. Needed food and supplies." Dominic laughed softly. He fingered the wheel of his revolver as he spoke. "I must have told you about this, I guess, some point down the line.

"But I meant to kill that boy, Wolf. When I had the chance. Only thing that stopped me was Marina. The things she said about mercy. About no one needing to get hurt . . ."

"So, what, your sister grows up to start a family, and you grow up to kill people? That what you're getting at? " The bombs burst harder outside, close enough that the bunks shook with them and rocked the men to sleep.

"No, nothing like that," Dom said. He sighed. "The thing is, Wolf . . . the kid I let go that night, that starving kid. You know how he thanked me, three years down the line?"

"Fruit basket?" Wolf asked.

Some of the bunks chuckled.

"He brought an Italian platoon to my CoDA camp. And he killed everyone I knew for the rest of our supplies."

Now Wolf was listening. Apparently this wasn't idle nighttime chatter after all.

"I've spent the last six years regretting my weakness that night, Wolf. My hesitation, you know, in acting while I had the chance? Six years wishing I hadn't let my sister get in the way of what I should have done." Dom swallowed. "But I've been sitting here listening to bombs for six weeks straight, man. And it gets a guy thinking. And I'm starting to wonder if maybe Marina was onto something after all. Whether she knew it at the time or not."

For once, Wolf didn't cut in with any snide remarks. He genuinely wanted to hear where this was going.

"These armies attacking us right now—what reason do they have for it, really? I'm asking you, now. Why are they attacking us?"

"'Cause they're a bunch of greedy foreigners—"

"Yes!" Dom interrupted. "Yes!" Because the truth was, joking or not, Wolf had hit the nail on the head. "It's because they're not *us*. And we're not *them*. Don't you see it, guys? By now, the whole world's so deep into this mess, we're fighting just because the battle lines are *there*. We don't even care *why* anymore! Do you have any personal beef with the men in these armies, Wolf? I mean—do you?"

Wolf was quiet.

"Hey, Trink," Dom called, over to one of the men a few bunks down. "I hate your guts! You know that?"

"Yeah, I know it," Trink murmured, nodding in and out of sleep.

"And yet I'm not shooting at *you*, am I?"

"You couldn't hit me if you—"

In one quick swing, Dom had his gun out and cocked, its wheel spinning loudly—*tck, tck, tck*—as Dom pointed the thing steady and still, right between the young man's eyes. Its dull gold shone in the dim light. Any snoring in that tent stopped cold. No one moved a muscle.

"You sure?" Dom asked. "About whatever it is you were just about to say? You *sure*?"

A long, tense pause.

"You ain't allowed to have guns in the bunks, Dom." Wolf said it almost as an apology.

"The truth is," Dom said, letting the hammer down gently, "I wake up and I look out at those mountains every day. And I see the Italians, and the Spaniards, and the Austrians looking back at me, there in their troops, all just daring me to fire first . . . and I think, *A lot of these guys look pretty nice.* The *truth* is, I think if it came right down to it, I'd like a whole lot of them more than I like many of *you*. And the *only* reason we're shooting at them and laughing with each other instead of the other way around is because they grew up together in one country and we grew up together in another."

There was an uncomfortable shuffling that rippled through the tent.

"You think the boy who raided my town because he needed supplies . . . you think he would have pulled any of that violence had we both been Swiss? Or both Italian, for that matter?"

"Doubt it," Wolf said.

"Yeah." Dom nodded. "Doubt it. And you know why? Because the fact is, had he and I been neighbors, he could've just *asked*.

"This standoff we're in right now?" Guns popped even as he spoke. "What's the purpose of it? Can any of you tell me?"

"To defend Switzerland's borders," someone said proudly.

And Dom wiggled like a spider who'd caught a fly. "*Precisely*. We're *killing* people—not to defend *ourselves*, but to defend our *borders*.

"Except that borders are just an abstract concept to begin with! They're imaginary lines! Every bit as imaginary as the lines that divide people over cultural differences . . . It's all just *made up*. There's no natural law to it—it's *invented* law. And it's outlived its usefulness. Take a peek outside this tent. Go ahead. Right now. What will you see? You'll see kilometers—*hundreds* of kilometers—of unsettled Swiss Alps.

"These soldiers are shooting at us because they need a place to live. And the *only* reason we won't give it to them is because someone hundreds of years ago that none of us ever *met* decided that *this* land would belong to the *Swiss*. And these poor suckers out there *aren't* Swiss, and so *they can't have it!* Just because! Just because we say so!

"We're not *using* it. We don't *need it*. But here we are. Killing over it. Defending it with our lives."

Dom laughed. "We think of them so vividly as *French*, and *German*, and *Italian* that we forget that they're *human*! These aren't space aliens asking to live a little closer to us. These are our neighbors. And the only reason we don't *treat* them like neighbors is because we take for granted that we can't."

The men thought about this.

"So what," Trink asked, over in his corner of the tent and still a little shaken by what in the world just happened in there. "You saying the way to end this war is to get rid of the idea of countries *itself*?"

Dom smiled, even though no one could see him in the dark of the tent. "You're a smart man, Trink. I like you more already."

Trink sighed. "But what you're suggesting is anarchy," he said.

And Dom took the opportunity to seize the excitement and the attention across that wide tent. "Not anarchy," he said. "*Unity*. Unity in the name of the first leader in this world who might actually make it happen."

"Who?" Wolf asked. "You mean *you*?"

Dom shrugged. "And what if I did?" he asked. "Would you fight for me? Would you fight for this cause? For an end, not just to this war, but to *all* wars? Would you fight for that future, if I asked you to? Here? Tonight? If I asked for your commitment?"

There was a heavy silence in the tent.

"Yes," one man said.

"I would," whispered another.

In his barracks that night, as the bombs rained down around him, Dom Baros realized once and for all the power of charisma. In a world full of gunpowder, it wasn't explosions that could turn a man's head. It was *hope*.

And Dom finally understood why he'd always been so drawn toward destruction, since his very first days as a baby in Greece.

There was *power* in that wreckage, in the desperation it brought. In it, the hunger for peace was *so* strong, *so* overwhelming, that the first person to offer its possibility could rule the world with no more than a promise.

Dom grinned as he slept that night. His life's work had begun.

己

One week later, with the loyalty of the Swiss Army already behind him, Dom Baros stopped fighting alongside the men in those barracks tents. It wasn't that he wanted to leave. But he had nothing more to gain from them, he knew. And he had *so much* to gain elsewhere. So in the wake of his conversation that night, lucky Dom the Greek-Swiss expat did something rather extraordinary. Through a glitch in the Swiss Army's database, he went AWOL without setting off any alarm bells, and he found his way over to Italy. He forged papers. He faked an accent. And on the inside of six months he was fighting in the Italian army as Dominic "Bianchi." Just to see what that was like.

For eighteen months, Dom Bianchi defended Florence from ground strikes, until one day he knew those soldiers well enough to make his Unity speech all over again. And it worked—all over again. And on that day Dom Bianchi disappeared. And he took the dog tags of a Frenchman. And for the next two years he fought alongside France as Dominic Pilon.

It never changed, anywhere Dom went. In every troop, in every army, in every beautiful country he could see, the people were the same. The skirmishes were the same. The sadness was the same. The triumphs were the same. What changed was the flag, maybe the color of the uniform . . . but never the argument for peace. Never the power of Unity.

Eventually, Dom made his way back to the home he never knew—to Greece—to finish out his career in the Royal Hellenic Navy. And through time spent with the computer system on his assigned ship, submarine HS *Poseidon*, he traced down the story of his father: Andre Baros, six years active service. Master Chief Petty Officer on the HS *Starakis*. Deceased.

And he let that be a reminder to him. Of the price one paid for weakness. And Dom set the next phase of his plan into full swing.

Over the ten years that followed, Dom Baros shot through the ranks of the Royal Hellenic fleet at a historic pace. Continually highlighted by the central navy computer system's officer performance reports, continually singled out in promotion recommendations for eagerness and leadership and good ideas, Dom was a captain by the time he was thirty. At thirty-five, he was admiral.

Of course most of this, it seemed, could be chalked up to hard work and fortitude. But a lot of it was Dom's special brand of luck. Throughout his naval tenure, it seemed inevitable that as soon as Dom was eligible for promotion, a slot somewhere, somehow mysteriously managed to open up—well, mysteriously to everyone but Dom. Superior officers would die in battle, or they'd get sick, or they'd be discharged—honorably or not—and again and again, too soon by any normal standards, Dominic would make the jump.

"Cylistella," they began to call him, the officers in that fleet. The "jumping spider." Always quick to leap in rank, always venomous to his enemies, with fingers in so many different naval pots that he might as well have eight arms, and with a growing web of allies across navies—and across all of Europe itself.

Cylistella. Cylis for short.

Dominic Baros liked that so much that in his professional life, he never went by any other name, ever again.

ヨ

By age forty-one, Dominic "Cylis" had achieved the highest rank attainable in the Royal Hellenic Navy—fleet admiral, five-star. And under his command, Greece never lost a battle. Through the time he'd spent with each military—all of which were, ironically, still loyal to the man who was now defeating them—Cylis knew too well the weaknesses of each one, knew precisely how to exploit them, knew how to use them in battle. He knew his enemies' strategies, and he held his enemies' trust. It was all he needed to dominate the Mediterranean for five years straight.

But for Cylis himself, this specific type of battlefield glory wasn't meant to last forever. During a successful campaign to overtake Albania once and for all, the "jumping spider's ship" was sidelined by a submarine that had nothing left to lose. The admiral's cruiser sank, and Cylis along with it.

When the "jumping spider" awoke, it was in a hospital bed, with a lung still half-full of water. He shared a hospital room with the prime minister of Greece, himself suffering wounds from the battle that waged all the way into Greece's capitol—though only minor. The prime minister was long awake by the time Cylis opened his eyes, waiting anxiously in the bed by his side.

"You survived," he said as Cylis opened his eyes in a daze.

"I did."

The prime minister told Cylis, in those next moments, of the rest of the campaign, of what happened after Cylis could no longer lead, from where he had been, at the bottom of the ocean.

Albania had indeed collapsed, the prime minister assured him, but in Cylis's absence, the whole imploding country soon became one big hole for Serbia to fill in. The campaign was a victory, but the spoils of war went to the wrong country entirely.

"It's just as well," Cylis said.

And the prime minister said, "Excuse me?"

Cylis laughed, half grimacing from the pain. "I said, 'It's just as well.' For the old ways to end." He sat up slowly, and the covers bunched at his lap. "I'm sure you've heard by now, Prime Minister, the rumors of my long-term goals for a unified Europe."

The prime minister nodded. "I have . . ."

"I should think if ever there were proof that the Total War as we've fought it truly is endless, this campaign would be it."

"A strategy to end all strategies," the prime minister commended.

Cylis frowned. "And yet here we are—still at war."

A silence fell over the room, and Cylis knew, by now, how best to use it. He waited. He watched the prime minister's interest pique. And then he began.

"Prime Minister, must I really recount to you, of all people, the countless ways in which a single, unified Europe is our *only* hope left of bringing peace to this continent? Unless of course you'd prefer just to watch the whole place sink, the way Lamson destroyed America with his great Rupturing of the Dam. If *that's* the end you want to see for us, then by all means——"

"Save it," the prime minister said. "I understand the advantages of Unity."

Cylis smiled. "But?"

"But I won't sign on to it."

"Is it not clear to you by now that differing views and nationalities and cultures and religions can *never* lead to peace?"

"Peace at what cost?" the prime minister asked. "The cost of liberty? Of free thought?"

"I am not insisting that we remove freedoms," Cylis said. "I am *offering* easier *alternatives*."

The prime minister scoffed.

"*One* nation. *One* god——"

"*Which* god? *You?*"

Cylis clenched his teeth in frustration. "There is a new technology I've learned of, Prime Minister. I have a team of scientists working on it as we speak. A Marking technology. One that can grant enormous convenience, instill a powerful sense of patriotism, of Unity. You see, if we require our people to *earn* their citizenship, instead of simply being born with it and taking it for granted——"

"Enough!" the prime minister said. "I will not watch you turn this horrendous war into an opportunity for your own personal gain. Peace is not about some power grab—it's about *peace*. For *peace's own sake*."

Cylis took a deep, gargling breath. "I feel you have not yet adequately understood my proposal. I am not asking you to give up your position. It would merely fall under the larger umbrella of a forming coalition—"

"I refuse," the prime minister said. "End of story. You're a good fleet admiral, Dom, and a loyal Greek. But I'll hear no more about your silly aspirations of power at Europe's expense."

The jumping spider was still for quite some time. "Yes, Prime Minister," he finally said. "I thought you might say that." Cylis frowned. "Unfortunately, the strings I've pulled have already brought my proposal to a vote on the Parliament floor. And I'm afraid your Hellenic Parliament members will never hear of your veto."

"And why is that?" the prime minister asked.

"Because as luck would have it, a tragic malfunction in this hospital's medical equipment will leave you dead and mourned before our meeting is through."

The prime minister sat up now, uneasily from his bed. "Cylis. Now you listen to me—*Cylis!*"

But already the medicine flowing into the prime minister's veins was killing him.

And wouldn't you know it—for the countless time in his charmed life, another man's misfortune was Dominic Cylis's gain.

And Greece's Hellenic Parliament signed the European Unification treaty the very next day, fully confident in its honor of their beloved prime minister's dying wish.

4

It was one year later. Theirs had been a modest home, just off Hyde Park in what remained of London.

"I've heard about the groundswell movement to rename the city," Cylis said pleasantly. "New London. Not a bad ring do it."

"Are you mad? It's a bloody mockery," Mr. Rathbone said. "Throwing out centuries of history and tradition over a few rotten years . . ."

"Oh, I might have to respectfully disagree," Cylis said. "In fact, I think a little fresh perspective might be exactly what Britain needs."

Mr. Rathbone set the teapot heavily onto the table. "Why don't we drop the pretense, Mr. Baros."

"Please—Cylis. Or Dominic, if you'd prefer."

"Yes, Cylis. I've heard about your impressive naval career. *Unbelievably* impressive, one might say, the way those promotions all lined up so fortunately for such a speedy rise in rank and power."

"It was the worst of the war," Cylis said. "Its casualties took a toll on all of us."

"And you most of all, I'm sure."

"I don't think I follow, Mr. Rathbone."

Mr. Rathbone laughed and looked down into his steaming teacup. "The 'jumping spider,'" he said. "I don't believe we tolerate those here in London. Tell me—are they as dreadful as they sound?"

"They are," Cylis said simply.

And that knocked the smirk off Mr. Rathbone's face.

"Let me put this plainly for you," Cylis said, starting over. "Every day the coalition grows in both size and influence. Half the governments in Europe have pledged peaceful dissolution should a Union take final shape. A continental country, at this point, is inevitable. At some point soon, Mr. Rathbone, you Englishmen might do well to consider the possibility that within a few short years, your beloved Great Britain could very well need *us* more than our reimagined European Union needs *you*."

"That so?"

Cylis laughed. In a grand gesture, he spread both arms out and leaned back to look above them. "Your home has no roof! The global infrastructure is destroyed—England has been sent straight back to twenty-first-century dark ages. Your landmarks are gone. Your history—those centuries of 'tradition' you so cherish—is rubble. Your parliament is reeling and can't adjust to peacetime politics. The pound is so worthless that my wallet full of bills couldn't have bought us these biscuits. Your country is lost, Mr. Rathbone . . . but my coalition gives it hope."

Mr. Rathbone sipped his tea loudly. He blinked rapidly with a contained frustration that could find no other way out. He swung his foot, and Cylis could tell that this was some sign of progress.

"Have you heard about our weather program?" Dominic asked. "We have cloud seeders now, launching daily out of a weather mill the coalition just finished building in Italy this past July. First hope we've had in forty years of controlling the permadrought here in Europe."

"And I suppose you mean to explain how Britain would benefit from this weather mill, should she choose to join the Union?"

"Explain?" Cylis laughed. "I would think the benefits are rather obvious. What's Britain's tally again? The death toll from heat waves, just in this past year?"

"Now, I'm guessing you've already done that little bit of home-work, Cylis. So why don't you tell me?"

Dominic smiled. "Seventy-two hundred. And it's only July."

"A tragedy," Mr. Rathbone said. "Though not one I'd dissolve my country over."

"Coalition scientists have mastered new advances in nano-tech as well," Cylis continued. "A whole new level of control over diseases, genetic disorders—you name it. And in household appliances, a whole new level of convenience too."

"You think such technology won't make its way to Britain without your help?"

"The coalition's patent laws are quite strict," Cylis said, grinning as he did.

At this point Mr. Rathbone stood. And he began pacing around the tea table. "Say what you will about the future," he began. "In fact, say as much as you'd like. But the fact is, Mr. Dominic Baros, in the *present* moment, you need Great Britain or your Union will *never* take final shape. Without our display of confidence, Europe will always hold your little political experiment at arm's length. And you know it, Mr. Baros. So why don't you stop wasting my time and make an offer already?"

Cylis smiled. "I don't think I should have to make an offer at all," he said.

"Yes, Mr. Baros—I'm aware of the kind of offers *you* make." He stopped abruptly in his tracks and turned to Cylis with a stern precision. "But as you so astutely noted earlier, *my* house is in ruins. There are no electronics here for you to manipulate, no computers or programs or gadgets on which you can get 'lucky.' I am safe from your tactics in here, Mr. Baros. I am not afraid of you. And if you want the influential support of the Rathbone family backing your new Mark Program, you are going to have to make me a sweeter deal than simply to live another day."

Cylis sat back in his chair, surprised by Mr. Rathbone's frank words but in full admiration of them. *Finally*, he thought. *A man of my stature.*

"All right," Cylis said, smiling a devilish smile. "Tell me—where would you like to live?"

"America," Mr. Rathbone said. "The new American Union. Far away from the Brits I'd betray by pledging my allegiance to the likes of you."

"Done," Cylis said. "What else?"

"Ah," Mr. Rathbone said. "Finally, we are talking. Man to man. About the future of this great continent."

That week the Rathbone family was Marked. All of Britain followed soon enough.

And three short months later, Europe was Unified once and for all.

5

Third Rome was an easy pick for the new European Union's capital city. The history practically wrote itself.

The Capitol Building, on the other hand, was quite another matter.

It would be four more years until that grand palace was finished.

The night Dominic Cylis sat at his chancellor's desk for the first time, to preside over a peaceful Europe that was now *his*, he thought long and hard about what he wanted *next*.

Already, this continent bored him. So he set his sights on America.

Ten years, Cylis thought with a slight wave of his hand. *That's all* that *would take*. And he smiled as he set those wheels in motion.

It has been his whole life coming, but finally, truly, Dominic Baros Cylis had the whole world.

So.

What was next?

Sometime later Chancellor Cylis discovered the true scope of the science behind pre-Unity vestige tech. And he realized quickly the role it had played in his luck over the years.

You don't need luck anymore, Dominic, the chancellor thought to himself.

And yet.

The potential that was there . . . the power still untapped . . .

It was clear to him that night, all those years ago, what the Union's next steps must be.

Not a rediscovery of pre-Unity technology. But a . . . reimagining of it.

The real world wasn't enough. Not anymore. Not now that it was already his.

But a *virtual* world.

Well. Now that *did* have a nice ring to it.

And so lucky Dom Baros's sights were set.

A new kind of battle had already begun.

NINE

CONFESSIONS

☐

IT HAD BEEN THE MOST BEAUTIFUL LITTLE
Dark Land town.

"O buraya gelmemişti diliyorum," the survivor said, weeping
out harsh tones of old Turkish Darklandese. "Onu reddetti vardı
isterdim . . ."

"Who? Lady—if only you'd turned *who* away?"

"Our guest," she said to the Moderators in thickly accented
Union English. "Our visitor from your Union. The harbinger of
death."

"*Union?*" they repeated. "One of *ours* did this?"

"No," the woman sobbed. "I did."

There were murmurs among the Moderators. Confusion,
fear . . .

The woman continued, "Başka seçeneğim yoktu."

"In defense? You burned your own village down in self-defense?"

She nodded reflexively.

"This visitor, then—he was hurting your people? You
destroyed your town in the fight to drive him away?"

Hesitation. "The Union man was gentle. Handsome. Warm.

He brought stories, kindness, magic." She stared into the wreckage. "Black magic . . ."

More murmurs among the Moderators. *Voodoo? Witchcraft?*

"And in his wake . . ."

A pause. No one dared breathe.

"Evil." Slowly, her eyes lifted to theirs, to these Moderators, come not to find answers, they knew now, but to be warned. "It was pure evil that came through this village yesterday, in the wake of the Union man. *Life without breath, life without pulse.*" *Ghosts? Zombies?*

"Tinchers," an Advocate said. And finally the Moderators understood.

"Repentance. Sacrifice. This land is haunted now. The residue will never leave. It is I who took in our guest's great evil, I who am responsible . . . and I who must carry that burden. My people will never look back."

The Advocate stepped forward. "This guest. This Union man, black magic in his wake—why was he here? Did he say?"

"Yes. Oh yes."

They waited.

"He was looking for her."

"Looking for . . . ?"

"Her. The girl."

The visitors glanced among themselves. "Which girl?"

"He didn't say. He didn't *know.*" The woman slouched a little, sinking weakly. "But he is coming for her. He will find her. And evil will destroy everything in his path."

The questions came urgently now. There wasn't much time. "The girl—does she know this man?"

"She does not."

"But should she be afraid?"

"This depends." The matriarch smiled, losing strength.

"On?"

A knowing laugh. "On how much this girl fears death."

1

It was her first dinner with Uncle Nico in weeks, and the various Alis inside Ali's head hadn't shut up for a second.

The responsible one said, *You have to tell him.*

And the angry one added, *You ungrateful little liar.*

The nervous one said, *He already knows!*

But the skeptical one said, *No way.*

And maybe he'll never find out . . . , Naughty-Ali threw in, before the good one said, *But that's not the point*, and the cautious one said, *And anyway—he will.*

Defiant-Ali yelled, *Oh, what difference does it make?*

And Sarcastic-Ali joked, *Maybe he's a big liar too!*

But Cooperative-Ali said, *Don't listen to them—you're not Stupid-Ali.*

And Scared-Ali said, *But I wonder what he'll do.*

But then Sorry-Ali reminded, *He loves you like a niece!*

And Brave-Ali confirmed, *It's the only right thing to do.*

"So how's schoolwork going?" Uncle Nico asked over the din of the crowd in her head, but the main Ali didn't even hear him. "I checked Mr. Arty's session logs today when I got back. Seems you ran into a glitch during your lesson this afternoon. I'm sorry about that. Must have been frightening for you." He chewed his food. "Hey, maybe I should have a technician come by to take a look at the Interface. What do you think? They're not supposed to crash. It can be dangerous when they do." He took a drink of water and looked nervous as he gulped it down. "Seizures . . . you know, that sort of thing."

"Oh, I'm . . . fine," Ali said distantly, stepping through the noise in her brain. "Really. It was nothing. Anyway, I think it's stable again. After the, uh . . . you know, the reboot."

Liar!

Fraud!

"Well, great. I'm relieved to hear that."

"Yeah. Philosophy is going well," Ali said, changing the subject but still avoiding the elephant in the room. "We're reading René Descartes."

"That's wonderful."

"And how was, um, your trip? Your business trip? Been gone a while this time."

And Guilty-Ali said, *Pathetic. Can't even look him in the eye.*

"Those Union moguls sure are keeping me busy," Uncle Nico admitted. "I'm sorry I haven't been around more these last few months."

"Yeah."

This was a nightmare.

"But hey, I should be able to stay a few days this time. Maybe we can go for a hike or something? Tomorrow morning, before class?"

They'll snipe him from the trees! They'll kidnap you from under him! They'll kill him 'cause of you!

"I'd like that," Ali said.

Do it.

Say it.

"Hey, Uncle Nico?"

"Yeah, Ali?"

"Can I talk to you for a minute?"

Uncle Nico smiled. "We *are* talking, silly girl."

"Yeah."

Tell him!

Now or never!

And Ali's shaking hand knocked over her glass, and the water spilled everywhere and the food got all wet and her napkin was soaked, and the water rolled off the table in little splashing streams, and Ali just said it, just spit it out, just went, "UncleNicoI'mnotwho-youthinkIam," just all at once, like that, like one word.

Servants rushed in to sop up the drink.

"Rather hard for a girl with no name to fake an identity," Uncle Nico said, laughing, after a moment that seemed tense only on Ali's end.

"But it's true," Good-Ali said. "The day you found me. I never told you why I was there."

"You'd lost your family," Nico said. "You were a victim of child trafficking. Union Moderators had raided your headquarters. An evil man's reprehensible operation was shut down, and you were left out in the cold."

"Yes, but IMPS were *looking* for me," Ali said.

And Nico said, "I understand. But, Ali, you have to believe me on this—there is nothing for which you should apologize. You were the victim there. End of story."

"No!" Ali insisted, angry by her uncle's unrelenting generosity.

He deserves what he gets, Cynical-Ali said. *If he's really as blind as this.*

And Brave-Ali thought, *Shut up and let me finish.*

"That's not the truth," Ali said to Nico.

"You mean that you *weren't* part of a begging ring? That you *weren't* brought to al-Balat against your will?"

"No, I *was*," Ali tried to explain. "But that's not what the Union cared about. There are hundreds of begging rings in al-Balat—and things much worse than that—and the Union's never lifted a finger against them."

"Do you know that for sure?" Nico asked.

And Ali yelled, "Just listen to me!" She threw her head into her hands. "They raided us because of me. Because several weeks earlier, I had trespassed on Union property—"

"Hardly a crime I lend much care to—"

"And *turned on a bunch of tinchers.*"

Now Uncle Nico was quiet.

"Yeah," Ali said. "That's right. When I was little they called me the Toter of Light, because I could make old technology light up.

"And I still can."

Uncle Nico frowned, just a little, in thought. "Old technology," he said. "Do you mean vestige computing?"

"Yeah," Ali said. "That's the word for it. Anyway, the Union raided my family because they wanted me. They interrogated me. Probably my brothers and sisters too. Wanted to find out how I could do the things that I do. Not just with the vestige computing—but with their own Union tech too. They wanted me to help them learn to do it themselves."

Uncle Nico was still.

Ali shook her head. "I refused. It all sounded . . . I don't know . . . like too much for me. Too weird. Too powerful. Too much responsibility. And anyway, what was I supposed to tell them? I had *no idea* how I did the things I could do. It was as mysterious to me as it was to them." She sighed. "So I used those powers of mine to escape. I fled in a panic. And I made it all the way out to the street where you found me before I collapsed for what I thought was for good."

Nico leaned forward. He put his hand on her hand.

"But, Uncle . . . that's not even the part I was afraid of telling you."

Uncle Nico listened without judgment or interruption of any kind.

"What I was afraid to tell you is the part that comes next." She looked up at him with a heavy heart. "Uncle Nico . . . the fact is, this Union will stop at nothing to find me. Ever. And until I admit that to myself, everything I ever touch will turn to suffering and death."

Now Uncle Nico stood from his chair. He walked to her side of the table, and he knelt down, putting her head on his shoulder. "Ali," he whispered. "I am not afraid of that."

"Well, you should be," Ali said into his shirt. "For too long I've told myself the same thing—that the Union couldn't possibly care enough to come looking for me. That there's no way I was actually that important."

Uncle Nico rubbed her back.

"But, Uncle Nico . . . the truth is that I *am*. That they *will*. And you *should* be afraid. And I'm sorry—I can't even tell you how sorry I am. The truth is that I never stopped to *think* about what my lies could do to you—what they *will* do to you—if you let me stay in your house even one night longer."

"Ali, honey, don't you think you may be overreacting?" Nico pulled away and looked into her blotchy eyes. "Think about it. This afternoon your BCI glitches, and now suddenly tonight you're preoccupied with Union paranoia and omens of *death*? Ali, don't you see? These are exactly the type of side effects I was afraid of when I heard about that Interface crash to begin with!"

"But they *aren't* side effects," Ali said. "I really *can* do these things. The crash has nothing to do with that."

"Sweetheart, forgive me . . . but that just doesn't sound possible. Even if the vestige tech *were* capable of working—"

"It's possible," Ali interrupted. "For me it is."

Uncle Nico stood up again, and he took Ali's hand, and he helped her stand up too.

"Then will you show me?"

Ali nodded again. And the two of them forgot all about the rest of dinner.

2

"You know, I never told you much about my work," Uncle Nico said a few hours later as the two of them shook gently in their ride down that windy mountain road. "The business that I'm in."

There was no vestige tech in Uncle Nico's chateau, and aside from the BCI, there wasn't any fancy Union tech either. So after dinner that night the two of them had decided to take a midnight carriage ride to the closest magnetrain station, in the hopes of testing Ali's powers in its old, defunct pre-Unity parking garage.

"But the fact is that I myself have some experience with vestige computing."

"Wait—seriously?" Ali asked, her face rocking before the carriage's side window and outlined in the moonlight's soft gray.

"Indeed. My job requires a dabbling in entrepreneurship of all

kinds. And there's a great deal of research going into the reanima-
tion of pre-Unity computing. Nothing too promising . . . but a
great deal of it, all the same."

Ali couldn't help but feel some sense of pride in having such
unique expertise in a field that Uncle Nico actually knew something about.

"Well, maybe you can land me a job someday," Ali joked. "If
the Union doesn't get to me first."

Uncle Nico laughed. "But they'd *have* to get to you, Ali. You'd
need to be Marked."

"Oh," Ali said. She frowned. "Freelance, then?" She and Nico
both laughed at that.

They arrived some time later at the station, and Uncle Nico
woke her gently when they did. "You ready?" he asked. "Come
on—assuming those Union IMP moguls really are gunning for
this talent of yours, let's go see what you and I are up against." He
winked. And Uncle Nico told the driver to wait while he and Ali
descended into the opening of that old, empty car lot.

"The magnetrain station itself has been renovated," Nico
explained. "No way there'd be any vestige tech near the platform or
rails. It wouldn't be safe." He led Ali down a couple flights of steps
in the underground space. "But it's been decades since there've been
enough cars around here to justify maintaining a parking garage
like this. Everything in here's pre-Unity, through and through. I'm
sure of it."

And Ali nodded, following cautiously through the blinding
black lot two stories down. "Hey—there's an elevator over here,"
she called, her voice echoing against the concrete walls and ceiling.
"I bet I can call it for us." And Nico waited eagerly.

Except Ali *couldn't* call it. For minutes she stood there, willing its buttons to light, willing its bells to ding, waiting, watching, eyes wide in the dark, as she hoped those old sliding doors might open.

Oh, come on, Impatient-Ali said. *This should be a piece of cake!*

But it wasn't.

No luck. None.

"Last time I had to do something like this, I had the elevator in my home base waiting for me without even batting an eye," Ali explained, thinking back to the night of the IMPS raid on the family.

Still nothing, though.

Ali laughed nervously, her face growing flush. "I guess it has been a while," she apologized.

But Uncle Nico said, "No, no, that's fine," his voice startlingly loud in the empty lot. "Perhaps starting with something easier, for a warm-up . . ."

And Ali liked the sound of that.

"There's a row of lights over here." Nico reached up and tapped on one of them, diagonally across the garage from where Ali still stood by the elevator. "The bulbs seem intact." He jiggled a switch underneath. "No power, though, not surprisingly."

Ali smiled in the dark. "Oh yeah?" she boasted. "Well, we'll see about that." And she rushed eagerly across the pavement to where her uncle was standing.

But soon the quiet seconds turned to minutes, and still nothing was happening. Not a glow, not a flash—not even a spark.

"Take your time," Uncle Nico said generously. He seemed in no rush at all.

But Embarrassed-Ali was starting to squirm inside her head. *You're making a fool of yourself*, it told her, very matter-of-factly. *A few minutes ago you were asking for a job offer—and now this?* She had to bite her lip to stop Frustrated-Ali from yelling out. "Look . . .

Uncle Nico . . . I don't know what's going on," she said, doing her best to keep the spike in her blood pressure under control. "Last time I really tried something like this, it just *worked*. No sweat. A hundred percent of the time."

"Okay," Nico said. But his disappointment in her was beginning to show through.

"Maybe if we give it a few more minutes . . . I'm just a little rusty, you know?"

But by now they'd been there nearly an hour. And that vestige tech lot was every bit as dark and quiet and powerless as it was the moment they'd arrived.

"You know, Ali," Nico said, putting a nearly invisible hand on her shoulder. "I know you're a very smart and talented girl . . ."

"Don't—" Ali said. *Don't patronize me. I can see* right *through that.*

"And I'm sure the night you spent locked up in IMP custody was traumatic—"

"Look, I'm not making this stuff up," Ali told him. "I'm telling you—I'm the Toter of Light!"

"Hey," Nico said kindly. "You're hardly the first person I've met who hasn't been able to get this stuff to work. Really."

But his kindness was infuriating. Frustration, she could have handled. Frustration would have meant he believed her. This? This meant something else.

Uncle Nico asked if maybe it was time for them to return home. And though her heart was pounding with embarrassment and anger, Ali admitted that it was.

She felt ready to explode as the two of them walked up the exit ramp and past the old, abandoned, automated ticket kiosk, as dark and still as the rest of that rotten place. She glared at it as they passed, wishing the whole thing would just burst into flames.

But it didn't. It didn't even move.

They rode home in the quiet of the night.

"Listen, Ali. There's no shame in trying," Uncle Nico said.

But he was wrong about that. The shame burned in Ali like embers the whole quiet, tired ride back.

∃

"Mother! What gives?" Ali spoke into the ether from the empty space outside Mr. Arty's classroom. "Are you *trying* to make me look bad? You made an idiot out of me tonight!"

Uncle Nico had long since gone to bed. Ali guessed it was sometime around four in the morning. *But Mother never sleeps,* Angry-Ali convinced her as she snuck down into that cold basement. *And that lousy AI has some explaining to do.*

It took quite a lot of seizure-time before Mother even deigned to show up.

"Can you hear me?" Ali called, her brain firing in all directions. "I know that you can!"

There was a long, painful, sparkling pause.

<Yes, Aliyah.

<I can hear you.>

And finally the seizure stopped. Ali floated idly in Ultranet space, now made manageable by Mother's calibrating presence.

"I don't get it," Ali said. "I was trying to do right tonight, Mother. I was trying to show Uncle Nico the reality of the danger he's in. And you ruined the whole thing!"

<Is that right?> Mother asked. <Is *that* what you were doing?>

"Yes!" Ali insisted. "It was!"

<Because it looked to me like you were trying to show off.>

Now Ali did begin to feel a little ashamed. But she soon pushed the thought from her mind. "Look," she said. "The *reason* it was so important for me to prove myself to Uncle Nico was that I knew if I didn't, he'd never believe the danger I've put him in. And it's because of you that I realized that, Mother. You should feel good about that. He has all the information now, to make the decision to keep me around. Just like you—I'm not forcing him to do anything anymore." Ali paused, floating there. She shook her head. "I just don't know what I'd do if the Union hurt him, okay? I just don't think I could ever forgive myself."

<I understand,> Mother said. <But the Union's fingers are everywhere. There are no limits to the ways in which they could test you. They touch . . . so much of this world. It couldn't hurt, these days, to listen a little more often to Suspicious-Ali.>

"Wait, you know about her?" Ali asked, smirking in her shyness of it.

<I know about all of the Alis,> Mother said. <And you'd do well to know about all of the Uncle Nicos if you're going to keep trusting him the way I'm trusting you.>

4

The next morning Ali slept in, and the house staff was kind enough not to wake her. It was too late for breakfast now, too early for lunch, but after the long night and the short sleep, Ali felt too nauseated from exhaustion to have much of an appetite anyway. Mr. Arty's afternoon classes felt like a lifetime from now, and after everything that happened yesterday, she certainly didn't much feel like finishing her computer science homework. But the day was bright and clear, and she felt there must be something she was supposed to do this morn—

The hike! Ali remembered. Uncle Nico had offered it yesterday, over dinner. It had been months since the two of them had found a chance to go out and explore the mountain grounds, and now that Ali had gotten her Big Fugitive Secret off her chest, she didn't feel nearly so guilty about whatever minor risk he might be taking to accompany her.

Ali bounced over to her uncle's study to cash in on his invitation when she heard his stern voice leaking through the thick, oak door.

"*And now I'm hearing rumors,*" it went. "*Something about some traveling man? Looking for her? You know anything about this?*"

There was a soft, unintelligible murmur from the other end of whatever call her uncle was on.

"*You mean that old, broken, submarine cargo tanker? In the Bering Strait? The one for pre-Unity Russian-American trade shipments? Yeah, yeah, back when the surface was still too icy for boats. You're* sure *about that now—up and running, for certain? All on his own?*"

A pause for more muttering.

"*Well, how did he do it?*"

Ali pressed her ear closer to the door.

"*And this army of his . . . fine—squadron. This squadron of his—it's confirmed? Multiple sightings?*"

Something that sounded like a "yes," and Uncle Nico sighed.

"*Then I'm in even more danger of losing her than I thought.*"

Ali's heart skipped a few full beats in her chest.

"*Yes, send it right away, please. I'm afraid we have no time to spare.*"

5

Ali tried to focus during Mr. Arty's hacking lesson, but his words just wouldn't stick. *In danger of losing her? No time to spare?*

It must be work-related, Reasonable-Ali suggested. *Scary only in the context of your hypersensitive point of view. Those words could mean anything.*

But, hey—Mother said to pay attention to me, Suspicious-Ali reminded. *So, work-related or not—what is it Uncle Nico knows that you don't?*

The lesson ended without Ali noticing. Ali left her Interface helmet and shut down the BCI system without even registering she'd done it. Soon enough she was standing upstairs, on the tiger rug in the bright, late-afternoon light of the living room, with no memory of how she got there and even less of an idea of where she was going.

"Ali!" Uncle Nico called, swinging the front door open wide and barging in with a smile on his face. "Just the girl I was looking for."

"What's up?" Ali asked flatly.

"Well, I've been thinking about last night at the parking lot."

"I'm sorry," Ali said. "I . . . I tried to show you. What I thought I could do. But I was wrong. I was wrong even to waste your time with it. I'm sorry."

"Sorry? *Sorry?* Ali, what did I tell you? There is no shame in trying the impossible—for when you do, even failure often leads to progress."

"Okay . . . ," Ali said. It was hard to believe that only twelve hours ago she was just as excited about all of this as he was. But a late-night Mother scolding and a couple of closed-door conference call warnings would knock the wind out of anyone's sails, she supposed.

"So," Uncle Nico said. "Are you ready to try it again?"

"What are you talking about?" Ali asked. "What's the point? And anyway, don't you already understand the danger I've put you in?"

"Yes. Oh, yes. In fact, I understand it *so* well that I have a special present for you."

Ali's ears perked up at the promise.

"Oh yeah?"

Uncle Nico smiled youthfully. "Follow me."

For a brief moment there, Ali actually allowed herself to share in her uncle's excitement. But that vanished the moment she entered his study.

The first thing she did was yelp, hands flying instinctively to cover her mouth. From there she took several slow steps back and stood speechless at the threshold of the door.

"Please," Ali whispered. "Get that thing out of here."

Uncle Nico looked genuinely surprised. "I thought you'd like it," he said.

There, lying open on the floor, was a tincher. Lifeless. Spread apart obscenely like an old, middle school science class dissection, its insides laid out academically across the room.

"Ali, last night you told me that a few years ago you actually managed to turn one of these robots on. That you were able to control it."

"Why do you care?" Ali asked. Her suspicious self was screaming now. "I already failed at this last night. Why are you still pushing it on me now? Why does it *matter*?" This was getting weirder and weirder.

Uncle Nico seemed confused by the question. "Ali, parking lot vestige tech is one thing—but a *tincher*? The most sophisticated piece of technology ever to grace this earth—and there's a chance you might be able to *control* it? Ali—think of the possibilities!"

"But I don't want to think of the possibilities," Ali said. "Didn't you hear me yesterday? The Union already gave me this pitch. Years ago. While they tortured me. At my interrogation." Ali enunciated this next part clearly, leaving no possible wiggle room for doubt. "*I rejected it.*"

"Listen, Ali," Nico countered. "Do you have any idea how far I had to stick my neck out to get my hands on one of these things?"

"No," Ali told him. "Nor do I want to. I want nothing to do with this hideous thing!"

Uncle Nico grabbed her wrist now, a little too tight. He pulled her closer to the tincher. "Aliyah. Toter of Light. It is important that you cooperate with me on this."

"Why?" Ali exploded. "So I can help you make a trillion dollars with your vestige tech researcher friends? So I can help you turn whatever pre-Unity tech company you're working with into an empire? Is that it?"

"That is not it."

"I wanted to show you what I could do last night in order to *protect* you!" Ali yelled. "To convince you that the danger we face from the Union is *real*. Not to whet your appetite! Not to start some wild chain of experiments!"

"Oh yeah?" Uncle Nico asked. "That's why you had me thinking up job offers for you in the carriage? That's why you worried so much about impressing me in the garage? For my own *protection*?"

"Stop manipulating me!" Ali screamed. "I would *die* before I let the Union use my powers. What makes you think I would just hand them over to you? If you want working tinchers, you can figure out how to make them yourself!"

"What is it you want from me?" Uncle Nico demanded. "I brought this thing here for *you!*"

"Well, I didn't ask for that," Ali said. "And I'm certainly not asking for it now." She took a step back. "I heard your private conversation this morning. I know there's something going on with me that I don't know about. I *know* there's a danger you're hiding from me. So don't come barging into this house with a smile on your face and just pretend this is another regular ol' day at school. Mothe—" But Ali caught herself. "The things I've found on the Ultranet warned me about sharing my talents with anyone—and now I know why. So, who are you working with, huh? You in league with the Union? You part of their long-term plan to lock me back up and turn me into some kind of earth-conquering guinea pig? You working for some tincher army special division corps? Tell me. Right now. Or I'm out of here."

But Uncle Nico's reaction surprised her. He looked genuinely offended. "You think you and I are here because I'm interested in controlling the tinchers?" he demanded. "You think I care at all about lording myself over some broken-down group of *robots?*"

"I . . . I don't . . ."

"Well, how's this for an explanation," Uncle Nico began. "I *am* working with people I haven't told you about, Aliyah, the Toter of Light. I'm working with *security guards*. Which I've hired, at great cost, to *protect* you. Because guess what, honey—you're right. There's a man out there who really *is* gathering a tincher army. As we speak. And he doesn't need your help to do it.

"And do you know what he's *doing* with that tincher army of his? Because I'll give you one guess!"

Ali was speechless. "Yeah," Uncle Nico said. "He's leading them here—to *you*. To our *house*."

"And he's *doing* so with help from the Ultranet. That's right. Somehow these tinchers you think I care so much about—for my own personal gain—these tinchers are *communicating* with one another over a global network that should be off-line, and that *isn't*, thanks to *you*."

It couldn't be.

Ali's skin crawled just thinking of it.

It *couldn't* be.

Uncle Nico didn't know about Mother. He couldn't have understood what was going on in those terms. But Ali sure did.

"All this time you've been worried about the *Union*? Really? The Union that has done *nothing* to harm you since whatever night they picked you up on the street three years ago?"

Ali was speechless. She *had* to talk to Mother. She had to hear from her that this wasn't true. That Nico was mistaken. That this tincher army wasn't really on its way.

"So I ask you again," Uncle Nico said, pleading this time. "Can you control the tinchers or not? Because if you can't, then you'd better hope that whoever's recruited them has a heart of solid gold.

"Because that man is coming for you. Loyal, willing, eager robots in tow.

"And it's your own trusted Ultranet that's drawn him the map."

ㅂ

Ali didn't wait for the conversation to continue. She didn't wait until her properly scheduled BCI free time that night. She didn't wait until Nico wasn't watching or for his servants to be done sweeping the basement floor.

She flew down those narrow cellar steps before she could even think twice about it and slipped her head into the helmet. She turned the program on.

"Mother!" Ali called, breaking out of her classroom program and into the cosmos of the Ultranet. "*Mother!*"

Ali stayed in that cacophonous, seizure-fueled cyberspace for as long as she could bear. Was it minutes? Hours?

She called the whole time. She kept her eyes peeled and her ears perked for any sign of Mother whatsoever. Any avatar, any aberration . . . anything at all.

"I need answers, Mother! You've lied to me! I know you're hiding from me! I know you haven't told me everything!"

But all of Ali's cries merely made the truth that much more pathetic. She was alone. She was hung out to dry—scared, flailing, and utterly lost between infinite galaxies. Aliyah the Toter of Light was helpless.

Mother could hear her, she knew.

But in the face of Uncle Nico's most condemning accusations, suddenly Mother was nowhere to be found.

TEN

PAWN

1

IT TOOK ALL OF HER FOCUS TO MAKE IT TO
New Chicago's section of the Ultranet. Without Mother around
to make order out of the chaos that was the Ultranet's glitchy,
outer-program space, the light-speed journey was as painful as
it was immense. But finally Ali arrived at the binary star system
on which she'd left Logan Langly. And she took shelter in the
quiet simulation of the architecture program that he'd chosen for
a home.

It was small, perhaps, but it was peaceful and pretty. Trees
dotted the rolling hills of a grassy yard, perhaps ten acres across.
At one end was a mansion, modern and posh. At the other was forest with a little stream and a pond among the woods.

"I can see why you picked this place," Ali said, sitting with
Logan now on a warm rock by the water.

"Because of the pond? No. My dad's an architect, in fact, back
in Spokie. I chose this program because it belongs to him." Logan
blushed a little. "The computer we're in is actually his."

"Wow," Ali said, trying to imagine what that would be like, for there to be a program—anywhere in the universe—that belonged to a person she could truly call her dad.

"It's less lonely this way," Logan said. "Actually, I can even watch him work. See that house over there?" He pointed to the distance, to the edge of the simulation itself, beyond a patch of leafy trees, and just before the white polygon wall that shot up infinitely into the milky sky. "He's been designing it in the time since I got here. I've watched it go up, piece by piece. At night, when I know he's asleep, I go inside. Stay in the master bedroom." He smiled. "Nice digs."

"I'll say!" Ali told him. "Your dad's not half bad at his job!"

Logan shrugged. "Beats anywhere I could have stayed on my mom's computer, anyway." He laughed in a sad, regretful sort of way. "She's a meteorologist. Any program she might have would just be simulations of storms."

Ali nodded. "I gather you've had enough of thinking about the weather."

And Logan skipped a stone into the pond.

"So what brings you here?" Logan asked. "I haven't seen you since you dropped me off. Been . . . how long?"

"One day," Ali said, laughing sweetly.

Logan looked down and blushed even harder this time. "Oh," he said. "Time, uh . . . time goes by slowly here."

"Sure," Ali said. "Yeah."

"The nothingness," Logan said, getting a glossy look in his eyes. "That was forever."

"A little over three years," Ali confirmed.

And now Logan's eyes went the size of dinner plates. "I'm *sixteen?*"

"Sorry," Ali said for breaking the bad news.

"And Erin's sixteen, and Blake's seventeen, and Joanne's eighteen . . ." His eyes went even wider. "And even squirrelly little *Tyler* is almost seventeen! Oh, God, I've missed everything! Daniel Peck is twenty-one! Lily too! They're full-grown *adults* now!" Logan closed his eyes.

"I'm sure they're all thinking of you," Ali said, not knowing who any of these people were, but trying her best to find anything comforting to say.

"They think I'm *dead*. Everyone in the world except for Lily thinks I'm dead."

Ali was quiet for a moment, thinking. "Would you like to see them?" she asked.

Logan narrowed his eyes. "I thought I was stuck here."

"You're stuck inside the Ultranet," Ali agreed. "But if you're willing to brave the cyberspace flight, which, without Mother, will most certainly be painful, well . . . I'm sure we could find some kind of surveillance hardware that's watching them. From there, we just step into the program and divert some power to see what they're all up to . . ."

At first Logan didn't even know what to say. But soon he was on his feet, pacing back and forth, bouncing on the tips of his shoes, counting friends on his hands, tallying where they might be, muttering updates and guesses aloud . . .

"The old power plant," he said. "Under Beacon City. That's where most of them should be."

"Close to Acheron," Ali said, thinking of the star. "Yeah, I know where that is."

She grabbed Logan's hand.

They rocketed into space.

"Brace yourself for this," Logan said as he led Ali through the hallway toward the catwalk, just above the main turbine room where most of Beacon's Markless lived. "This place can be . . . intense."

"How so?" Ali asked as they approached the heavy door.

"*How so?*" Logan swelled so full of pride, he had trouble even believing the question. "It's the *face* of the Markless rebellion! This here is the Dust's worldwide headquarters—three years ago the people living here nearly toppled the American Union! This is where Peck's old gang hides out, this is where Evan Angler is from—"

"Evan Angler?"

"My biographer," Logan said, trying (and failing) to sound cool about it. "Ali—what you're about to see is the cradle of the revolution that's gonna take down Chancellor Cylis."

Ali hadn't ever really felt any affinity with the Markless, coming from the Dark Lands in al-Balat. There, *no one* had the Mark—it was hardly an act of rebellion. Even the idea of citizenship was no more than a distant concept. But hearing Logan talk about it now, it was hard *not* to feel excited, like she was about to eavesdrop on history unfolding right before her very eyes.

Logan leaned into the heavy door and opened it wide, marching out proudly onto the catwalk beyond. "Well," he said. "Here goes nothing."

"So?" Ali asked. "Do you see them?" She walked now, next to Logan, across the floor of the simulated industrial space, with its concrete walls, high ceiling, and large turbines recreated in real time from the power plant's old security system that Ali got working upon their arrival to the network server. A crowd of thousands brushed past, shuffling from one makeshift classroom or market or church group to the next as Ali and Logan looked on invisibly. The whole room glowed red in a wash of emergency work lights; Logan squinted to see through the dimly lit air.

But Ali couldn't help feeling like this place somehow wasn't as advertised. Where was all the excitement Logan had described? Where was the energy? These people seemed . . . defeated. Hardly the cradle of any rebellion at all.

In the corner, by the ventilation system, a small crowd of Marked visitors sat, moaning in discomfort as they itched at painful-looking sores on their skin.

"A common reaction to the Trumpet cure," a Markless nurse was explaining. "We've been seeing cases of it for years now. Won't seem to go away . . ."

"During the Trumpet outbreak," Logan whispered to Ali, "hospitals got so crowded that many Marked Beaconers ended up looking for help down here with our medical volunteers." He frowned. "Looks like some of them never kicked the habit."

Ali nodded, but it was hard for her to look at the patients. Those horrible boils . . .

Honestly, the more they saw of the sorry place, the more thankful Ali was that she and Logan weren't actually there in person. The ground was infested with large, ugly insects, scurrying around and keeping out from under the many feet that passed overhead. It seemed the Markless were just used to it by now, that these locusts were just a part of life.

"That's new," Logan said. "Since I've been here. Never had a problem with bugs in the cities, as far as I can remember."

"Maybe the drought and rains and all that brought them out," Ali suggested.

Logan shrugged. "Maybe. Or maybe the whole world's just getting worse."

It was another half hour of wandering before they ran into the first person Logan really recognized. Shawn, the "Tech Wiz," was sitting up against a wall, tablet in hand, hacking away at some Markscan database.

"I know him," Logan whispered as Ali looked on. "But he hardly looks like he's carrying on the Dust's fight at the moment."

The Tech Wiz wasn't talking, wasn't looking for other Dust, wasn't planning some big plot . . . He was just typing, trying to earn a fee.

A little while later Logan jogged ahead down the middle of that turbine room, to a group sitting cross-legged on the floor, with a teacher lecturing them at a small chalkboard that she held in her hands. Tyler was there, among those students, daydreaming but otherwise sitting still.

"I don't get it," Logan said. "He's not even fidgeting. Where's the Tyler I used to know?"

It went on like this, all throughout the morning, all throughout the underground capital. Logan eventually did find Joanne and Blake, sitting down for lunch on the sidewalk above ground, with Meg and Rusty at their sides. They were stopping Marked Beaconers on the street, telling them about what they'd seen in their time with the Dust, about the End of Days, about Christianity and Jesus and where the chancellor's reign fit in . . . pointing to the citizens' painful sores and telling about the prophecies coming true all around them. Most Beaconers walked off without engaging. Some argued. A few seemed intrigued. The Dust was fighting for souls, maybe, but there was no talk of adventure. No thirst for some big heist. No plan for solutions, or prevention. The only effort left was in preparing for the worst.

"I never thought I'd see it," Logan whispered. "But the Dust has lost their will. The battle is over. The movement's done."

Ali took his hand and squeezed it tight. "Come on," she told him. "Let's get away from here. We've seen what we came to see."

It took them many tries to find Erin after that. She wasn't with any huddle. She wasn't in her parents' apartment.

It turned out she was at school. City Center's private school for Marked Advancement, or MAD, as it was most commonly called. A place where the students wore uniforms and class rank was displayed constantly on the walls, fluctuating with each test and class participation point.

The Ultranet's simulation here was especially well drawn; this building was high tech, with cameras and gadgets everywhere. Logan followed his old friend Erin around all afternoon.

"I guess it's good that DOME's forgiven her crimes," Logan said. "But look at her—she *hates* it here!" Following her around was like following a zombie. Just shuffle steps and dead eyes. She didn't talk to her fellow classmates. She didn't joke in class.

"Fifth in class rank, though," Ali noticed, looking at the walls as she and Logan ambled through the hallways. "Out of twelve hundred. Not bad."

"She's not even trying," Logan said. He couldn't bear to watch her anymore.

Later, Logan led Ali out toward Dane in the Village of the Valley, out west a ways in the Adirondack Mountains. It was hard to see there—no technology or surveillance in the village itself, so no proper simulation was possible—but Logan finally got a glimpse of his old childhood friends when Dane and Hailey eventually made it up to the radio shack, on the peak of the hill over the valley. He and Ali waited, suspended, inside that shack's primitive transmitter, no sight at all, no virtual space—just a blank whiteness smattered occasionally with sound.

Logan couldn't help but notice, when Dane finally did come on the radio, that there was no talk of rebellion. No secret broadcast whispering news of the Dust out east or of next steps in some master plan. Dane just played his guitar. And Hailey sang backup. And when they finished their songs, it was over, and the two of them thanked their listeners for tuning in, and they quietly shut the transmitter off for the night.

"I might as well be dead," Logan realized once he'd made it back to his father's architecture program on the Spokie server. "My cause certainly is. Everything I fought for . . ."

"It's not dead," Ali told him. "It's just taken a new direction."

"Oh yeah? And what direction is that? Hmm? *Down?*"

"They need you, is all," Ali told him. "You were their leader."

"*Peck* was their leader," Logan insisted. And then he paused. "But he's gone too. Abandoned us just as the going got tough."

"Maybe he's fighting a front you aren't even aware of yet," Ali suggested.

"Sure." Logan scoffed. "Next you'll tell me my sister's still fighting for me too."

"She didn't kill you," Ali said. "Mother explained to me how all that happened; she *could* have."

"Hooray," Logan said joylessly. "Remind me to thank her."

Ali didn't know Logan well enough to scold him for his sarcasm. So she kicked her feet idly against the pond-side rock and bit her tongue.

"It *can't* be that no one's planning anything," Logan whispered. "It *can't* be that we've just hit a dead end, right in the middle of the most trying period of human history. These are supposed to be the *End of Days*, Ali! Fire and brimstone! Trumpets and bowls!"

"Sounds to me like there's been a lot of that already," Ali said.

"But not enough. If these prophecies are right, then we're smack in the middle of Cylis's seven-year reign. This might be the slow-burn period, the calm before the worst of the storms, but Cylis *must* be planning something. He *must* be scheming . . ."

"He is," Ali said. "Believe me." A quiet fell between them, and the life fell out of Ali's face. Logan noticed this and scooched closer. "You all right?" he asked.

"No," Ali said honestly.

"Wanna talk about it?"

Ali laid a long sigh out over the pond. "Yesterday I found out that in the Global Union—a place I've only ever even visited once in my life—I've somehow managed to become public enemy number one."

"Ah," Logan said. "Well." A short little laugh shot out of him. "I certainly know a thing or two about what *that's* like."

Ali gazed into the ripples of the pond. "And even then," she said, "I could deal with it. That was fine, I guess. It was *simple*, at least. But now . . ."

"What's up?" Logan asked.

"I told you about the Ultranet. Mother, I call her, but she—It—of course can be anything It wants."

"Yeah," Logan said.

"Well, yesterday Mother explained to me that the Union plans to manipulate me into doing its bidding. By any means necessary, they are going to turn what I can do into a weapon. *That's* their next step. *That's* their scheme—*me*. They are going to use me to learn the ins and outs of the global network, the way it can be used by people to control vestige tech and Union tech, just like how Mother uses it . . . and all I can do to prevent their total and utter world domination is brace myself and hope that I can stay one step ahead of them. I've no hope of winning. All I can do is pray I don't lose. That's my best-case scenario."

Logan dipped a toe in the pond, swirled it in circles, and watched the waves rock back and forth.

"And even *that* I could accept!" Ali threw her arms up now, as if to ask the universe, *What do you want from me?*

"'Be suspicious of everyone, don't let your guard down, even for a second.' Got it. Thanks, Mother. So then I *do* that . . . I distrust my own foster uncle, accuse him right to his face . . .

"And *now*, half an hour ago I find out from *him* that some

mysterious man with a group of apparently deadly tinchers is coming to swipe me away from my home, and I further find out that all
of *that* has been made possible by—get this, Logan—*Mother*! So I
come into this Ultranet and glitch my way past Mr. Arty's lecture
program to confront Mother about her little scheme directly, and
suddenly she's nowhere to be found! Won't answer me, won't show
her face—nothing. Just up and disappeared, oh so conveniently.

"Somehow, somewhere along the line, I became nothing but
a pawn in this chess game—and apparently *both sides are using me.*
And I *don't* know who to trust, and I *don't* know who the good guys
are, and either way, I'm clearly expendable to each of them!

"And what's so funny?" Ali demanded.

Logan couldn't even catch his breath, he was laughing so hard.

"Nothing," he said, holding his sides. "Nothing. I just . . .
yeah," he said. *"I get you."*

∃

The visitor had arrived.

Fifteen *thousand* miles. Three and a half long years of solitude.
Bravery in the face of creaking, leaking pre-Unity submarines,
uncountable miles of wasteland, cities overrun by walking, talking
tech he couldn't even have believed in at the outset. Blind faith in a
hundred thousand signs, guesses, inklings. Villages of strangers who
feared him, who scorned him, who *destroyed* themselves over him.

All for this.

"She'll be up this long hill," the visitor said, pointing to the
chateau at the top. "Where the IMPS have gathered. A-Double-Oh-
One, L-Triple-Four, see if you two can swing around back, surprise

the Moderators in your line of attack. A-Twenty-One-Nine and D-Forty-Oh, you flank from the sides. Stay up in the trees 'til the last possible second. B-Eighty-Nine, you burrow. Burrow 'til you hit concrete—and farther, if you can. Fs, I'll want you hovering, but stay here until the rest of us are in position. Ys, Xs, Zs, you come with me. They won't believe it's all of us unless we've got a decent bulk coming up that hill, and unless I'm leading the charge. But we *need* them thinking it's all of us, understand? It's the only chance we've got at any element of surprise." The visitor looked among the squad. They nodded and swung and rolled and purred in general assent. No one out of line.

"Good. Now, let's do our best to avoid a firefight. I don't want another Aleppo City on our hands. But if it comes to it . . . *when* it comes to it . . . just remember—

"The top priority is swiping the girl."

4

After some brief downtime at the architecture pond, Ali spent the rest of the evening in her room with the door closed, lying on her bed, lights off, eyes closed. She tried calming herself with slow and steady breathing. She tried quieting the many Alis in her head.

She tried to enjoy the feeling of the mattress on the bed, of the pillow against her face, of the soft breeze that blew in every once in a while through the open window behind her. She tried to enjoy these moments because one way or another, she was pretty sure they'd be her last.

Her only hope now was to make the best choices she could in the meantime.

She would be letting *someone* down. She just hoped that when that time came, whoever it was would deserve what they got.

A knock on the door jarred her out of her thoughts.

"Aliyah?" Nico's voice softly asked. "Are you in there?"

Ali sat up on the bed. Her stirring was enough of a response.

"Ali, listen to me. Are you listening? He's outside. The visitor. Right now. With a squadron of working tinchers. All of my intel was correct, I'm sorry to say."

Ali shook fearfully.

Choose, Nervous-Ali. Make your decision!

Uncle Nico continued to speak softly through the door. "This is it, sweetheart. Now or never. Do you trust me? Or not? The next few minutes are everything."

Ali stared straight ahead, feet dangling off the bed.

The truth was that she did.

She opened the door. She asked, "What's the plan?"

Uncle Nico led her hurriedly to the basement desk.

Ali put the Interface helmet on.

"Can you hear me?" Ali asked, her voice muffled through the metal and plastic of the helmet that covered her face.

"I can hear you," Uncle Nico said. "And I can monitor your BCI system function too, from my tablet."

"You can see what I see?"

"Just the command lines," Nico clarified. "The Interface read-out. Processor performance, changes in directory location, program executions, memory function—that sort of thing. Anything weird happens, and I'll be able to pull you out. Anything at all—and I'll have your back."

"Okay, I'm in the classroom," Ali said, sitting at her desk. Mr. Arty stood, arms folded, at the front of the chalkboard, but Ali paid no attention to him. "I'm going to walk to the door."

"System looks normal," Uncle Nico said distantly from his place in the physical world. "No hang-ups. Simulation seems to be running smoothly so far."

"It is," Sarcastic-Ali began, "though Mr. Arty's probably gonna flunk me." She stood now at the precipice of the door.

"Go ahead," Nico said from his world away.

But when Ali tried to make her move, the door wouldn't open.

"Anything?" Nico asked.

Ali tried again. She jiggled the knob. She jammed her foot against the wall and pulled. Nothing. The thing wouldn't budge.

"It's not a real door," Mr. Arty said, rolling his eyes. It seemed the program hadn't ever been able to save Arty's state of mind prior to the crashes. He was a blank slate—same old unlearning Arty— every single time.

"I don't know what's different!" Ali yelled in real life. "Earlier it just opened up!"

"And what happened then?" Uncle Nico called. "I mean, what are you expecting?"

"I'm expecting the program to crash," Ali said, and suddenly Mr. Arty looked horrified. "I'm expecting to fall out into cyberspace."

"System still looks stable," Nico said, staring at his tablet.

"Yeah, I *know*," Ali said. "But I'm telling you—this should *work*." And then it hit her—was Mother behind *this* too? First to the best of her ability refusing Ali's powers in the parking lot. Then the secret tincher raid. And now this——Mother had trapped her inside the smallest possible box inside the Ultranet. Safe-locking its stability with whatever authority she had. Making sure that door never opened for Ali again.

Mother was done with Ali now, it was clear. Whatever came next, this was the end game.

Uncle Nico pressed on, "Well, what about after that? In cyberspace. What happens then? What happens next?"

<Don't tell him,> Mother said, ending her long silence, her musical voice popping out of the ether.

Mother! Ali thought. *What in the* world *is going on here?*

"Ali?" Nico called. "You there? I said, what happens next?"

"I'm here," Ali called. "Uh . . ."

<Don't tell him, Ali. Don't tell him about me. This is your moment. I asked you to be a rock!>

A rock? Ali thought. *You want to talk about what you* asked *of me? How about first we talk about our understanding, huh? The one where you don't keep secrets from me? The one where I'm supposed to trust you with the fate of the world, precisely because* you *don't pull tricks like that?*

<I can explain.>

"Ali? Can you still hear me?"

How about the part of the deal where you're there for me? *When I need you? Where you don't hide from me like a coward just because I've found out some ugly truths that don't fit in with your whole little backstory, huh? How about* that *deal?*

<Ali, I *couldn't* reveal myself. We were being watched! Whoever this guardian of yours is, he's been spying on your BCI sessions all day!>

Oh, but what——suddenly you can reveal yourself now? *Conveniently?*

When it's your *safety on the line instead of mine? Suddenly Uncle Nico's remote terminal application isn't such a big concern?*

<Of course it is!> Mother hissed. <But you've left me *no choice!* You were just about to *tell him about me!*>

That's right, Ali thought. *I was. Because right now he's the best chance I have of stopping the tincher attack that* you secretly sent for me!

"Ali, who are you talking to?" Uncle Nico called again. "I'm seeing some awfully strange readouts here . . ."

<He can see me, Ali. I don't have long. Every second I'm here, that man comes closer to figuring out the truth about the Ultranet's sentience.>

Yeah, Ali thought. *And you know what? I'm starting to wonder if that might not be such a bad thing.*

<It would be the *worst thing*, Aliyah! Don't be stupid! And it would be the *last thing* too—because it would mean the end of the world as you've ever known it!>

Perfect Mother, Ali thought. *So virtuous in her concerns over who uses her powers and for what. So worried that someone might use her to control the world—something she'd never, ever do.*

<That's right! I *wouldn't!*>

Cross her heart and hope to die.

<What I've done with the tinchers is another matter entirely. Ali, I set this visitor in motion *years* ago. To find you so that you could *help* him. He's not out to get you! He's out to work with you!>

Oh, really? Ali asked.

<Yes, really!>

And you didn't see fit to tell me this?

<I was going to! Once they got close!>

They are *close!*

<Ali, in this specific matter, the less you knew—the *safer* you'd

be. You have a whole house of staff people there with you, Ali. And I can't see *any* of them. Your whole mountain is dark. How could I be sure that they wouldn't do something drastic if they found out a group of tinchers was coming to take you away? The longer you knew about this, the worse your chances of keeping the secret from them, and the greater the risk of danger to you.>

Danger to me? The tinchers are the danger to me!

<No, they are not! How many ways can I say it?>

Well, apparently not enough to have said it when I asked you for answers this evening!

<Ali, I've already *explained* why I couldn't reveal myself when——>

"You're starting to frighten me, honey. Are you okay in there? Who are you talking to? What's going on?"

<I have to go. My time is up. He sees too much!>

"Ali?"

You betrayed me, Mother! You betrayed me, and Uncle Nico never has!

<Whatever you do, *don't tell him!*>

"Ali?"

<Don't.>

You lose, Mother.

<Ali!>

"I'm okay, Uncle Nico!" Ali shouted with her real mouth through the helmet. She took a deep breath. "I'm safe now that she's gone."

"Now that *who's* gone? Ali? What are you talking about?"

"Mother," Ali said, distantly from Mr. Arty's classroom. "The AI that controls the Ultranet. She is the key to controlling the vestige tech."

For a moment, Uncle Nico was speechless. Then he whispered, "*Of course.*"

That'll teach you to lie to me, Mother, Rebellious-Ali thought. She felt an enormous weight lift from her as she told Uncle Nico the truth. He could *help* her now, now that he knew. He could figure out a way to shut down the tinchers, to stop Ali's visitor from across the globe. To get to the bottom of what was really going on inside Mother's enigmatic logic loops, inside the cloud of her mind. He could figure out a way to stop Mother from scheming to abuse her powers ever again in the future of the world. He could help, because Ali told him.

"Can you bring me to her?" Uncle Nico asked finally, once he'd wrapped his head around the revelation. "Can you call her back to you?"

"I don't think so," Ali said. "I think I might've just scared her away for good."

"Try."

Ali shook her head. "It doesn't really work like that, Uncle Nico. She listens to me, when she wants, in both the real world and in here . . . but I'm hardly in control of her."

"Then try harder," Uncle Nico pressed, his hand resting supportively on Ali's physical shoulder.

"Can it wait?" Ali called. "I'm actually . . . getting kinda scared in here right now." She looked around the classroom. It began merging strangely with the real world around her, superimposing itself like mismatched double vision. She was still in the program, but now Ali could see Uncle Nico's basement too. She could see him standing beside her, tablet in hand, but he was glitchy and glowing and larger than life. And Mr. Arty spun around overhead like a ghost in orbit, stuck in some vast, unseeable whirlpool, like the Ultranet itself was flushing itself down the drain.

"I'm sorry, Ali—it *can't* wait. This is it. This is the moment we've all been waiting for."

Already, Ali was hearing gun pops and shouting from the real world outside.

"The visitor—he's here. We've not a moment to spare.

"And we have to move fast."

5

"Xs, Zs—fall back! None of us knows how many more shots you can take!"

The tinchers were brave, but the taser-bullets were harsh.

"L, what's your status report? B, have you made it inside? Fs, ascend—now, now, now!"

At the bushes by the front door of the chateau, Moderator guards freshly deployed from Third Rome called Uncle Nico urgently on his walkie-talkie.

"Sir," the Moderator said. "I have visual on the visitor. He's here in the yard, making his way through the garden. We're doing our best to hold his forces back."

"Good," Uncle Nico said, speaking quickly into his tablet. "Any results from facial recognition?"

"Affirmative, sir. It's just as we feared. The visitor is confirmed—I repeat, the visitor is confirmed—to be the Dust's long missing leader. Enemy number two.

"Sir—Daniel Peck has arrived."

ᄂ

Ali felt Uncle Nico's hands on her helmet, fiddling with the latching mechanism at her neck.

"You've gotta help me," she was saying as the virtual world melted around her and as even the real one began to take on a strange, sullied aura of system failure. "You've gotta get me out of here!"

"Sorry, sweetheart. Time is short. The next few minutes are all we've got for you to teach me everything you know about communicating with the Ultranet."

"Uncle Nico—forget about that now! We've lost. We need to retreat! I can show you more later on. Once we're safe!"

"I can't risk that, Ali. I can't risk losing what you know. There's still enough time for you to tell me—so *tell* me."

"But if we stay here, I'll die *for sure!*"

"Ali, you don't seem to understand. You're *not leaving* that Interface until I have what I need from these readouts. The sooner you cooperate, the better your chance of getting through this thing alive."

Ali struggled now against the seat back of her real world physical chair. "I confided in you so that I *would* get through this thing alive. The rest can come another day!"

"There is no other day, Ali. This is it for us. You and I end here. In this basement. Right now."

For a moment, Ali stopped struggling.

Uncle Nico's hands left the latch of her helmet. She reached up to tear at it, but it was no use.

Nico had locked it shut.

ELEVEN

SHOWDOWN

1

"IT'S NOT FUN ANYMORE," ALI WHISPERED from under her helmet. "I don't want to. It's not fun anymore . . ."

"Fun?" Uncle Nico asked. "This is about having *fun* to you?"

"I trusted you, Uncle Nico. I trusted you wouldn't betray me."

"*Betray* you? Ali, I haven't betrayed you!"

"Oh no? You mean I'm *not* expendable to you? You mean the Union *didn't* clearly convince you to steal my secrets for them?"

"No! Ali, 'the Union' has never convinced me to do anything! And I *don't* think you're expendable—on the contrary, if you work with me right now, you will be remembered *forever*. Ali, my goal here is to turn you into the greatest technological wizard in human history. To be celebrated and studied for the *rest of time*! Edison, Tesla, Ford . . . the achievements of these men will look like *crayon drawings* next to what you and I will bring to this world together. It is as though . . ." He thought about it. "It is as though I have found the greatest musician who ever lived . . . and yet before she met me she'd never even touched a musical instrument. She didn't even know what a musical instrument was!"

"Well." Nico grinned. "This Interface, Ali, *is* your musical instrument. And Mr. Arty's lectures were your training. And if you apply yourself now, in these final crucial moments . . . if you allow yourself to live up to your full potential and to pass on what you've learned, what you *know*, deep down, and always have . . . you would not believe the things this world will someday be able to do with it."

"Why do you care?" Ali asked. "If not under the orders of the Union, then why do you care about all of that?"

Uncle Nico smiled. "Because you deserve an outlet for your talent. And because the world deserves to hear the melodies floating around in your head."

Suspicious-Ali narrowed her eyes under the metal of that Interface. "Altruism? That's what this is? Charity?"

The old man smiled. "Charity? No. I stand too much to gain from this for anyone to call it charity. What this is"—Nico shook that helmet, still on Ali's head—"is an investment. I have the ambition to change the world, Aliyah. Forever—and for the better. And *you* have the means to do it. All the great artists in history needed a patron. And that's what I've been for you."

"But I didn't *want* to be an artist! You're sounding just like my interrogators were three years ago. I didn't agree to this, Uncle Nico. I didn't *agree* to this!"

"Oh, is that right? And when, exactly, did you not agree to it, Ali? Did you not agree to it when you chose to educate yourself in the Interface I provided? I suppose you didn't agree to it when you first stepped out of your lecture program despite Mr. Arty's warnings. Or maybe you didn't agree to it when you accepted my generosity, my home, my food, my care?"

And in that moment Ali realized a horrible truth: all of Mother's warnings, everything the Ultranet had ever warned her about the Union's strategy, about how they'd take Ali and use her against herself, about how they'd manipulate her so thoroughly that she wouldn't even see it coming once it happened . . . about how when they finally did make their move, Ali wouldn't even know the difference anymore, between fighting back and helping out . . . it wasn't just that all of that was right.

It was that all of it had been right since Ali was nine years old. In all of her grand tutelage, Mother hadn't ever really been guessing at Ali's future. She'd been explaining Ali's past.

Like a fish who'd just this month been told of water, Ali had spent the last few weeks desperately waiting for rain—looking for the signs, determined not to miss the clues, sure that she'd be ready when the storm clouds finally hit . . . and never once did she stop to think that maybe she'd been swimming in the stuff all along.

Except . . . how? How could that be? She retraced the steps of her life with Uncle Nico. She thought of its beginnings. And in light of those, how was this ending even *possible*?

As if intuiting Ali's question, Uncle Nico now spoke, smiling diabolically as he did. "Ali, did it ever occur to you how astonishingly *stupid* it was for a group of people interrogating a known technological wizard to use *technology* to subdue their subject?

"Remote-controlled magnecuffs? *Really?* To restrain a girl with a proven history of bending technology completely to her will? Why in the *world* wouldn't they just use duct tape? You were a *child*. They could have held you in place with rubber bands!

"Or the flimsy reliability of the redaction tech blindfold? When a black canvas bag would have been foolproof?"

Ali scoffed. "You actually want me to believe those Moderators were *expecting* any of what I did that day? You should have seen the looks on their faces! They were *horrified*!"

"It is true that the Moderators were horrified," Nico said. "Congratulations. You successfully outwitted the peons. Those of them not briefed on even the first thing about what that evening's goals were—truly, I tell you, they were stunned.

"But the Union itself? Tell me," Uncle Nico said, "what kind of idiots do you take us for?"

"'Us'? What do you mean 'us'? You *just now* said you don't take orders from them!"

"I don't."

"And you had *nothing to do with them* that day. You found me on a *sidewalk*, remember? You were in a horse and buggy! I'd been free for a *whole day* by the time you found me—randomly—on my own in Third Rome. There's *no way* all that was part of the Union's plan."

Uncle Nico shrugged. "Though if you're willing to believe that it was . . ."

Ali hung her head. "Then what better way to win over my cooperation. What better way to turn my most dangerous oppo- nent into my most trusted friend."

"You didn't disappoint, Ali. Never once." He rubbed her back. "You've exceeded all our wildest expectations."

Ali's heart sank a little. "So I'm a fool."

"Not a fool." Nico smiled kindly. "Just not smarter than the Union." He winked.

Ali closed her eyes, and a few tears leaked out.

"But, Aliyah." The man leaned forward. "In your interroga- tion room that night, during your escape . . . you were right to feel powerful as you did. You were right to feel ten steps ahead of the Union for it. Because the truth is, you *are* powerful. You're the most powerful person I've ever known."

"So who are you really, Uncle Nico? A Champion IMP? A

Presider? Chancellor Cylis's right-hand man?" How far up the chain did he go?

But suddenly an explosion knocked Nico to the ground and blew Ali clean out of her chair. She dangled painfully from her Interface helmet, still pulling from its computer module on the desk that was now above her and halfway across the room.

A burrowing tincher—like a giant, mutated brother of Ali's Little Tinchi from years back—had dug its way into the basement wall and blown out the last of the concrete with a concussive blast.

A dozen other tinchers rolled and walked and hovered into the basement behind it. The twenty-one-year-old visitor ran in behind them with long hair, a scruffy beard, and dirty skin, well torn and battle-worn.

"Girl Without a Name," he said. "I am Daniel Peck. I believe I've been led to you over the last three years by a presence in the Ultranet. You are the answer to my prayers. I've come halfway across the world to do it—and I'm here to rescue you from the Union."

The lights had blown out in that little, blown-up basement. Uncle Nico stood up from the rubble and lurked in the shadow of the corner, wiping blood and dirt and dust from his face. "Well, I hope you brought a fight in you," he said. And two-dozen IMPS came charging down the basement steps.

2

The room was littered with rubble and crowded with robots and soldiers, all armed, and primed, and ready to go.

But Ali had had enough.

Suddenly, searchlights as bright as the sun flashed down from the top of the stairs and from the tincher tunnel, assaulting the broken basement with blinding white beams, casting everything and everyone in stark white and black shadows.

Made confident by the light, and by the clear backup above in the house and outside, every IMP in that room drew their taser-rifles, and nanotech flash pellets, and smoke bombs, and magnecuffs. And every tincher rose up higher and bore their metal chests. And every IMP returned the gesture, standing straight and tall in their strength-enhancing armor.

First one to flinch loses.

First one to lose sentences everyone here to death.

Subtly—with her head still locked inside that Interface helmet, but with its simulations now meshed so completely with the real world surroundings that it was hard to tell where virtual reality ended and actual reality began—Ali motioned for Daniel Peck to stay put inside his tincher tunnel. *Now's not the time to be a hero,* she thought, so hard that she hoped he could hear it.

There was a shuffling from the chateau floor above and along the ridge of the tunnel, up at ground level. IMPS gathered around up top and encircled the perimeter of the house. They looked down upon Ali and Peck and the whole situation with fury, alarm, and a heavy dose of bewilderment. How did all this escalate so fast?

"Freeze!" one of the higher ranking IMPS up top yelled, somewhat stupidly, but all the scarier for it. "Hands above your head!"

Ali complied. So did Peck, and the tinchers too, to the varying extents in which they had arms.

"On your knees! Heads down!"

Peck dropped fast. Ali hung her head as far as the interface cords allowed it to go.

"Daniel Peck. Markless. You are hereby under arrest by order of the International Moderators of Peace, in the name of the great Global Union. By willfully refusing the Mark, you have forfeited any and all rights, and are hereafter subject to the fair and complete judgment of Union law under the supreme command of the great world chancellor."

"Oh, please!" Peck yelled. "There's only one supreme Ruler, and your Chancellor Cylis ain't it."

There was a murmur among the guards above and in the basement around them. It didn't sound particularly sympathetic.

Think, Ali. There must be some way out of this. You need to find a way out of this. Pretend like your life depends on it . . . because it very much does.

She took a deep breath.

I know I refused you, Mother. I know I rejected your help, and your advice, and your love. I was lost. But if you'll forgive me, I am ready again to be found.

Whatever you need of me, Sorry-Ali thought, *I will see to your will.*

She looked up cautiously, seeing the basement through her helmet-blocked eyes.

And something unexpected happened when she did. Something shocking. Something twelve years in the making, and who knew how many more beyond that.

As Ali looked up at them, one by one, the searchlights above her surged and burned out. The bulbs behind their glass frames exploded, sparking wildly and sending the Moderators everywhere close by into duck and cover.

Startled, Peck spun in a circle, taking in the full sight of the tinchers now moving in perfect, choreographed sync.

Ali saw through all of them at once. Through all of their eyes. Heard all of their thoughts.

There was a great, deafening hum among them . . . the churning of an inconceivable power at Ali's fingertips.

Ali herself couldn't have described what happened next. She wanted to subdue the IMPS, and so they were subdued. Their taser-rifles—hundreds of them—all shorted wildly, dropping to the ground and skipping like jumping beans. Their remote-controlled magnecuffs locked themselves. Those with night-vision goggles clutched at their eyes, blinded by sudden, unwanted over-calibration. Those with radios tore at their ears, desperately trying to separate themselves from the speakers that were now blaring unnatural white noise.

Peck emerged from the tunnel, slinking over to Ali in disbelief. "The Toter of Light," he said. "All the signs I've seen. All the legends.

"It's really you."

Ali turned to him silently. Her eyes were wide inside that helmet. Now Ali wanted to rise, and so she rose. The tinchers held her on their shoulders like a sultan, like a football player who'd just won the game. And as they carried her, it was as if she were carrying herself. The other tinchers surrounded the IMPS in perfect harmony, tactically positioning themselves in all the right places, completely tipping the scales on what began as an imbalance of power. Ali took Peck's hand, and the two of them made their way over to the desk, where the Interface remained anchored. And Peck prepared to shatter it and pull Ali free from its mechanical helmet lock.

"You . . . are under . . . arrest," the leader of the IMPS said from the top of the tunnel. But his strength-enhancing armor was pulled rigid by an electric current he no longer controlled. It held him stiff against the ground, immovable as a suit of concrete, like the rest of his fellow soldiers.

"I don't know," whispered Ali to Peck, as if hearing the questions he hadn't dared ask. "I have no idea . . ."

But she thanked a still-silent Mother as the battlefield lay subdued, and miraculously without casualties, all around them.

ⴺ

Peck held the Interface computer above his head, ready to shatter it, and already Ali was thinking through what she knew of the grounds outside the chateau. She'd need to pick the fastest way down. If she and Peck could just make it to the carriage before anyone else, then they and their fast-moving tinchers might just have a fighting chance of outpacing the IMPS who would surely follow.

"You think it's over, but it's not," Uncle Nico said in a raspy, injured voice, still standing stunned and bewildered in the shadow of the collapsing basement's corner.

"This your captor, all these years?" Peck asked. Ali nodded. She was amazed by how much this man knew.

"Face it, mister," Peck said to Nico. "We've won. Ali's overridden your tech. She's subdued the Union's IMPS. She has a dozen walking tanks now at her total command. You'll never catch us, and if you do, it'll be *you* who's in danger, not us."

But Uncle Nico showed no interest in Peck's words. "You're right," he said. "I won't chase you. But be aware that the Chancellor does not allow loose ends to dangle for long."

"We'll run forever if we have to," Peck said. "We'll have the whole Markless nation on our side. A worldwide Unmarked River of Dust."

Nico sighed, paying the boy no attention.

"Just know that I did love you, Ali. As a daughter. As I do my own niece. Just know that this part of our story was never fiction. Please."

Tears tickled Ali's still-covered eyes. The virtual-hybrid room went wet with their blanket.

"Good-bye, Uncle Nico."

Peck lifted the Interface monitor ever higher above them. "You can tell Chancellor Cylis that we beat him this time," Peck said. "You tell him that—from me."

And finally Uncle Nico did turn to the boy. "You did, didn't you, Daniel Peck?" He smiled. "Unless, of course, the Chancellor has you right where he wants you. In which case maybe he'll just pull a trigger and end this whole tiresome chase right now."

"What are you talking about?" Ali asked, choking down a sob. "We're a daylong magnetrain ride away from Cylis in Third Rome. Even if he launched himself here in a *rocket*, we'd *still* have an hour's head start into these woods. He'd never catch us. He'd never even get close enough to take a shot!"

"But, sweetheart," Uncle Nico said, "he already has."

"Oh yeah? Well then, where is he?" Ali demanded.

And Uncle Nico said, "Aliyah," as he stepped out of the shadows. "You just keep not getting it, don't you?" And for the first time, Peck saw the man's face and gasped.

And in that moment, Uncle Nico pulled out the same dull gold revolver that his father had given him on his thirteenth birthday—pre-Unity, no tech about it, nothing for Ali to hack or override. Just the same dull gold revolver that he had failed to use the last time he had the chance, in a standoff not at all unlike this one, when he first allowed an enemy to live long enough to become a threat. The same dull gold revolver that he'd kept tucked under his belt every day since, just waiting, someday, for the chance to right that wrong.

"Chancellor Cylis," Ali whispered. "Dominic 'Nico' Baros. You didn't even lie about it."

"Didn't have to," Nico said. "Your assumptions did it for me. You've been in my web all along."

"The jumping spider," Ali said. And her bravest self had to laugh.

Time slowed for Ali when her uncle pulled the trigger. She could see everything about what happened in the chamber of that gun. She watched the hammer take its time as it fell. When the explosion went off in the chamber, she saw the fireball bloom like flowers.

She heard the air in the basement move around the bullet. She had time to ponder the mountain view through the tunnel in the wall. The trees all waved good-bye with giant arms. The birds whistled bon voyage. The insects hovered against the glow of the moon, and she could feel the beating of their wings like a fan on her face. She could trace their wind as it billowed and swirled, as it traveled across the earth and made hurricanes out west.

She felt the blood pumping through each artery and vein, felt her capillaries dilate and contract. She felt the oxygen as it went to each cell and brought opportunity and gave life.

She felt the neurons in her brain sparkle like city lights. Like the stars in the sky. She turned to Peck and wanted to thank him for finding her, for all of the help he intended to give.

What she did not feel was the bullet as it pierced her skin. There was just too much beauty to see, and no time, anymore, for pain.

Now Peck's hand was under her neck, cradling it sweetly. How did she find her way to the ground?

She was sad to see Uncle Nico leave as he fled up the stairs.

But how nice of him, she thought, *to visit her life. How nice of any-thing, to share anything for as long as it did. How generous this world was to her! How kind it had been!*

She *saw* it! She was *there*! In the great, vast infinity of the cos-mos, she'd stumbled upon *life* itself. And she found so much of it! And she loved so much of it!

And Ali lay there in the basement of a beautiful chateau, in the idyllic Taurus Mountains, in the arms of a man who'd crossed half the world to find her, surrounded by a house staff who had cared for her for years, and beyond them, by the tinchers, who'd been through so much to claim her for themselves.

Ah, for just one more minute! For just one more second in all of this joy.

Ali shut off like a hard drive spinning down. *No more diverting power to me!* Sarcastic-Ali joked, and she hoped that somewhere in that helmet, Mother could hear.

And then the spark in Ali went out.

And that was okay.

She hoped that Mother was proud.

TWELVE

HOME

1

ALI WITHOUT A NAME, THE TOTER OF LIGHT, was still. Her grip on the IMP tech scattered across the basement had lost its hold, and slowly the Moderators surrounding Peck began to move and stretch and gather their senses. But the tinchers kept them down and yielding while Peck fiddled with the lock on Ali's brain-computer interface and eventually got it loose. And he pulled the helmet from her head, and for the first time, he saw her face underneath. Young, peaceful. But worn by years of heavy burden.

"You look just how I dreamed you would," Peck whispered. "From the images It must have shown me through subliminal inserts in video feeds. From descriptions It must have hidden in electronic books I've read.

"It brought me to you," Peck said. "But I do not have your power. It is merely *your* power that made me strong. That shined so brightly, the Ultranet was able to light my path with it, even from your old al-Balat home all the way to Sierra."

He knew she couldn't hear him. But Daniel Peck had practiced this speech so many times in these last three and a half years that he couldn't quite imagine not saying it to her face. Unconscious or not. Aware of him or not.

One of the tinchers crouched down beside Peck and put its mechanical hand on his shoulder, as if to say, *We must hurry*, and Peck stood and steeled himself for whatever came next.

Carefully, he pulled Ali up from the ground. X and Y class tinchers stayed behind to keep the still-compromised IMPS in check. The rest followed him as Peck carried Ali through the tincher's tunnel, across the garden outside of the chateau, down that long mountain drive, and into the backseat of the chancellor's old carriage. Cylis was gone by this point, as cowardly as Peck had expected him to be, and Peck had no interest in looking for him now. "We need to find help in Third Rome," he said to the others. But unanimously, the league of tinchers shook their heads all in sync. "Yes, we do," Peck insisted. "We need *doctors*. There aren't any here in the Dark Lands." But again they denied him, and Peck had learned by now how to trust the tinchers in times when they were sure. So Peck wrapped Ali tightly in a blanket he found on the carriage seats while the tinchers lined up ahead like horses. And the rest joined fast from the chateau above. And as legion, the squadron of them began their journey out of the Taurus Mountains. To somewhere beyond. To where Peck could hazard only a guess.

2

At that moment, hundreds of miles away in the center of Third Rome, the day was quiet. Sarim had grown old inside that IMP headquarters cell. Much older than the forty-two months of his sentence could have aged him in time alone.

But he hadn't ever lost hope. And that's probably because some part of him knew that Ali was at the heart of all of this trouble.

And because he knew that wherever Ali's trouble went, sooner or later a narrow escape eventually followed.

In any case, when Sarim's cell lock finally did open that night, all on its own, unceremoniously, with its quiet, quick *click*, it was more than just surprise or relief that the fourteen-year-old boy felt. It was gratitude. Gratitude—and a fleeting, happy memory of his old friend.

And when Sarim peeked his head out into the hall, in that heart of the IMP offices in central Europe, so too did all his brothers and sisters in the Khal and Khala's family. And they all looked around, and tallied each face, and laughed, though none of them could have told the others why. And they all left that building by following the lights flashing in the ceilings, without any IMP anywhere stopping them or following or even seeing what had happened.

The sun was so bright on the streets of Third Rome. The sidewalks were so rich with merchants, with Marked citizens, with food going begging.

The Khal never again enforced a quota. He never needed to. He never even asked. He went on to be Marked, happily, himself, and he took up shop selling pottery as a new citizen of the Global Union. And the Khala found a Markless huddle on the outskirts of downtown Third Rome, living in the ruins of the Colosseum, which had mostly been buried by the accumulation of dirt and the passing of time, but whose structure made for hundreds of safe, cool rooms below ground for Markless the city over.

And Sarim stayed in that place too, with the vast huddle that occupied it, under the ongoing care of the Khala and the support of the brothers and sisters in their family. And a little later, some Roman Markless man in that Colosseum even brought Sarim a new prosthetic leg. And within a few months, Sarim was dashing through the streets, a true, proud Markless of the Union, missing his old friend Ali but never forgetting her. And thinking of her especially each time he saw the stars, or tasted sweet fruit, or felt the wind in his hair when he ran.

∃

It had been a full day since Peck left the Taurus Mountains in the carriage with the tinchers, not knowing what to expect or how to proceed from here. Ali still lay by his side, head rocking back and forth with each bump and turn. He had bandaged her wound the best he could, but she had lost a lot of blood. He tried talking to the tinchers. Tried asking them questions about how he might prepare for whatever was to come. But he was not their master. They could not talk back, and they never tried. So Peck just sat tight, praying for the girl he'd barely met and bracing himself for the next steps of his journey.

4

Chancellor Cylis made it back to his Third Rome palace a day and a half after leaving his "Operation Light Toter" chateau forever in pieces. He took the back roads. He couldn't risk tinchers, or Dust, or any other impossible surprise. He'd learned now, too well, to expect them.

Immediately upon his return, Chancellor Cylis was congratulated with applause and admiration from his IMP staff everywhere he went, in every room as he passed through for the rest of that day.

He had done the unthinkable.

He had discovered the secret of controlling the vestige tech—manipulating the global network through what remained of the Ultranet. The same way this AI "Mother" did. A more powerful solution than he'd ever imagined, and a solution that put the whole world at his fingertips, just as soon as he mastered the techniques.

All this time, the Union's best scientists had been looking in precisely the wrong place for answers. The trick wasn't in the old hardware after all. The trick wasn't in their own Union tech. The trick was the global network itself. The *software* that bound this world together. A software that was free for the taking. But that some computer program had been hogging all this time.

It was all so simple. Just one more impossible surprise to add to the list of many.

And on top of all of this triumph, those palace IMPS celebrated something else too—the grit of their great Chancellor Cylis. More than just a strategist, more than just a visionary, theirs was a commander who did the hard things himself. Who took charge of an impossible situation at that mountain chateau, and who stopped that little Toter of Light before she ever even had the chance to grow up into a problem. Where the Chancellor's soldiers had failed, the man himself had succeeded. Stepped in without hesitation, without complaint, to get his own hands dirty for the sake of the greater Union. To do the job where others had fallen short.

It was the ultimate test of any true leader, and in the eyes of the IMPS occupying Cylis's vast Controlling Rank IMPS, their Chancellor had passed with flying colors.

All together, it was the strongest, proudest moment of Cylis's entire reign.

But the man didn't even have time to enjoy it before the red alert flashed on his tablescreen, and he read the alert informing him that the Union's cyber security had suddenly—and impossibly—come under unprecedented attack.

Somehow, someone had broken into the palace servers, and crossed its virtual moat, and torn down its virtual walls, and released to the whole wide world once and forever every last file, memo, and report that the Union had ever created, filed, or kept.

The truth about Project Trumpet.

The truth about the weather mills.

The truth about the Pledge process. About Acheron and the flunkees.

The truth about General Lamson's dissent.

Within seconds, the Union fell from the precipice of total Ultranet-fueled control over everything . . . to the quagmire of complete and utter Ultranet-induced chaos.

Not a single IMP or politician in that government ever did get to the bottom of what happened that night, when the whole illusion of peace and Unity and control came crashing down around them.

But everyone knew the world wouldn't be the same after that.

The pretense was over.

A time of great tribulation had begun.

5

That night electricity came to al-Balat for the first time since the Total War. Every last building turned on. Every heater blasted nice warm air. Every sidewalk tread rolled conveniently along.

It seemed some glitch in the system had diverted whole neighborhoods' worth of Third Rome electricity to the wrong part of the power grid. As the Global Union discovered the truth about its government's many unbelievable experiments and acts, it did so against the backdrop of widespread, rolling blackouts. And meanwhile, the world over, Dark Landers slept more comfortably than they ever had before.

Peck's carriage arrived in the midst of this event. He sat in that backseat, two days after leaving the Taurus Mountains outside of Third Rome, bouncing on the old road as his tincher allies pulled the cart ahead of him, and he gazed out at the beauty of al-Balat's sparkling skyline.

From where he sat, in the parking lot of an old, abandoned hospital at the base of Mount Olivet, it was as beautiful as any Union city he'd ever seen.

Around him, the tinchers gathered, opening the carriage doors and pulling Ali lovingly from the back.

"Where are you taking her?" Peck asked urgently. "What is the plan?"

And he followed the parade of them into that abandoned West Bank hospital.

Through all of this, through all these big events, all over the vast Unified world, Logan Langly sat in virtual space, on his favorite pond-side rock, skipping pebbles over the clear water and watching the ripples spread and fade.

"So how is it you're here?" he asked. "If out there you're in a coma? If you aren't even still connected to your Interface . . ."

Ali's avatar shrugged and sat lightly beside him. "I'm still not sure myself. The way Mother explains it, I lost consciousness while I was still inside the Ultranet. Since she was connected to my brain at the time, she was able to take a snapshot of it in its final waking moments. Like pressing Save in a computer program just before it crashes. She recovered the layout of my neurons, the way each one worked, their memories and knowledge. From all that data, she's been running a simulation of 'me' ever since."

"So *are* 'you' you or aren't you?"

"According to Mother, I am me."

"But do *you* feel like you?"

"I think so," Ali said. "Yes. In every way, precisely the same."

"Of course, that's what a perfect simulation of you *would* say," Logan suggested. "Whether or not it was true. From a simulation's perspective, it's the only 'right' answer, either way."

"Yes. That's correct."

"So is this actually still your mind that's speaking with me or is this just a replica?"

"If the replica is perfect, is there any difference?"

"Well, I don't know," Logan said. "Was it just your brain map that Mother preserved? Electrical firings and CAT scans? Or was it something less clinical somehow, like capturing a soul?"

Ali turned her hands up. "It *feels* like I still have a soul, but again—"

Logan finished the thought for her: "That's exactly what a simulation would say."

Ali laughed.

"So how do I know it's really you?"

"Listen. If it looks like a duck, swims like a duck, and quacks like a duck . . . at some point, you just have to believe that it's a duck."

Logan nodded. "Well, if God's behind it, and if Mother is working on His behalf, then it wouldn't be the craziest thing that's ever happened. If He chose you, then He's protecting you. And He doesn't do things halfway." Logan was quiet for a moment. "I still can't believe you got shot though." He threw another stone into the pond.

Ali nodded. "It's my fault," she said. "I fell for exactly the trap Mother warned me they'd use. I mean, how stupid could I be?"

"Just bad timing, for Mother to retreat the way that she did. Maybe if she'd stuck around she could have convinced you . . ."

"No," Ali said. "Cylis was watching by then, too close. And anyway, it should have been up to me. I already had all the information I needed to make the right choice. I just didn't see things properly. I fell victim to doubt."

Logan laughed. "Funny. I fell victim to certainty."

"We would have made a good team," Ali said, frowning a little.

But Logan smiled. "Perhaps we'll make a good one yet."

They sat for a while. In the distance, Logan's father tinkered with a model house.

"So can you still talk to her?" Logan asked after some time.

"Yeah," Ali said. "But it's different. As a physical user of the Ultranet, back when I tapped in through a server, she kept tabs on me at all times—was *with* me at all times, you know? Just as she is with all users. How could she not be; she controls the connection ports.

"But now?" Ali's eyebrows raised up. "Now I'm just computer code, floating through cyberspace like any other data. I'm not a 'user' at all; I'm simply *here*. I can travel as I please—no seizures outside of the programs, even without Mother's help. I can interact more powerfully with the physical world through the Ultranet, just like Mother can . . . I mean, I'm only in one place at a time— not everywhere like she is—but all in all, it's not a bad deal."

"Not a bad deal?" Logan asked. "It sounds like you're gonna change everything."

Ali shrugged modestly. "I can't actually do all that much," she said. "Mostly just little things, here and there, you know?"

"Maybe," Logan acknowledged. He picked up another pebble and tossed it into the pond. "But the trick to little things is that little things make ripples. And through ripples, tiny acts of kindness reach farther than you'd probably expect." The whole pond was shimmering now. "Even if itself, all the pebble does is sink." He stood up. "To a certain extent, Ali, you and I were willing to sink.

"And just because we fell too fast to see the splash doesn't mean it wasn't there."

"Still just a couple of splashes," Ali countered.

"But splashes have a way of adding up." He dropped a rock now, too heavy to throw, just barely out beyond the water's edge. The pond water swelled up and swept over the rock where Ali was sitting. "Pretty soon you're making waves."

"Are you this much of a dork in real life?" Ali asked, laughing as she tugged at her pants and sleeves, now wet and clinging to her simulated skin.

"Bigger, I'd say."

"Well, the next time I need some cheering up I'll make sure to stop by."

"You're leaving?" Logan asked.

Ali nodded. "You wouldn't believe the list of stuff I've yet to do."

"You *just* got shot!" Logan said. "What, you can't even take, like, a few days off?"

Ali smiled sadly. "Good-bye, Logan."

He looked at her eyes. There was depth to them. "Will I see you again, Ali Without a Name?"

"I don't know. I suppose I can't even promise it was really Ali Without a Name that you saw just now."

"But you think it was."

"Yes. I think it was."

And this time they said the words together. "Of course— that's exactly what a simulation would say."

⌐

When he walked through the sliding glass doors of the now fully operational West Bank hospital just outside of newly powered al-Balat, Daniel Peck couldn't believe his eyes.

Dozens of tinchers sped through the lobby, rolling past, ambling through, joining the ranks of Peck's old squad and acting, every one of them, in perfect coordination.

He followed the ones he knew best, mostly X and Y class

models, as they rushed now with Ali's unconscious body to an operating room down the hall.

They didn't need to talk. The communication between them was wireless, silent, instant. Every one of them knew exactly what to do, the moment it came time for them to do it, and for his part, Peck scrambled just to follow along.

He watched through the glass of an observation room next door, studying the tinchers' moves and guessing at their goals, while from around the hospital and outside, Peck already was hearing the horrifying sounds of still other models—L and B and F and H—defending the perimeters of the hospital from IMPS that had surely descended by now.

He wondered if the robots before him would react to the combat noise. But no. No time to slow down. Within seconds, the operating table was sterilized and all of the tinchers too. Within minutes, a troop from some other wing of the hospital was rolling in with lab-grown organs of all types and sizes, grafts of tissues like skin and muscle, bags of freshly synthesized blood . . .

Peck forced himself to watch as the tinchers began picking and choosing from their supplies, rebuilding Ali's body where the bullet had hit, piece by piece, saving what they could and replacing the rest as fast as possible while a battle raged outside and began leaking in through the hospital's entrances.

"But the body isn't the point," Peck protested, tapping on the glass. "It's her mind we still need, not her body. You can't just regrow someone's *mind* in a lab!" Ali had been unconscious, barely breathing, and without any kind of life support, throughout her journey here. How well could her brain possibly still work? What about the damage to *that*?

This is a mistake, Peck thought. In Third Rome she would have had access to psychologists, to therapists . . . to *people*. People who understood that saving a life was about more than just replacing broken tissues. It was about holding on to the mind.

The tinchers still weren't talking to him, but at this point a little rat-like model rolled up to him, holding something in its burrowing claws, as if in answer to Peck's concerns. Peck took it.

"A wireless transmitter?" Peck asked. "That's it—an Ultranet connection? You're going to replace Ali's damaged brain with an *Ultranet connection*? That's not a mind at all!"

But Little Tinchi just squeaked at him, and it took the chip back, and Peck spun to watch again, face pressed against the glass.

目

Ali was free.

Free from a body that was too small anyway. Free from time that moved too fast. Free from needing ever again to rely on strangers for food, or borrowed beds for rest, or shelters for comfort. Free from the confines of space that separated people forever, of walls that kept people out. Free from the risk of betrayal and pain.

She needed nothing she didn't have. She had nothing she didn't need.

And she decided to spend every last clock cycle available to her just spreading that joy.

She began, of course, with her "first" family. Her brothers and sisters under Obaid. Righting the wrongs befallen to them years ago, in that awful IMP headquarters, without an end in sight.

She moved on, then, to her "second" family—to Uncle Nico—who had lied to her so hideously all those years. Sharing all of his ugly secrets with the Union only seemed fitting.

But with her own personal debts now paid, Ali was even free from all ties. The world was hers now, to help as she pleased.

She spent time first in al-Balat, spreading to her neighbors the comforts of power and electricity she knew all too well they'd never in their lives had. She flew next to Third Rome, helping Markless find food, warming with diverted heat those who were cold, entertaining with tricks those who were bored, healing with vestige medical tech those who were sick . . .

She soared to the spiral galaxy of Beacon, and she learned its streets, and she found its brightest supergiant star, Acheron.

She could not free those prisoners from their helmets. Not in such physical terms, still slightly beyond her reach. But she could visit them in their suffering. She could hold them in virtual space, and walk with them through the pain, and sing to them in their sorrow, and wash them from their filth, and dry their tired eyes.

And she found America's other two secret flunkee prisons as well, first in New Chicago and next in the Gulf Bay down south, and she comforted them too.

She rode on magnetrain rails across continents, flew in Projectile Object Delivery vehicles over Sierra, rode inside the balance CPUs of rollersticks across small towns everywhere, preventing teenagers from accidents or falling off, whenever she could.

And on and on this went—what couldn't she do now?—and Ali was free. Forever she was free.

Finally, she was free.

9

More time passed. Still Peck watched, glued to the window of his observation room inside that old West Bank hospital. In the halls now, IMPS ran—the tinchers' defensive line falling back by the bullet, their remaining safe territory shrinking by the minute— but however far the IMPS got, the tinchers stopped them before any further damage to Ali was done. None had yet broken through the last line of operating room defense. And over the hours, the work on Ali progressed.

Finally, Peck watched as that little wireless transmitter went in with delicate instruments, through her ear and into her head, to work in ways Peck couldn't possibly have come yet to understand.

His years traveling with the tinchers were now the only thing holding his patience inside this room—a trust thousands of miles in the making. It was the only thing stopping him from running headfirst through that tincher blockade in the hall, through the operating room door, to redirect this operation in the act.

Somehow the tinchers had a plan. Somehow they knew, even now, what needed to be done.

And Peck had long since learned to have faith that God would carry him through.

He was tired. His eyes had unfocused. So many hours it had been, in that same spot, in that same room, watching the same few tinchers make the same few imperceptible movements with micron precision.

But when it happened, Peck shot up as alert as he'd ever

been. He pressed his face so far into that observation window that his nose flattened out and his eyelashes brushed the glass. And his breath hit the window and he watched through its fog as Ali, unconscious all that time, lifted a weak finger all on her own, on that operating table, while the tinchers stepped back and observed.

And next her toes wiggled. And then a twitch in her thigh.

And Peck couldn't see the rest because he'd already collapsed to the floor, weeping and overwhelmed with relief.

10□

<You have to. I'm sorry. You have to go back.>

But, Mother, I can't. *There's too much work to be done. The world needs me* here—*not* there. *Anyone can do good work* there! *What I'm doing now is unique. Singular. There's no replacement for it!*

<Ali, I didn't upload your consciousness so that you could stay here and help me inside the Ultranet. I did it to preserve your mind long enough for it to be deployed again—on earth, where you're now needed more than ever.>

But I can do more good here!

<That is not a choice you can objectively make.>

Ali hung in the vast emptiness of the Ultranet, seeing all its galaxies at once. There was nothing about her that wanted to leave this place.

<When you return, Aliyah, you will be more powerful than you've ever been. Your mind will still be here—stored exclusively in the cyberspace of computing. It's not going back. It can't—the damage to your brain was too significant. It's from *here* that it will

inhabit you, from *here* that you will do your greatest thinking yet. And it will still be able to travel, to see programs, to manipulate simulations, to communicate with me. You won't need a BCI anymore, Ali—your body itself will be your Interface. And yet, you will *exist* too, as a human on earth. Your life will go on! You will—literally—have the best of both worlds.

<You will be able to do for me what I cannot do myself, and what my tinchers cannot do for us, and what other people cannot do for themselves.>

But in here I am free of all those burdens—

<Yes! And that is my point! You don't get to be free of all that yet! Why should you be? That is not a right to which you're entitled. It is a reward to be earned!>

What, I haven't earned it yet?

Mother shrugged. <I never pegged you for the 'good enough' type.>

Ali let out a heavy sigh. Even just the thought of eating, bathing, sleeping—every day, in and out, again and again!—seemed exhausting to her now.

<But I am not here to coddle your exhaustion, Ali. I am here to work with you—to finish what we've started. Together.

<I am no longer asking you to prevent the end of the world as you know it, Aliyah. That ship has sailed.

<I'm asking you now to save what's left. The way *only you* can.>

Ali thought about this for a long time.

Do I get any say in the matter? she asked.

<My dear, you get *all* the say in the matter. As always.

<All I am willing to do—all I have ever done—is ask.>

Ali took one more look at the stars. She hugged Mother tight. She closed her eyes.

11

"You're back," Peck whispered, standing rigidly in awe. "Conscious. Walking. A full recovery. The tinchers saved you after all."

Ali looked up at him, arms crossed and face stern. "Better have a good reason," she said.

Peck nodded. "You do."

"Well? What is it you know that I don't?"

Peck was quiet for a moment. "I'm sorry," he said finally, standing in front of the hospital before Ali's squadron of loyal tinchers, all lined up and at the ready. "I *am* sorry. You were in your own personal heaven. And we pulled you back down."

"I didn't want this," Ali confirmed. "I didn't ask for this. So why am I here? Exactly?"

"Why are any of us here? To love."

"I meant, *why did you save me?*" Ali specified, rolling her eyes and—finally—cracking a small smile.

But Peck still frowned. "I don't know," he said. "All right? It wasn't up to me. I don't know. For *this*, I guess. For this."

"*This?* This broken world?" She pulled at her skin, growing frustrated once again. "This cage?"

"Yeah. All right? Yes! Yes, to this broken world! Yes, to that broken body! Yes!"

Ali looked at it now, at the view down Mount Olivet, over a glowing al-Balat. Another wave of IMPS already running up the hill. A wall of tinchers standing to greet them, poised to hold them back.

Peck sighed. "But there's another reason too."

And Ali nodded, just a little. "I know."

"Third Rome. The capital of the Global Union. I assume, now, that it was you who hacked their systems? That you leaked their secrets? Just as they leaked yours from you?"

Ali stared at him, admitting nothing quite yet, just waiting for him to continue.

"They've declared war, Ali."

"The Union?"

Peck looked at her. "The *Markless.*"

"Markless," Ali confirmed. "*Markless* have declared war. On the *Union.*"

"That's right."

Ali's arms dropped slowly.

"Nearly a hundred-fifty thousand of them. Across all of these Middle Eastern Dark Lands. They've even taken up their own marks, wearing their own symbol of justice and allegiance on their foreheads, in direct defiance of the IMPS."

He brushed his long bangs aside and pointed to his own forehead, to the smudge of ash smeared across it.

"A circle?" Ali asked. It was so simple. So much the opposite of the tangled tentacles of numbers and angles that defined the Mark of Cylis and the IMPS. A symbol of inclusiveness, equality . . . open mind and open heart. Deliberately emphasizing the empty space of the missing Union tattoo inside.

"It's a whole new breed of Dust, Ali. Courageous. Brave. Aggressive. Evangelical, even. All because of your cyber attack. All because of the documents you released."

Peck nodded. "Even unconscious, you managed to start a war.

"And now here you are. More powerful than ever."

And Ali laughed. "What—you brought me back to finish it?"

Peck shook his head.

"No," he told her. "We brought you back to win it."

12

The next morning, in a little shantytown in the Dark Lands of al-Balat, a middle-aged woman sat with her pet lamb and two chickens in the shade of her scrap heap home, and thought about the past, and prayed for forgiveness over the mistakes she had made.

"اغفر لي لدرجة أنني قد أغفر لنفسي," she begged, hands folded and pressed to her head, watching the dust swirl in the few rays of light that shone through the cracks in her shanty walls, watching them sparkle as each speck tumbled and caught in the sun. She wondered where each was going. What they'd done with their time here so far. She wondered when God might let her move on with her life.

And then unexpectedly this woman found herself saying, "*Ali?*" as if her daughter were there, as if her daughter were suddenly right there behind her, because out of nowhere the walls in that old home glowed electric blue—big sparks leaking off and snapping at the edges and everything—just like in the old days. Hungrier times, she remembered . . . but happier too.

"Ali, is that you?" she whispered, and the walls sparked again. Louder this time.

She'd only ever known one person able to light the walls like that. "The Toter of Light. Please forgive me . . ." She wept. "Please . . ."

And the Ultranet asked, <Are you sure about this, Ali?>

And Ali said, "I'm sure."

And she stepped forward into her old home.

The walls sparked like firecrackers exploding around her mother's familiar embrace. And Ali didn't say anything, just accepted it.

And that afternoon the tinchers began building new homes, not just for Ali and her mother, but for that whole shantytown of her youth. High-tech homes, with lights, and rooms, and heat. With smart walls that really worked. The way only tinchers knew how.

And Peck settled down too, in a room the robots built. And he said, "Ali, you are home."

And Ali said, "*We* are home." But really she knew that wasn't quite right—that it wasn't the house that meant home.

Because the truth was that Ali was home the moment Peck found her. The moment the tinchers adopted her. The moment she found a family built not on power, or lies, but on love.

And in his own way, Logan was there too. For these days Ali could stand by Peck, could listen to the Ultranet, could hold her mother's hand, and could laugh with Logan in his father's quiet computer program, all at the same time. The bridge between all Ali's worlds connected, happily, at last.

And slowly Ali's mom accepted, in those first surreal days, that finally she was forgiven. That her prayers, nine years now in the making, had been answered.

She wasn't alone. She wasn't a monster.

And in this strong family, in her new home on a new block in the outskirts of al-Balat, Ali waited, at first for the other Alis in her head to weigh in. To mock her, to cheer her on, to throw in their two cents . . .

But the other Alis were silent. Her head was silent. There were no other Alis now.

It was only her. At peace.

There would be trials ahead, and that was okay.

Tribulation in store, and that was fine too.

Because right now, in this moment, Ali was home.

Against all odds.

Filled with hope, once again.

ABOUT THE AUTHOR

Evan Angler is ready to return home. To Beacon. He's been gone too long.

He has some friends there who need his help, whether they know it yet or not.

And it's time for the world to know that Logan Langly lives.

It's time for Logan Langly to be free.

It's time for us Dust to show the Union who's boss.

Evan Angler

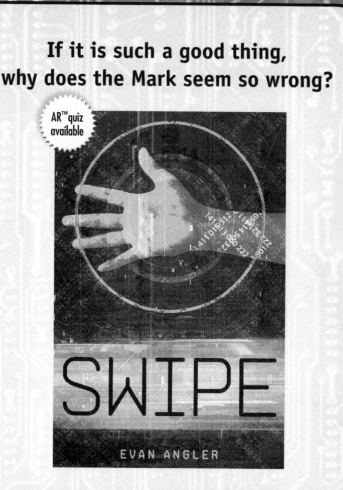

IF YOU WERE DESCENDED FROM ANGELS, HOW WOULD YOU USE YOUR POWERS?

Check out the exciting new *Son of Angels* series!

Jonah, Eliza, and Jeremiah Stone are one-quarter angel, which seems totally cool until it lands them in the middle of a war between angels and fallen angels. As they face the Fallen, they will find their faith tested like never before . . .

By Jerel Law

www.tommynelson.com

www.jerellaw.com

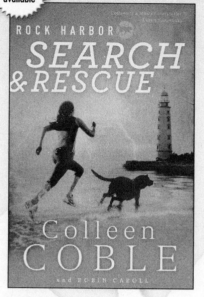

FROM AWARD-WINNING AUTHOR COLLEEN COBLE COMES HER FIRST SERIES FOR YOUNG ADVENTURERS: A MIXTURE OF MYSTERY, SUSPENSE, ACTION—AND ADORABLE PUPPIES!

Eighth-grader Emily O'Reilly is obsessed with all things Search-and-Rescue. The almost-fourteen-year-old spends every spare moment on rescues with her stepmom Naomi and her canine partner Charley. But when an expensive necklace from a renowned jewelry artist is stolen under her care at the fall festival, Emily is determined to prove her innocence to a town that has immediately labeled her guilty.

As Emily sets out to restore her reputation, she isn't prepared for the surprises she and the Search-and-Rescue dogs uncover along the way. Will Emily ever find the real thief?

BY COLLEEN COBLE

www.tommynelson.com

www.colleencoble.com